Lost in Time

a Blue Bloods novel

MELISSA DE LA CRUZ

HYPERION
New York

First Edition
1 3 5 7 9 10 8 6 4 2
G475-5664-5-11196
Printed in the United States of America
This book is set in 12-point Baskerville.
Designed by Tanya D. Hughes

ISBN 978-1-4231-2129-9
Reinforced binding

Visit www.hyperionteens.com

SUSTAINABLE FORESTRY INITIATIVE
Certified Fiber Sourcing
www.sfiprogram.org

THIS LABEL APPLIES TO TEXT STOCK

For my family

I tried to say "I miss you tonight."
And they claim you've already died.
—stellastarr*, "Lost in Time"

What on earth can you do . . .
but catch at whatever comes near you
with both your hands,
until your fingers are broken?
—Tennessee Williams, *Orpheus Descending*

Never Say Good-bye

Schuyler did not sleep the entire evening. Instead she lay awake, looking up at the crossed wooden beams on the ceiling, or out the window to the view of the Duomo, which shone a rosy gold in the dawn. Her dress was a crumpled pile of silk on the floor, next to Jack's black tuxedo jacket. Last night, after the guests had left, after cheeks were pressed affectionately against hers in loving good-byes, and hands had blessed and patted her ring in a gesture of good luck, the new couple had floated over the cobblestone streets back to their room, buoyed by the happiness they'd found in their friends and in each other, in turns exhilarated and exhausted by the events surrounding their bonding.

In the dim light of the morning, she curled her arm through his, and he turned toward her so that they pressed against each other, his chin resting on her forehead, their legs entwined together under the linen duvet. She placed her hand on his chest to feel the steady ordered beating of his heart, and wondered when they would be able to lie like this again.

"I need to go," Jack said, his voice still rough with sleep. He pulled her closer, and his breath tickled her ear. "I don't want to, but I need to." There was an unspoken apology in his words.

"I know," Schuyler said. She had promised to be strong for him, and she would keep that promise, she would not fail him. If only tomorrow would never come; if only she could hold on to the night just a little longer. "But not yet. See, it's still dark outside. It was the nightingale you heard, and not the lark," she whispered, feeling just like Juliet had that morning when she'd entreated Romeo to stay with her, drowsy and loving, yet fearful for the future and what would happen next. Schuyler was trying to hold on to something precious and fragile, as if the night would be able to protect their love from the oncoming doom and heartbreak the day would bring.

She could feel Jack smile against her cheek when he recognized the line from Shakespeare. As she traced his lips with her fingers, feeling their softness, he moved his body over hers, and she moved with him until they were joined together. He placed her arms above her head, his hands gripping her wrists tightly, and when he kissed her neck, she shuddered to feel his fangs on her skin. She pulled him ever closer, clutching his fine baby-soft hair as he drank deeply from her blood.

After, his blond head rested on her shoulder, and she folded her arms around his back and held him tightly. By now, daylight was streaming into the room. There was no denying it anymore: the night was over, and it would soon be time for them to part. He gently withdrew from her embrace and kissed the wounds that were still fresh on her neck until they healed.

She watched him dress, handing him his boots and sweater. "It'll be cold. You'll need a new jacket," she said, brushing off dirt from his black raincoat.

"I'll get one when I'm back in the city," he agreed. "Hey," he said, when he saw her mournful face. "It'll be all right. I've lived a long time and I intend to keep doing so." He managed a quick smile.

She nodded; the lump in her throat made it hard to breathe, hard to speak; but she did not want him to remember her this way. She adopted a cheerful tone and handed him his rucksack. "I put your passport in the front pocket." Already she loved the role of bondmate, of helpmeet, of wife. He nodded his thanks and shouldered the bag, fiddling with the zipper as he tucked in the last of his books, not quite meeting her eyes. She wanted to remember him exactly as he stood, looking golden and beautiful in the morning light, his platinum hair a bit tousled, and his bright green eyes flashing in determination.

"Jack . . ." Schuyler's resolve faltered, but she did not want to make their last moment more funereal than it had to be. "I'll see you soon," she said lightly.

He squeezed her hand one last time.

Then Jack was gone and she was alone.

Schuyler put away her bonding dress, gently folding it into her suitcase. She was ready to forge ahead, but as she gathered her things, she realized a truth that Jack had refused to acknowledge. It was not that he was afraid of meeting his fate; it was that he would simply bow to it.

Jack will not fight Mimi. Jack will let her kill him rather than fight her.

In the clear light of day, Schuyler grasped the reality of what he *was about to do. Meeting his twin meant meeting his doom.*

It was not going to be all right. It was never going to be all right.

He had tried to hide it with his brave words, but Schuyler knew deep down he was marching to his end. That last night was the final night they would ever have together. Jack was going home to die.

For a moment, Schuyler wanted to scream, rend her clothing, and tear her hair in grief. But after a few shuddering sobs, she controlled herself. She wiped her tears and held herself together. She would not let it happen. She could not accept it. She would not *accept it. Schuyler felt a surge of excitement fill her veins. She couldn't let him do this to himself. Oliver had promised he would do his best to distract Mimi, and she was thankful for his efforts in securing her happiness. But this was something she had to do for herself and for her love. She had to save Jack. She had to save him from himself. His flight was leaving in a few minutes, and without thinking, she ran all the way to the airport. She would stop him somehow. He was still alive, and she planned to keep it that way.*

Jack was standing on the tarmac, waiting to climb the stairs to the private jet that would take him first to Rome, then on to New York. Two black-clad Venators were waiting for him at the plane and looked at Schuyler curiously, but Jack did not look surprised to see her suddenly appear at his side.

"Schuyler . . ." He smiled. He did not ask what she was doing there. He already knew, but this time his smile was sad.

"Don't go," she said. I cannot let you face your fate alone. We are bonded now. We will face it together. Your destiny is mine as well. We shall live or die together. There is no other

way, *she sent, letting him hear the words in his head.*

Jack began to shake his head, and Schuyler said fiercely, "Listen. We will find a way out of the blood trial. Come to Alexandria with me. If we are unsuccessful and you have to return to New York, then I will share your fate. If you are destroyed, then so am I, and my mother's legacy is meaningless. I will not *leave you. Do not fear the future; we will face it together."*

She could see him weighing her words, and she held her breath.

Her fate—and perhaps the fate of all vampires—was in his hands. She had made her case, she had fought for him, and it was his turn now to fight for her.

Jack Force had a dark destiny before him, but Schuyler Van Alen hoped—she prayed—she believed*—that together they could change it.*

SEVEN MONTHS LATER

ONE

Paradiso

They left Alexandria just as the masses arrived to escape the heat of Cairo. "We always seem to be going in the wrong direction," Schuyler said, watching the traffic crawl, inch by inch, on the opposing freeway. It was the middle of July, and the sun was high in the sky. The air-conditioning in their rented sedan barely worked, and she had to place her palms right in front of the passenger-side vents just to cool down.

"Maybe it's the opposite. Maybe we're actually going in the right direction this time." Jack smiled and put a little more gas on the pedal. In comparison to the hordes descending upon the beach city, the traffic leading into the capital was light, and for Egypt, they were practically cruising, if that was the correct way to describe the chaotic scene on the highway. The Alexandria desert road was notorious for fearsome bus crashes and fatal accidents, and it was easy to see why: cars sped wildly, bobbing in and out of lanes at whim, while massive trucks looked as if they would pitch and roll every time they swerved to attain the slightest advantage. Once in a while someone would hit a random speed bump—either a huge unmarked crater or debris that had never been cleared—and traffic would screech to a halt without warning, causing a massive pileup. Schuyler was thankful Jack was a good driver; he seemed to know instinctively when to speed up or slow down, and they weaved through the careening vehicles without a scratch or near miss.

At least they weren't driving at night, when cars didn't even have their headlights on, since Egyptian drivers believed headlights burned through gas too quickly, and so made do without them. It was fine for vampires, of course, but Schuyler always worried for the poor humans who were barreling through in the dark—driving blind, like bats fluttering in a cave.

For seven months, she and Jack had lived in Alexandria, wandering through the picturesque cafés and airy museums. The city had been designed to rival Rome and Athens at their height. Cleopatra had made it the seat of her throne, and while there were a few traces of the ancient outpost still visible—a scattering of sphinxes, statues, and obelisks—there was actually very little that remained of the ancient world in the bustling metropolis.

When they'd first arrived, Schuyler had been filled with hope, and heartened by Jack's faith and presence, she was certain they would soon find what they sought. Florence had been a decoy, and Alexandria was the only other possibility regarding the true location of the Gate of Promise according to her grandfather's files, which had documented Catherine of Siena's travels from Rome to the Red Sea. Schuyler's mother had trusted her with the family legacy: to find and protect the remaining Gates of Hell, which kept the world safe from the demons of the underworld.

They had checked in to the Cecil Hotel, a favorite of Somerset Maugham's and one that had been popular during the British Colonial era. Schuyler had been charmed by the 1930s-style caged elevator and its splendid marble lobby, which oozed old Hollywood grandeur. She could imagine Marlene Dietrich arriving with a dozen trunks, a footman to carry her feather-trimmed hats alone.

Schuyler began her search at the Bibliotheca Alexandrina, an attempt to recreate the great library that had been lost over two thousand years ago (or so the Red Bloods thought, as the library still existed in the New York Coven's Repository of History). Like the original institution, the grounds of the Bibliotheca sprawled to include acres of gardens, as well as a planetarium and a conference center. A wealthy and secretive local matron had been instrumental in its foundation, and Schuyler had been certain she had found Catherine at last. But when they visited the grand patroness in her elegant salon overlooking the Eastern Harbor, it was obvious from the beginning that she was human, and no Enmortal, as she was sick and dying, lying in a bed, attached to a series of tubes.

As she and Jack had walked out of the elderly woman's room, Schuyler felt the first flicker of anxiety that she was letting down not only her beloved grandfather and her enigmatic mother, but also the boy she so dearly loved. So far, finding the gatekeeper was turning out to be a difficult—if not impossible—task. Jack did not say anything that day, nor had he ever voiced any regret at his decision. Back in Florence, at the airport, he had escaped from the Venators and accepted her challenge, agreeing to her plan. She did not want to fail him. She'd promised she would find a way out of the blood trial, a way for them to be together, and she would. The gatekeeper, Catherine of Siena, would help them, if only Schuyler could find her.

Their life in Egypt had settled into a comfortable routine. Tired of hotel living, they'd rented a small house near the beach and concentrated on blending in as best they could. Most of their neighbors left the young good-looking foreigners alone. Perhaps they sensed the vampire strength behind their friendly smiles.

In the mornings, Schuyler would comb the library, reading books on the Roman era, when Catherine was first tasked with the charge of keeper, and matching it to the files from Lawrence's journal. Jack took on the footwork, using his Venator training to zero in on any clues as to her whereabouts, walking the city, talking to the locals. Enmortals were charismatic and unforgettable beings—Lawrence Van Alen had been very popular during his exile in Venice, and Schuyler was betting that Catherine, or whatever she called herself these days, was the same: a magnetic personality whom no one could easily forget. In the late afternoons, Jack would stop by the library, and they would head to a café for lunch, sharing plates of *mulukhiya* stew over rice or spicy *khoshary*, and then return to their duties. They lived like locals, having dinner at midnight, sipping fragrant anise tea until the wee hours of the morning.

Alex, as everyone calls the city, is a resort town, and as spring arrived and a breeze blew in from the Mediterranean, buses and boatloads of tourists arrived to fill the hotels and beaches. Their seven months together was sort of a honeymoon, Schuyler would realize later. A small slice of heaven, a brief and bright delay of the dark days that lay ahead. Their marriage was still young enough that they celebrated every month they were together, marking the time with little gestures, little gifts to each other: a small bracelet made of shells for her, a first edition of Hemingway for him. If Schuyler could keep Jack at her side, she believed she could keep him safe. Her love for him was a shield that would keep him whole.

Even as their relationship grew stronger and deeper, and they began to ease into the comfort of daily bonded life, Schuyler's heart still skipped a beat every time she saw him lying next to her. She would admire the silhouette of his back, the fine sculpture of his shoulder blades. Later, reflecting on their time in the city, she would wonder if somehow she had known what would happen, how it would end; as if no matter what happened in Egypt, whether she found Catherine or not, whether they were successful or not, she had known from the beginning that their time together would not last; that it *could* not last, and they were only lying to themselves and each other.

So she tucked her memories away for safekeeping: the way he looked at her when he undressed her, as he slowly pulled down a silk camisole strap. His stare was voracious, and she would be sickened with desire, she wanted him so much. The bright fire she felt was matched by the intensity of his gaze—just like the first time he had flirted with her in front of that nightclub in New York, and the dizzying rush of infatuation she'd experienced the first time they'd danced together, the first time they'd kissed, the first time they'd met for a covert tryst in his Perry Street apartment. The strong yet gentle way he held her when he performed the *Caerimonia Osculor*. In the days that would come, she would replay these moments in her mind, like photographs she would remove from her wallet and look at again and again. But in the present, at night when they lay together, his body warm next to hers, when she pressed her lips against his skin, it felt as if they would never be apart, that what she feared would never come to be.

Maybe she was crazy to think it would last, that any of it—their love, their joy together—would hold, given the darkness that had been part of their union from the beginning. And later she would wish she had enjoyed it more, that she had spent less time poring through books, spending hours in the library alone, less time removing his arms from her waist, telling him to wait, or missing dinner so that she could go over the papers again and again. She would wish for one more night spent in a roadside café, holding hands under the table; one more morning sharing the newspaper. She would cherish the small moments of togetherness, the two of them sitting side by side in bed, just the simple touch of his hand on her knee sending shivers up her spine. She would remember Jack reading his books, lifting his eyeglasses—his vision had been bothering him lately, the sand and the pollution causing his eyes to water.

If only they could have stayed in Alex forever—walking the gardens full of flowers, watching the hip crowds at San Stefano. Schuyler, who had been hopeless in the kitchen, enjoyed the ease with which a meal could be prepared. She had learned to put together a proper feast, buying premade platters of *kobeba* and *sambousek*, accompanied by *tahini* and *tamiya*, chopped salads and a roasted leg of lamb or veal, stuffed pigeon and fish *sayadeya* and chicken *pane* from the local market. Their life reminded her a little of her year with Oliver, and she felt a small pang at that. Her dearest, sweetest friend. She wished there was a way to still retain their friendship—he had been so gallant at her bonding—but they had not exchanged a word since he'd returned to New York. Oliver had told her a little of what was happening back home, and she worried about him, and hoped he was keeping himself safe now that she was not there to make sure he was doing so. She missed Bliss as well, and hoped her friend—her *sister*—would find a way to fulfill her part of their mother's destiny somehow.

As the months passed, Schuyler worked every angle, made more wrong guesses, and met more women who did not turn out to be Catherine. She and Jack didn't talk about what would happen if they failed. And so the days slipped by, like sand through her fingers, grit in the air, and then it was summer. News trickled in slowly of the world they had left behind—that the Covens were in chaos—reports of burnings and mysterious attacks. And with Charles still missing and Allegra disappeared, there was no one to lead the fight. No one knew what was to become of the vampires, and still Schuyler and Jack were no closer to finding the keeper.

Before they left Florence, they had ordered the Petruvian priests to keep MariElena safe, to let the young girl who had been taken by the Croatan carry her pregnancy to term. Ghedi had given them his word that the girl would not come to any harm under their care. Schuyler still did not believe what the Petruvians swore was true, that the Blue Bloods had ordered the slaughter of innocent women and children in order to keep the bloodline pure. There had to be another reason for it—something had gone wrong in the history of the world—and once they found Catherine, the gatekeeper who had founded the Petruvian Order, she would tell them the truth.

But as the days dragged on and still they did not find the keeper or the gate, Schuyler began to feel discouraged and lethargic. It did not help that it had been a long time since she had used her fangs. She had not taken a familiar since Oliver, and every day she felt less of her vampire self and more human, more vulnerable.

Meanwhile, Jack was growing thin, and dark circles had formed under his eyes. She knew he was having trouble sleeping at night. He would toss and turn, murmuring under his breath. She began to worry that he thought she was a coward for asking him to stay.

"No, you are wrong. It is a brave thing that you did, to stand up to your beloved," he'd said, reading her mind as usual. "You will find Catherine. I have faith in you."

But finally Schuyler had to admit defeat—that she had read her grandfather's documents incorrectly. She had to accept that Alexandria was another decoy, another red herring. They had walked the city's dark alleys and haunted its bright new megamalls, but had found nothing, and the trail was cold. They were as stumped as they had been in the beginning, when they first left New York.

Their last night in the city, Schuyler had studied the

documents again, re-reading the section that had made her believe the elusive gate was located in Alexandria.

"'On the shore of the river of gold, the victor's city shall once again rise on the threshold of the Gate of Promise.'" Schuyler looked at Jack. "Hold on. I think I'm on to something." When she'd first read the passage she had immediately thought of Alexander the Great, the conqueror of the ancient world, and she'd been certain that the gate was located in the city to which he had given his name. But during her seven months in Egypt, she had learned a little Arabic, and the answer was so clear she immediately berated herself for wasting so much time.

"Cairo—Al-Qahira—literally translates to mean *victorious.*" The victorious city. The victor's city. She told Jack as her heart beat in excitement, "The gate is in Cairo."

They left in the morning.

TWO

Inferno

*F*lying from New York to Cairo was a always a bit surreal, Mimi Force knew, sitting in her first-class seat and shaking the ice in her cocktail glass. For hours now they had been flying over endless desert—soft golden dunes of sand that went for miles—when suddenly an entire city rose from the dust, sprawling out in all directions, as immense and infinite as the nothing that had preceded it. The capital of Egypt was a golden brown sprawl of towering buildings jockeying for space; standing shoulder to shoulder, they looked as if they were stacked on top of one another like children's blocks, cut through by the green borders of the Nile.

Seeing the city gave Mimi a burst of hope in her heart. This was it. This time, she was going to get Kingsley back. She missed him more than ever, and she clung to a fierce bright hope that she would see his smile again, and feel the warmth of his embrace. His brave, selfless act during the

Silver Blood attack at her disastrous bonding had saved the Coven, but it had consigned his soul to the seventh circle of the underworld. She shuddered to think how he was faring. Hell was not for the weak, and while she knew Kingsley was strong and would endure, she did not want him trapped down there for one moment longer.

The Coven needed his courage and wits. Kingsley Martin had been their bravest and most effective Venator, but Mimi needed him more. She would never forget the way he had looked at her before he disappeared, with so much love and sadness; with the kind of love she had never experienced with Jack. She was certain her twin had never felt that way about her in all their time together. With Kingsley, Mimi had had a glimpse of what real love was like, but it had been snatched away so quickly she hadn't fully grasped its reality. How she had mocked and teased him—how much time they had wasted—why hadn't she gone with him to Paris like he'd asked before the bonding?

No matter. She had come all the way to Egypt to save him, and she felt euphoric at the possibility of their reunion.

Although, her ebullient mood threatened to fade with the many irritations that came with international travel. At customs she was told she didn't have the proper visa, and by the time she was waved through passport control and had collected her luggage, the driver sent by the hotel had picked up another guest. Mimi was left to fight the crowds to find a cab.

Once she had managed to hail one, she ended up arguing with the driver about the fare all the way to the hotel. He'd quoted a preposterous sum, and if nothing else, Mimi was not born yesterday. When they finally arrived at the Mena House Oberoi, Mimi got out, tossed her cash through the window, and simply walked away. When she told the hotel clerk what happened, the fool inquired why she had not used the hotel's driver.

Mimi was tempted to snarl and throw something, but she remembered she was supposed to be eighteen now. She was Regent of the Coven, and it would not do to stomp around the place like a spoiled teenager.

Exhausted from the trip, she had fallen straight to bed, only to be awoken by the housekeeper, who'd arrived to turn down the bed and fluff the pillows. The maid was lucky she had brought chocolates.

But now it was a new morning, a dazzling new day, and with the view of the pyramids glinting in the sun, Mimi prepared for the most important day of her life.

The witch would not lie to me, Mimi thought as she brushed her hair until it shone like spun gold. *"Helda made an exception once, and since then the Orpheus Amendment has stood. The same rules apply."* Ingrid Beauchamp, the mousy librarian from North Hampton, New York, who could see the future, had told her, albeit reluctantly and only after humiliating groveling on Mimi's part, that there was indeed a way to release a soul from beyond the seventh circle of the underworld. It was why Mimi had allowed herself to be dragged to the eyesore of the Hamptons last week to consult with Ingrid in the first place. The witch might have disliked her, might have thought the arrogant young vampire was nothing but an annoyance, but she would not have lied to her. The witches followed a set of rules older even than the Code of the Vampires. Mimi was sure of that as she sat in her warm bed for just another minute longer.

The past seven months had not been easy, and Mimi had barely held it together. The death of the Nephilim had done little to assuage the growing fear and instability in the Coven; the Elders were about to revolt; talk of dissolution and hiding underground was gaining more ground every day; but the Lennox brothers' betrayal grated hardest of all. Instead of securing her traitorous brother, as she had ordered them to do, they had disappeared into the ether, with only a lame excuse for their resignation—something about hunting down more of the demon-born Nephilim hidden around the world, with the Venators from Shanghai—a noble enough cause, surely. But orders were orders, and insubordination was cause for an arrest warrant. Not that Mimi had any more Venators to send after them. The few that were left were too busy protecting the rest of the Coven. News from the outposts was grim: vampires were being slaughtered in every corner of the world—a fire in London during a Conclave meeting, more young ones found drained in Buenos Aires—the Silver Blood menace, far from being extinguished, had only grown.

The Dark Prince remained trapped behind the Gates of Hell, but it seemed to make little difference, as the Covens, mired in fear and infighting, were in danger of self-destructing on their own. Lucifer had struck at the heart of the Blue Bloods when he'd sent his nemesis, the archangel Michael, to the white darkness that had claimed Mimi's own true love. As for Gabrielle, supposedly Allegra had woken up and left the hospital, but her current whereabouts were unknown.

Overwhelmed and overworked, Mimi had decided that she could not lead the vampires alone. She wanted him back. She had nothing to live for otherwise, and only Kingsley Martin—of the cocky grin and sexy drawl—could help her rebuild the Covens and create a true haven for the vampires, now that her cowardly twin had abdicated his duty in order to be with his half-human whore. If Mimi believed the rumors, Jack had actually made that creature of Abomination his bride. His freaking *bondmate*.

Not that Mimi felt any ounce of love for Jack anymore, but it was still humiliating to hear that he had gone through with it. Broken their bond and cast his lot with that freak. First Gabrielle had broken her bond to wed her human familiar, now Abbadon was doing the same. . . . What was next? Did nothing matter anymore? What about the Code of the Vampires? Should they just toss that into the Black Fire as well? Were they to live like indulgent Red Bloods now, who made and broke their vows without a shred of thought or guilt? Perhaps they should just give up, forsake civilization and the old ways, and live like barbarians.

On Oliver's advice, Mimi had gone to Egypt in December to make her first attempt at breaking Kingsley out of Hell, secure that when she returned to New York, Jack would be in chains. But the Venators stationed in Italy had reported that Jack had slipped away from them in Florence, and they had no idea where he'd gone. Mimi was surprised, as she had believed deep down that Jack would return to face his crime on his own honor. He was no coward, and she was sure that, at the very least, he would respect the Code and defend himself at a blood trial. Obviously, she was wrong. Perhaps she did not know him as well as she thought. Perhaps his new bride had made him soft—encouraged the delusion that he might live a life of peace without any consequences for his actions.

It didn't help that Mimi's first trip to Egypt had been a bust, and she had returned empty-handed. Her mother had convinced her to go back to school, so in May she had graduated from Duchesne—accepted her crown of white flowers and stood in the tiled courtyard in her tea-length white dress, gloves, and satin shoes, like she had in other lifetimes. It was a farce, just like all of the Committee events—the old Blue Bloods clinging to their social calendar and their seasonal rituals as their world fell to pieces. Mimi never felt older in her life than she had that day. "The future is before you," the graduation speaker had told the assembly. "You are full of promise and have the ability to change the world." Blah, blah, blah. What a bunch of bull. The future was over. There was no future without the Coven, without the Code, without Kingsley.

Before leaving for Cairo again, Mimi had given instructions to the remaining conclave to contact her should something incredibly stupid or terrible happen to them while she was away. They could not disband the Coven, as she had taken the keys to the Repository with her, which unlocked the cycle files contained in the House of Records, along with the remaining sacred materials. The cowards could go underground, sure, but they would leave knowing they had little hope of returning in a new cycle; and not everyone was strong enough to live as an Enmortal.

Mimi walked onto her expansive balcony to get a closer view of the three pyramids of Giza, grand and intimidating in the near distance. She had wanted to stay as close to them as possible. On a clear day, one could see the Giza pyramids from many points in the city; they appeared as looming triangular shadows just beyond the skyline. But here the pyramids were so close she felt as if she could almost reach out and touch them with her hand, and she felt closer to Kingsley by just looking at them. It wouldn't be long now.

She yawned, feeling fatigued from her arrival the day before, still sluggish with jet lag, when the phone buzzed. She hit the speaker.

"Breakfast on the terrace?" asked her Conduit, Oliver Hazard-Perry. "I saw they have *t'aamiyyas* today."

"Mmm. I like those fried little cakes." Mimi smiled.

When Mimi walked to the buffet, she found Oliver sitting at the table in front of the gardens facing the pyramids. He was wearing a linen safari jacket, a straw fedora, and desert boots. He stood when he saw her and pulled out a chair for her. The hotel restaurant was crowded with affluent adventure-seeking tourists—Americans spreading *fül*, stewed chickpeas (a "breakfast chickpea" Mimi thought, amused), on crisp pita bread; English families consulting maps; groups of Germans laughing boisterously at pictures taken on their digital cameras. A general hum of self-satisfied smugness pervaded the ritzy hotel atmosphere. Mimi had learned that it didn't matter what country she was in, all five-star hotel buffets were the same, with offerings of expensive cold cuts and delicate pastries along with the custom-omelet stand and a selection of "native" foods, catering to the same preening sector of the international bourgeoisie. She had traveled all over the world and yet could never escape the denizens of the Upper East Side—from Mount Kilimanjaro to the Arctic Circle, the privileged tribe could be found beached on the shores of the Maldives or scuba-diving in Palau. The world was flat, all right, and best traversed in Jack Rogers flip-flops.

"Don't you look like you just stepped out of an Agatha Christie novel," she told Oliver, placing her napkin on her lap and nodding to the waiter to pour her a cup of their strong black coffee.

"Planning my death on the Nile already?" Oliver asked with a smile.

"Not yet," she growled.

"Because I'd like to get a bite to eat first, if that's all right with you." He nodded toward the sumptuous buffet. "Shall we?"

They filled their plates and made their way back to their table. Mimi cast a skeptical eye at Oliver's plate, which towered precariously with stacks of eggs, strawberries, waffles, toast, pita, cheese, croissants, and bagels. Boys were such food-shoveling machines, but maybe he had the right idea. Who knew when they would be able to get another meal? She tried to eat but could only pick at the tasty little morsels on her plate, as she had butterflies in her stomach and had lost her appetite. No matter: before she left New York she had visited her current familiar and had "blood-loaded" for her trip, like a marathon runner filling up on carbohydrates the night before the race.

"Pity we're not staying long," Oliver said, taking a hearty bite from a flaky biscuit. "I heard that at night there's some sort of laser light show at the pyramids. The concierge says it's narrated by the Sphinx. Which begs the question, if the Sphinx could talk, what would it say?"

"Amazing what Red Bloods will do to something so sacred. Is there no limit?" Mimi asked.

"It could be worse. There could be a Sting concert, like last time," Oliver reminded her.

Now, that was truly a disaster, Mimi thought. When they had arrived in Cairo the first time, the area around the pyramids had been chaos—not only unbearably hot, trying to push through the crowds so they could get to the entrance, but all the while Sting was up there belting out those run-of-the-mill saggy middle-aged yoga melodies. She shuddered at the memory. Rock stars should not age. They should die before they turn thirty, or disappear into their châteaus in Mustique, returning only with doorstop-size tomes full of their heroin-fueled misadventures.

"You could stay," Mimi offered, before she could change her mind. "I can go down alone, like before." She could find another way to fulfill the exchange, she thought. He didn't have to do this. Oliver was a bit of a prig, a bit of a stiff, but he was sweet and thoughtful, and it had been his idea to visit the white witch; and thanks to him, Mimi now knew exactly what she needed to get Kingsley out of the underworld.

This is your last chance, she thought.

Oliver sopped up some egg with his toast. He had made a heroic effort and his plate was almost empty. "You said you needed someone to come down with you. And besides, it's not every day I get to visit Hell. Do I get a souvenir?"

Mimi snorted. If only he knew. Oliver *was* the souvenir. There was something the witch had told her about her mission that she had kept from him all this time. *The Orpheus*

Amendment demands a sacrifice in payment for the release of a soul. A soul for a soul. Oliver had made it all too easy, Mimi thought. Truly, it was unfortunate to lose him just as she had started to like him, just as they had become friends of a sort, especially after he had practically saved her life not too long ago. Okay, scratch "practically." He'd saved her life, and he was a proven asset to the Coven, uncovering clues that had led to the hidden Nephilim in the end. He was a good guy, and a good friend to Mimi. Still, it had to be done. She would have to ignore her growing fondness for him if she was going to get Kingsley back. There was no contest. It was just so *convenient* of him to have volunteered to make the journey with her, and Mimi was never one to look a gift horse in the mouth. Besides, human Conduits lived to serve their vampire masters, didn't they?

THREE

Beatrice

*A*llegra Van Alen had visited San Francisco many times in her past life cycles, yet had avoided the city in her current one, almost as if she were allergic to it. Whenever Conclave business had called for a trip out West, she'd always found a way to wriggle out of it, find someone to take her place, or a way to handle issues by conference calls.

But now that she was twenty-one years old, and, in the fall of 1989, newly awakened to her full memories and powers, she did not see the harm. She had graduated from college in the spring, standing tall and proud with her brother at the dais, clutching her alumni pin (diplomas would be given out later through the registrar). Amazing that she had accomplished that much, considering her high school education had been cobbled together from a jumble of prep schools of varying academic reputation. After abruptly leaving

Endicott Academy her junior year, she had refused to return to Duchesne, and instead had aimlessly hopped around the Northeastern private-school corridor, sometimes switching midsemester on a whim.

Cordelia had been certain there was no way Allegra would gain admittance into the prestigious university that had just rolled out the red carpet for Charles. But her mother had somehow forgotten the power of a fancy name, or the pull of the family's illustrious history (along with its generous donations over the years), and an acceptance letter had been sent. College had been a blur of parties and drama, and Allegra had thrown herself into campus life with gusto, showing an energy and motivation that had eluded her during her peripatetic high school years. It was as if she was finally getting over the terrible mistake she had made at Endicott—of falling in love with her human familiar and putting her bond at risk. Allegra had accepted her destiny and position in Blue Blood society, and Charles was pleased.

It would not be long before she would be bonded to her twin and claim her rightful heritage. Allegra was looking forward to another productive lifetime with Charles, the two of them leading the way, setting examples for the rest of their kind, as they had done since the beginning of time. They had had many names over the years—Junia and Cassius, Rose and Myles—but they would always be Michael and Gabrielle, protectors of the Garden, the Uncorrupted, Archangels of the Light.

She was in San Francisco because of Charles. The two of them were rarely apart these days, and when he'd asked her to come with him, she'd said yes. He'd left early that morning to meet with a group of local Elders about an emergency concerning their newest batch of vampires. Allegra had been worried, but Charles had assured her it was probably nothing but the usual issues that came with Transformation. There were always a few kinks here and there: some would awake to the memories too early, causing confusion or catatonia; others would have trouble controlling their bloodlust. The Elders were a jittery bunch.

Allegra and Charles were staying in Nob Hill, in one of the many luxurious apartments and residences around the globe that were now at their disposal as heads of the Coven. Since she had time alone, Allegra had decided to spend the afternoon wandering around the pretty neighborhood, reacquainting herself with the hilly streets, doing a little shopping, pausing to admire the view. She'd crossed Union Square and wandered into a tiny jewel box of an alley called Maiden Lane—a charming side street filled with small boutiques and art galleries. She walked inside the nearest one.

The gallery assistant, a chic dark-haired girl wearing red-rimmed spectacles and a spare black dress with an interesting neckline, greeted her upon arrival. "Hi there. We just put the show up. Feel free to look around."

"Thanks," Allegra said, thinking she would just have a quick peek around the place. Charles was the one who collected art; he'd started as a boy and had built an impressive collection over the years. His taste ran toward what was currently popular and expensive—he bid heavily on the trendy artists of the day. Their mansion back in New York was filled with Schnabels and Basquiats, paintings strewn with broken crockery and street-style graffiti. She could understand their value, but the pieces were not something she cared to live with for the rest of her life.

The Vespertine Gallery seemed to specialize in the new wave of realistic paintings, and Allegra examined several portraits before a particular one caught her eye. It was a tiny little canvas, five inches square, and the painting was of a teenage girl sitting on a hospital bed, with her head in a bandage. Allegra looked at it again, not quite believing what she was seeing. It was all there—the plate of cookies, the wicker furniture. The girl had a bemused smile on her face, as if she couldn't quite understand what she was doing in a hospital. The painting referenced religious iconography—a golden halo surrounded the girl's head, and the bright colors of the room were painted in a style similar to illustrations found in medieval prayer books, with delicate images of saints and angels. The painting was called *Always Something There to Remind Me.*

Allegra gasped and turned bright red, feeling as if someone were playing a cosmic joke on her, and she almost stumbled on her heels as she turned away from the piece. It couldn't be . . . could it? But it had to be. . . . That song had been a secret joke between them. . . .

"Do you know his work?" the pretty young gallery assistant asked, suddenly appearing at her elbow. The girl had an obsequious smile on her face, as if she instinctively knew when "looking" turned into "shopping."

"I'm not sure I do," Allegra said, her heart pounding underneath her thin cashmere sweater. Her face felt hot and her mouth had turned dry. "What's his name?"

"Stephen Chase. He's a local. Got a rave review from *Art Forum* on his show last season. Amazing work. Everyone is talking about it. He's made quite a splash."

Allegra nodded, unable to do more than that at the moment. Stephen Chase. Now, there was a name she would never forget, although when she'd known him he'd gone by his middle name, Bendix. It was Ben's painting, of course. She knew it the minute she'd seen it. "How much?" she asked, before she could think it over. But there was no doubt. Once she saw the painting, she had to buy it.

The gallery assistant named a tidy sum, and murmured something about extra fees for framing and shipping services, should they be required.

"I'll take it," Allegra said, rooting around in her pocketbook for her credit card. "And I'd like to take it now. With me, I mean."

"How wonderful! It's an amazing piece. Congratulations. But I'm afraid I can't let you have it just yet. The show runs until next month, and we'll be shipping everything to the buyers after. I hope that's all right?"

Allegra nodded, even though she was disappointed. She had wanted to own it right then, tuck it into her suitcase and spirit it away so she could study it in private.

Everything from that fateful year came flooding back. Ben had not forgotten her after all. The painting was from the day they'd met—the day she'd been hit on the head with a field hockey ball and had been sent to the clinic. They had been roommates of a sort, sharing the same television. He had broken his leg, she remembered now, and had asked the field hockey team—her team—to sign his cast. It all returned to her in a flash as if it were yesterday.

"How long are you in town?" the assistant asked, as she ran Allegra's credit card and checked her ID.

"We leave tomorrow."

"Too bad. There's a dinner party for him on Saturday night, and he loves meeting his patrons."

Allegra's mind raced. She could ask Charles if they could stay for a few more days. He had mentioned wanting to attend the opening of the new Olmec exhibit at the de Young. Of course he would want her to accompany him, but perhaps she could manufacture some sort of excuse and slip away to the party instead.

"My schedule is flexible," she told the clerk. "And I would like to thank him for this piece. . . ."

The gallery girl gave Allegra the address, writing it down on her receipt. "Wonderful! He'll be thrilled."

Allegra was not sure if "thrilled" was the right word. She remembered the last time she'd seen Ben: it was the first time she had marked him as her familiar, the first time she'd drunk his blood and taken him for her own. Then she'd disappeared off the face of the earth. She never thought she would see him again. Correction—she had *hoped* she would never see him again. Not after the terrible vision she'd seen of their future—a future she'd been running from for the last five years.

Every fiber of her immortal being, and all the knowledge she carried in her soul, told her to hop on the next plane out of the city. It was dangerous to see Ben again. She had fallen for him once, and her heart was in the right place now. She loved Charles, and they would renew their bond as they had since the beginning of time—since they had journeyed from Heaven's kingdom to bring hope to the Fallen. Her heart was pledged to love her twin, as before, and yet it was this same stubborn heart that argued to stay, that would not let her leave.

She would see Ben on Saturday night, she was sure of it. If there was such a thing as destiny, Allegra felt it pulling her in a new direction, one that would lead her far from the life she had planned, far from the Coven and the angel she had loved for eternity. Allegra thought she would feel tormented with anxiety and guilt, but instead, as she left the gallery, she felt a strange emotion—one she had not felt in a very long time: she felt happy.

FOUR

Knives in the Market

he Zambezi rest stop was unlike any Schuyler had ever seen. Not only was it a sprawling complex of restaurants and parks, with groups of large families picnicking in the grass, enjoying the afternoon air, but it also housed a full African-style safari. The affable staff explained that zoos were now common in a number of rest stops catering to the commuter crowd that traveled between Egypt's largest cities. The owner had designed this one to mimic the African veldt, complete with zebras and lions.

"Apparently on Friday afternoons there's a lion hunt," Jack said, reading the brochure. "They put a pig in the lion pen, and the lioness—"

"Stop!" Schuyler said, trying not to laugh. "That's *horrible.*"

They smiled and held hands across the table, careful not to display any more public affection than that. Schuyler's ability to shift her features, along with her many-layered wardrobe, let her blend in easily, especially with the black silk scarf around her hair. During her time in Egypt she had noticed that not every girl chose to veil, although of course there were some women in full head-to-toe burkas. But most wore stylish brightly colored head scarves with regular jeans and long-sleeve T-shirts. The wealthy women dripping with jewels had sleek salon blow-dried hair, and did not wear scarves at all. The only inconvenience Schuyler had found living in Egypt was that she could not travel alone without taking on the appearance of an older woman, which tired her. Not that it was dangerous, but young women simply did not walk the streets by themselves. They either traveled in groups or with a male relative. Schuyler and Jack wanted to call as little attention to themselves as possible, so they tried to follow the local customs.

They finished their late lunch at the rest stop and were back on the road, fighting the crazy traffic once again.

When they arrived in the city, Schuyler found Cairo as overwhelming as she had the first time they'd arrived in the country, the streets and sidewalks extremely crowded, loud, and polluted, teeming with people and cars and the incessant honking of horns. With some difficulty, Jack returned their car to the rental shop, and they found a cab to take them to a hotel. Since they were trying to be careful with money, they headed downtown, where Schuyler had heard there were more affordable options, rather than the high-end hotels along the east and west banks of the Nile. The budget hotels were located in old dilapidated apartment buildings on busy, noisy streets. There were several grubby backpacker dives that Jack rejected, although Schuyler told him she did not mind. Finally they settled upon a small hotel on a relatively quiet block, whose lobby looked cleaner than the others around it.

Jack rang the bell, and after a long wait, a sleepy manager appeared from a back room. "Yes? How can I help you?" he asked grumpily.

"We'd like a room," Jack said. "Would you have any available, sir?"

"For how long?"

"A week for now, maybe more. Is that all right?"

"She is your wife?" the clerk asked, casting a suspicious eye on Schuyler.

"Yes," Jack said tersely. He held up his bonding ring so the clerk could see it better. Schuyler tried to look modest and demure as the clerk eyed her warily. Jack rapped on the counter. "Will this be a problem, sir?" His voice was polite, but Schuyler could sense the annoyance behind it. She knew Jack did not like using the compulsion on humans, but it had been a long drive and he was getting irritable.

After taking a long time counting their cash, the clerk finally produced a key and led them to the second level. The room was plain but clean, and Jack and Schuyler went straight to bed so they could be up early the next morning.

The next day, Jack set off to speak to members from the local Coven. "I'm going to make a few calls. See if I can find anyone who can help us track down leads about Catherine," he said. "You rest for a bit. You look tired, love." He kissed her and was out the door. With his blond hair hidden in a cap and his green eyes shielded in wraparound sunglasses, dressed in light khakis and a white Oxford shirt, he looked capable and ready; yet Schuyler felt fearful for him. She knew he would be safe—as Abbadon, he was the one everyone should be afraid of—but she could not help it, she was afraid for his life. She knew she'd done the right thing in helping him change his mind about meeting the blood trial, but she worried it would not be enough—that somehow, some way, Jack would be snatched away without warning, and she would never see him again.

While he was out, Schuyler studied the rest of her grandfather's journals. She could never read them without missing Lawrence. She could imagine him prodding her, challenging her to find the real, hidden meaning behind the cryptic words. "Usually what we are looking for is right in front of us," was one of his favorite maxims.

Jack returned in the afternoon. He removed his hat and rubbed his eyes. "The Conclave's headquarters has been abandoned. But I was able to track down a human Conduit who used to serve an old friend of mine. He said the Coven has been under attack for the last month and the vampires are getting ready to leave the city. Bad news all around." He looked despondent for a moment. The news that another Coven was going underground was hard to hear, Schuyler knew. "Anyway, I asked him if he'd ever heard of someone called Catherine of Siena. It was a long shot, but sometimes legends last a long time in older parts of the world."

"So you found her?" Schuyler said hopefully.

"Maybe. He gave me a name: Zani, a holy woman with a huge following. We're meeting a guide who can take us to her temple at the souk in an hour." He looked at her directly. "There's something else."

"What is it?" Schuyler asked, her inner alarm bells ringing, as Jack looked so somber.

"I think my sister is here. I can feel her. . . . She's looking for something."

Schuyler rushed to his side. "Then we'll go."

"No," Jack said. "Somehow I sense she's not here for me."

"We can't risk it. . . ."

"Yes we can," he said gently. "I am not afraid of Mimi or her wrath. We will meet with the holy woman. You will find your gatekeeper."

They set off, navigating their way on foot through the topsy-turvy streets of Cairo, where there were no crosswalks, traffic lights, stop signs, nor turn lanes; and along with the cars, buses, and rickety microbuses, the roads were clogged with donkey and horse carts, bikes and scooters headed in opposite directions. Just as on the highway, everyone on the streets pushed and shoved their way through. Schuyler noticed a car in the middle of the road, its owner fixing a flat tire—he had not thought to move it to the side, and so everyone else had to go around him. Using their vampire speed, they quickly zigzagged through vehicles, and arrived at the marketplace in good time.

The Khan el-Kalili was a winding labyrinthine souk that was once the center of commerce in Cairo during the Middle Ages, but now mostly existed to serve the tourist community, with dozens of shops selling Pharaonic memorabilia and Egyptian trinkets: scarabs, crystal pyramids, Queen Nefertiti tea sets, and gold and silver cartouches with your name inscribed in hieroglyphics. Formerly organized into districts, the shops were now mostly jumbled together, with rug merchants next to computer shops. Only the goldsmiths, coppersmiths, and spice dealers still kept to their historic places.

Schuyler walked quickly, matching Jack's pace, attempting to ignore the peddlers who thrust their wares in her face and tried to persuade her to come inside their shops. She would not let him out of her sight. He was convinced Mimi was not after him, but Schuyler was not as certain, and she didn't trust Mimi to leave them alone. They tried to stay together, but the crowd was dense and they were often separated by the aggressive shopkeepers who came between them, holding up an "authentic" trinket of some sort.

"Very pretty very pretty ring yes? From authentic jade

stone. One hundred percent made in Egypt!"

"No, sorry," Schuyler said, trying to hold on to Jack's hand and feeling his fingers slipping from her grasp as a shopkeeper inserted himself between them.

"Miss miss miss . . . come see . . . alabaster vase from the tombs themselves. Very rare. Very rare," another said, holding up what had to be a cheap ornament most likely made in China. Where was Jack? Schuyler looked around, trying not to panic.

"Ankh? Ward off the evil eye, miss. . . . Come see. Come inside, many more for you. Very nice."

"No, no, sorry . . ." she said, brushing through and trying to make her way past a crowd of Russian tourists who had stopped to gawk at a copy of Tutankhamen's gold coffin. *Jack?* She sent.

I'm here. Don't worry. Jack appeared by her side, and Schuyler could breathe again.

"Miss! You want, here—perfect sapphire match your eyes!"

"No, sorry. Please . . ." Schuyler said, pushing the man away. "Goodness, they're persistent," she said.

"They're always a little more desperate in the off-season. Ah, here's the shop," Jack said, stopping in front of a small storefront that sold all sorts of religious ornaments, from crucifixes to menorahs.

"Who's this guide?" Schuyler asked.

"Roberston said it's one of Zani's followers, like a high

priest in her temple or something." He motioned to the Yankees baseball hat on his head. "He's supposed to look for the Yankee," Jack explained with a wry smile.

"You buy! One hundred percent authentic!" a particularly aggressive shop owner demanded, waving a Persian rug in Schuyler's face.

"No thank you, sir . . ." she said, trying to bat him away.

Next to her, Jack was accosted by another shopkeeper trying to sell him a hookah. Jack was being polite, but Schuyler was just about to lose her temper with her persistent rug salesman. She tried to dodge him, when she noticed Jack had disappeared again.

"Jack?" she called, feeling her anxiety triple. She was sure he was fine, of course, but Mimi *was* in Cairo. He had said so himself—and Schuyler began to feel a cold dread in her stomach. "JACK!" *Jack?* she sent. *Where are you?* When she turned, her wristwatch caught on the rug, unraveling part of the wool.

"You buy! You break, you buy!" the shopkeeper screamed. "You buy!"

"Jack!" Schuyler called, brushing the salesman away. Had he found the guide? Where did he go? Why wasn't he answering her call in the glom?

"Miss! You buy this! You broke, you buy! One hundred dollar!" The rug merchant gripped her arm and yelled into her ear.

Schuyler pushed him away, sending the tubby fellow

crashing into a display of lamps. "Oh my god, I'm so sorry," she said, which enraged him even more, and now there were two shopkeepers demanding payment for broken objects.

Starting to feel as if she had been set up, she looked around wildly for Jack, and when she finally saw him, she was horrified to find a hooded assailant coming up from behind him, sunlight glinting off a silver blade. The market was so busy, no one noticed. Tourists and shoppers walked by, oblivious to the danger around them.

She was paralyzed, too frightened to scream, but at the last moment, Jack turned around and swiftly disarmed his attacker and gained the upper hand. But then he looked up in her direction and suddenly released his hold.

What was he doing? Schuyler was about to call to him when a black hood was thrust over her head and she found herself being dragged, kicking and screaming. The noise of the market and the chaos created by the enraged rug and lamp sellers drowned out her cries, and she was pulled away from the crowd into a quiet back alley.

Her attacker kept a solid hold around her neck, but Schuyler ordered her mind to calm, and reached for the hilt of her blade. In a flash, she was gripping its golden handle.

"Your friend has already surrendered his weapon," a cold female voice said. "I suggest you do the same."

Schuyler dropped her mother's sword.

FIVE

The Pyramids of Giza

*T*here was a sleek black limousine waiting at the hotel entrance, and a uniformed chauffeur greeted them with a bow and held the door open as they neared it. "Much better," Mimi said, thankful that she wouldn't have to play the cab-fare game today at least.

"I thought it would be." Oliver smiled. "After you."

Even if the pyramids were located practically at the hotel doorstep, the car moved at an ant's pace through the crowded streets. While popular perception held that the pyramids were located in the middle of a vast desert landscape, lone pylons against a blank sky, in reality they were located next to the crowded Giza suburbs, and the scene at the complex was distinctively carnival-like, packed not only with tourists from all over the world, but schoolchildren on field trips, souvenir hawks, spitting camels, and flag-waving tour guides. If Mimi cared to do her memory exercises, she would recall that it had always been this way. The pyramids had been built by Blue Blood pharaohs as oculi in the glom, lighthouses for the spirits, *ka*, to find their way home. But ever since they had been constructed, the Red Bloods had descended upon them like moths to the light, marveling at their size and beauty. The vampires had found it odd, but from the beginning, the pyramids had always been tourist attractions.

The driver parked them as close as he could to the entrance of the site, and they exited the car. Mimi shielded her eyes from the sun's glare and looked up at the magnificent structures. They were immense, each stone larger than the tallest man. She remembered that they had been much more beautiful in their original incarnation, covered with polished white limestone blocks. It was a pity they had been stripped over the millennia for use in other building projects. Only the second largest pyramid, Khafra, still had limestone casing at its peak.

Across from the pyramid complex was the Giza Hut, as everyone called the Pizza Hut located across the street. During their first trip to Cairo, Mimi and Oliver had caught lunch there, and Oliver had taken a photo that showed the cheerful modern restaurant logo next to a window with a view of the tombs. You didn't have to be a Blue Blood to appreciate the delicious irony or the piping-hot pizza.

It was sheer luck, of course, that Mimi and Oliver had discovered this entrance to the underworld at all. Oliver had studied the repository files and concluded that the Gate of Promise was located in the city of Alexandria, but when they landed in Cairo, Oliver suddenly changed his mind when a fellow traveler called the city the "Big Mango," which led to a conversation about the roots of the city's name. He hadn't been able to hide his excitement when he discovered that Cairo was called "the victorious city." *The victor's city on the shore of the river of gold*, Oliver had explained, reading from his notes. Not that Mimi had understood a word about all that Gates of Hell hullabaloo. They never did make it to Alexandria, as Oliver had been convinced the gate was in Cairo, and Mimi had followed his lead.

As they walked through the crowded bazaar, Mimi ruminated on their relatively easy path down to Hell. Wasn't this one of those famous gates her brother's bondmate was looking for? From the so-called Van Alen Legacy? Could it be possible that Jack was nearby? She could sense something in the air, something in the glom that felt like his signature, but she wasn't sure. It had been so long since they had been able to communicate telepathically, so long since she had been able to read his mind. Mimi felt the old bubbling of hatred rising like bile in her throat. Whenever she thought of her twin, her mouth turned dry, like ashes and sand. She would have his life one day, she promised herself. He owed her a blood trial, a combat to the death. But she pushed aside her venomous thoughts for now. Descending into the underworld required her full attention.

Even if her and Oliver's journey would not require a Death Walk—that far more dangerous venture that only highly skilled Venators could manage, since one had to hide the spirit trail in order to mimic death—it was still far from easy and no doubt would be hard on her human companion. Mimi planned for them to walk into the glom with their physical selves intact; there would be no division between the mind and the body. DeathWalkers had the ability to be anywhere in the underworld at any time. This way, she and Oliver would be much slower and easier targets, but they didn't have much of a choice, as Oliver was human and unable to separate his spirit from his physical shell. She had no ambition to become a DeathWalker anyway. It was much too risky.

But first they had to reach the gate, of course. The best way to reach their destination was on horse or camel, and once again, Oliver proved his worth, as he had already arranged for guides and two beautiful black Arabian horses to take them to the tombs. Mimi had won many equestrian ribbons and was quickly trotting her horse, while Oliver looked a little awkward in the saddle and had more difficulty controlling his mare. "I should have let my mother talk me into riding lessons instead of ballroom, huh?" He grimaced.

Mimi clucked her tongue. "You need to hold the reins a little tighter. Show her who's boss."

They picked their way past the public entrances near

the great pyramid of Khufu, the largest of the three, and another one by the Sphinx, which, unlike the pyramids, looked smaller in real life than it did in pictures.

There wasn't much to see inside the pyramids, which were essentially empty tombs and not for the claustrophobic. The path to the underworld was located in Menkaure, the smallest pyramid. They left the horses tied to a tree, made sure the guides had food and water for them, and walked toward the entrance.

"Off-limits. Private tours inside are that way, miss," a guard said, blocking their approach and pointing to the other pyramid.

"We're just going to be a second," Mimi said, using compulsion to make him look the other way. Truly it was so easy: the Red Blood mind was so malleable. When he turned, she unlocked the doors with a spell, and Oliver led them inside and down the underground stairs.

The Gates of Hell had been built upon the Paths of the Dead by the Order of the Seven during Caligula's reign, to secure the earthly domain from the demons of the underworld. The gates kept the Silver Bloods trapped behind them, but anyone could walk in from the other side and into Hell if they knew the way; although Red Bloods usually had to wait until the end of their lives to reach the Kingdom of the Dead.

Mimi pulled Oliver through the living glom, the alternate world hidden from the physical one. "How are you feeling?"

she asked, as he doubled over, clutching his stomach.

"Nauseous. But I'll live," he said, wiping his mouth with his handkerchief.

For now, at least, Mimi thought.

In the distance stood a small metal gate, not unlike a garden gate, secured with a hook latch. "That's it?" Oliver asked skeptically. "That's the Gate of Promise? It looks like it keeps children out of a pool."

"Yeah, well." Mimi shrugged, unhooking the lock. "I think it looks different to everyone. From the other side it looks like a fortress. You ready? You might feel a little sick."

"Even more than I do now? You should have told me to pack a barf bag." Oliver wiped his brow and took a few deep breaths.

Mimi rolled her eyes. She held the gate open, and they crossed the threshold together. One step felt equal to a mile, or seven leagues, and after a few paces they were in Limbo, the first circle of Hell's Kingdom. The space between the worlds manifested as a vast desert landscape, not dissimilar to the one they'd just left, with a lone road cutting through the sand, but without the pyramids.

"It's easier on the transition if it looks like where we came from," Mimi explained.

Oliver thought it looked a bit like the Mojave Desert in Death Valley, rocky and abandoned. There were palm trees in the distance, and tumbleweeds blew along the highway;

the heat was oppressive, and he was sweating through his safari vest.

"Let's go," Mimi said, jangling keys to a red Mustang convertible that had materialized by the side of the road. "Get in, I'm driving. I know the way."

"Of course you do." Oliver coughed, but he followed her lead.

Azrael, Angel of Death, had come home.

SIX

Portrait of the Artist as a Young Heir

*A*llegra arrived late to the party. She had spent too long standing in front of the mirror, wondering what to wear and feeling nervous. Nothing she'd brought from New York felt right: she hated all her clothes. Charles had gone to the exhibit opening as planned. Allegra had been able to convince him she did not feel like making social chitchat that evening and preferred to stay in and catch up on her reading. Luckily, he had been too excited about the chance to see the remarkable collection of ancient South American art to press for her company. Charles enjoyed the social whirl, enjoyed basking in the attention of a worshipful Coven, and she knew he would not miss her.

The minute the door closed behind Charles, Allegra stormed her closet. The last time Ben had seen her she was sixteen years old, fresh-faced, brimming with youth and life and energy; and while she knew that five years was not such a long time, she did feel older, much more aware of her beauty and the reaction it engendered from the opposite sex. She wore her hair shorter now, cut close to the scalp, almost boyish, and Charles hated it—he'd adored her long golden tresses, had loved winding his fingers through the gossamer thickness. He had been disappointed when she'd returned from the salon with her new haircut.

But Allegra loved the liberating relief: no more of that heaviness behind her neck—she had always been too hot in the summer—and no longer did traffic screech to a stop when she ran across the street, nor did heads turn when she walked down the sidewalk, her golden hair flowing behind her like a sail. She enjoyed being a little less conspicuous, a little more forgettable, a little more ordinary, almost as if she were someone else for a change. But now, as she rubbed the blunt edges of her chopped crop, she fretted that maybe Charles was right, that without her hair she did not look like herself; that shorn of her best asset, she looked dull and plain.

She decided upon an old standby, a white silk shirt, a pair of men's Levi's, a thick leather belt, and battered cowboy boots.

The party was in a hilltop mansion in Pacific Heights. Allegra slipped past the gilded doors and took a champagne flute from a waiter carrying a silver tray. She made her way through the good-looking, moneyed crowd—women in fur and velvet, men in Japanese-tailored jackets. The party was centered in the living room, a comfortable book-lined space with a breathtaking view of the Golden Gate and a real Monet above the fireplace. Yet for all the rare antiques and remarkable art on display, it still managed to be warm and welcoming at the same time.

"You look so familiar. I'm Decca Chase. Welcome to our home." One of San Francisco's premier society matrons, who also happened to be Ben's mother, smiled at Allegra. "You're the girl in the paintings, aren't you?"

There were more of them? Allegra wondered. She had only seen one at the gallery. "Mrs. Chase," she said, "it's so nice to see you again."

"So we have met before!" Ben's mother said with delight. She was tall, like her son, and shared his all-American, rangy good looks, and was impeccably dressed in swaths of white cashmere. Allegra recalled something her prep-school roommate had told her, that Ben's mother was an heiress to a great San Francisco fortune, and his middle name came from his mother's side of the family.

"I went to school with Ben. At Endicott," Allegra explained, feeling a little intimidated by her friendly host.

"Of course you did! He'll be glad to see an old friend." Decca Chase swiveled through the party, holding Allegra's hand, and finally stopped in front of a tall boy in a shabby blue jacket who was regaling a large and adoring crowd with a fascinating story that had them snorting into their cocktails. "Look who I found," she said triumphantly.

Allegra suddenly felt very self-conscious and wished that she had attended that museum opening with Charles. What was she doing here? She didn't belong here. His mom was being so nice it was painful. Maybe she could simply disappear from the party and no one would ever remember she was there. But she felt rooted to the spot, and Ben was turning around to greet her.

He looked exactly the same—tall and golden-haired, with the same friendly, happy grin, the same sparkling blue eyes, his entire personality as clear and sunny as a summer afternoon. "Legs!" he said. It hurt Allegra to hear that old nickname a little, and to hear him use it so easily. He gave her a hearty embrace and a quick peck on the cheek, as if they were just old schoolmates and nothing more. . . . As if she had never marked him, had never taken his blood and made it hers.

She wondered what had possessed her to come tonight. Why had she come? What had she feared? Had she come to see whether he was ruined somehow—whether she had destroyed him? Was she disappointed to find she had not? No. She had done right in leaving Endicott when she had, after she'd been warned by the vision. Look, he was better off without her. He was the same old Ben, with his ruddy cheeks and dimpled smile. He was wearing a frayed rep tie as a belt—still the same old preppie. The jeans were nattily paint splattered, of course. But if there was any pretense or calculation, she could not find it in him. He was natural and friendly, so hard to dislike, one of those boys whom everyone loved, which was why Charles had loathed him from the beginning.

"Ben, hi," Allegra said, returning his kiss on the cheek, her smile masking the riot of emotions she felt under the surface.

"No one calls me that anymore," he said, taking a sip from his beer glass and regarding her thoughtfully.

"No one calls me 'Legs' either, but you," she said faintly.

Ben grinned. "I'm only teasing. Call me whatever you want. Or don't call me at all," he joked. The crowd around him dispersed, as it was obvious the gorgeous new girl—and Allegra should never have doubted; she was still stunning even with the short haircut—had his entire attention.

"Well, you kids get reacquainted. I should go see what your father is up to; make sure he hasn't eaten all the caviar puffs," Decca Chase said, looking contentedly at the two of them. Allegra had forgotten his mother was there. She and Ben watched her move easily through the crowd, pinching an elbow here, laughing at a joke over there, the consummate hostess.

A waiter slid by to refill Allegra's champagne glass, and she was glad for the distraction. She did not know what to say to Ben. She still didn't know what she was doing here. Only that the opportunity had arisen to see him again, and she had grabbed it, like a drowning man reaching for a life preserver. "Your mom is cool. You never said she was cool."

She remembered that he'd said his parents didn't have much time for him growing up. Perhaps they were making up for it now, with this splashy party.

"I forgot to mention it." Ben grinned. "Oh, right. I did give you the Poor Little Rich Boy act, didn't I?"

Allegra laughed. He could always make her laugh, and she had missed their easy camaraderie. "Nice house," she said, raising her eyebrows at the Picasso above the dining table.

Ben rolled his eyes. "My parents," he said. "The worst thing about having money is that I don't get to be a starving artist."

"Is it that bad?" Allegra said, with a slightly mocking tone.

"Oh, it's the worst," Ben said cheerfully. "I get to eat well, and my mom uses her connections to get everyone to write about me or buy my work. It's rough, I'm telling you."

Allegra smiled. Ben's background was just part of him. He was not responsible for who his parents were—he was just lucky to be their son.

Ben looked at her closely. "You cut your hair," he said, his brow furrowing.

"Thought it was time for a change," she said, trying to feel brave. God, he hated it, she could tell. Why had she ever cut her hair? What was she thinking?

"I like it," he said with a nod of approval. "By the way, the gallery told me you bought a painting."

"I did." She nodded, noticing that there was a group of people hanging around them, waiting for Ben to release her so they could pounce on him.

"Good, I need the money."

"Liar." She motioned to his adoring crowd. "I think I'm keeping you from your fans."

"Ah, screw them." Ben grinned. "It's really good to see you, Legs," he said warmly. "You want to come by the studio tomorrow? See a couple of other things? I promise I won't try to sell them to you. Well, maybe not *all.*"

He wanted to see her again. Allegra's heart skipped a beat. "Sure. Why not." She shrugged nonchalantly, as if she would only stop by if she had nothing better to do.

His face lit up and he looked downright jolly. "Great! I'll have the gallery give you the address."

Finally, one of the hovering guests, an older gentleman with a trimmed beard, grew tired of waiting. "Stephen, excuse my interruption, but you must meet one of our best clients—he's thrilled with your work and is insistent on buying the entire collection."

"One sec," Ben told his dealer. "Sorry about this," he said to Allegra. "Work calls. But stay. Enjoy the party. Some of the old crowd is here—a bunch of Peithologians, at least. You'll find them at the bar doing shots. Old habits die hard."

Then he was gone, taken away by his guests who had come to celebrate his success.

Ben was happy, friendly, fine. He was *fine*. Allegra resolved to feel happy for him, and glad that she had done the right thing in nipping their little affair—whatever it was—right in the bud. As she wandered in the direction of the bar to find her old friends, she couldn't help but smile to herself. She was glad he'd liked her hair.

SEVEN

Mirror Images

Their abductors led them away from the souk, and Schuyler was shoved inside a vehicle that quickly sped away over bumpy roads. She thought she could feel Jack's presence next to her, but she wasn't sure. The hood they had thrown over her head was disorienting—not a normal dark cloth, but one that was made to subdue vampire sight; yet another weapon in the Venator arsenal. She wasn't sure how much time had passed, but finally she was pulled out of the car and led indoors. Schuyler began to feel frightened, but she wanted to be strong.

Are you all right? asked Jack's calm voice inside her head. *If they harmed you I will tear them apart limb by limb.*

So Jack was here. Relief flooded over her as she answered him. *I am fine. Where are we? Who has taken us?* Her mind raced—Venators from New York? Or had the Countess's forces regrouped?

Before Jack could answer, the hood was removed from her face, but it was quickly replaced by a knife underneath her chin, and her assailant was pulling her hair so that her neck was vulnerable. Jack was sitting across from her, similarly subdued, his hands bound. His glass-green eyes glinted in anger, but he kept his fearsome power in check. He could have killed them with a word, but once again, he had been restrained by his weakness—his love for her. With Schuyler in danger, Jack was effectively powerless, and she hated that most about herself, that she could be used to control him.

The girl who held a knife at Schuyler's throat was a beautiful Chinese Venator, dressed in a uniform denoting a high command, with three silver crosses embroidered on the collar.

"Hold. This is one of ours." Her companion, a stocky boy with an open face, gestured toward Jack. "General Abbadon. This is a surprise. Deming, did you not recognize him?"

"Rujiel," Jack said, using the Venator's angel name as he carefully and expertly removed the bindings around his hands as if they were made of string. "I did not realize the West Winds had cast their lot with traitors. I am disappointed to find you and your brother answering to Drusilla's command."

"We are no traitors," Sam Lennox replied sharply. "The Countess might have turned the European Coven, but we do not do her bidding. And neither do we work for your sister anymore."

"Good thing, too, or you'd be on the next plane back to the city," Ted said with a growl.

"Well then, would you kindly ask your friend to let my wife go?" Jack asked. "If it is true that we are not in opposition, there is no need for this animosity."

The Chinese girl looked questioningly at Sam, who nodded, and she withdrew her knife.

Schuyler exhaled. "My mother's sword. Where is it?"

Another girl—with the exact same face as the Venator who'd accosted her, tossed her the blade, and Schuyler caught it deftly and let it shrink down to size, then put it in her pocket. The Chinese Venators and the Lennox twins were an interesting match. Mirror images of each other, they moved with complementary grace and dexterity, like a well-oiled machine fueled by centuries-old expertise. They looked battle-hardened and weary.

Jack took charge of the situation—naturally assuming that the mantle of leadership fell on his shoulders—and introduced everyone. "Schuyler, these are Sam and Ted Lennox, also known as the brothers Rujiel and Ruhuel, the Angels of the West Wind. Good soldiers. They were part of my legion a long time ago. I believe they were last on Kingsley Martin's team in Rio. And if I'm not mistaken, these charming ladies are Deming and Dehua Chen. I remember you two from the Four Hundred Ball." He motioned to Schuyler. "This is Schuyler Van Alen. My bondmate."

"The famous Jack Force," Deming said, her voice

dripping with contempt. While the Lennox twins might have deferred to Jack as their old commander, it was obvious she did not feel a similar respect. She was stronger and fiercer-looking than her twin, Dehua, who had a gentler demeanor. Schuyler had no doubt that Deming would have slashed her throat without hesitation. "I remember you as well," Deming told Jack. "They said in New York that you had run away with Gabrielle's Abomination and broken your bond with Azrael. I did not believe it was true." She looked at him with such distaste that Schuyler fully understood for the first time the enormity of what Jack had given up for her—his lofty, honored place in the vampire community, his pride, and his word. In the Venator's eyes he was nothing more than a lowly coward, someone who had broken a heavenly promise.

"Careful. I do not care for that word or that accusation. I will not have my wife insulted in such a manner." Jack spoke softly, but his words carried the weight of a threat.

"It is the truth," Deming said. "Gabrielle's mistake was bad enough, but you have made it worse by breaking your oath and taking up with her spawn."

"You will apologize for your rudeness!" Jack ordered, leaping to his feet.

Deming stuck out her chin, looking as haughty as a Chinese empress. "You forget we no longer answer to your bidding. Azrael kept her honor. Where is yours?"

"Let me show you." Jack smiled and reached for his sword.

In a flash, the two had crossed blades, and sparks flew from the heavenly steel.

"Do not threaten my sister," Dehua warned, unleashing her weapon as well, while Sam and Ted Lennox did the same.

"Careful, Abbadon," Sam said. "We are not your enemies, but we will protect our own."

This had gone far enough. Schuyler jumped between the warring angels, her hands outstretched so that all were forced to lower their swords.

"Jack, it's all right. Deming, you don't know me, but I'm hoping that we can all make peace somehow. There's something more important at stake here than any of us," Schuyler said. "Please. If we fight between ourselves, we lose everything."

Deming glowered, but Jack backed down. "You are right as usual," he said to Schuyler, with a soft look on his face. He turned back to his adversary. "I warn you, *Kuan Yin*, that I will insist on my wife receiving your utmost respect. But I apologize for threatening you."

Weapons were quickly holstered, and the couples reunited—Sam and Deming and Ted and Dehua instinctively going to each other's sides. They looked at the newcomers warily, unsure what to do with them.

"Well then," Jack said, as if nothing had happened. "If you four are not here to drag me into the Countess's service, or bring me back to my sister for the blood trial, why did you ambush us?"

"We hunt Nephilim," Deming said. She pointed her sword at Schuyler, and for a moment it looked as if another fight would break out. But the Venator said simply, "Her glom signature was muddied, a mixture of divine and human, like theirs. We thought she was one of them."

EIGHT

Checkpoint Charlie

*O*liver remembered the trip to the Mojave. It had been one of those last-minute excursions. His parents had friends who lived in Palm Springs, and their kids—a couple of spoiled California teenagers, Brentwood bohos with shaggy hair and expensive toys—had asked if he wanted to see Death Valley with them. There had been talk of looking for an abandoned ghost town, and Oliver had jumped at the chance to go, since anything was better than sitting around while the adults got drunk on Pimm's Cup and talked about tennis tournaments.

At first he had worried he'd made a mistake. The dirt roads through the canyons were flooded from a rainstorm, and what was supposed to have been a two-hour trip became an eight-hour odyssey and a bit of a nightmare. But thankfully, his hosts had turned out to be good-humored and up for the adventure, instead of sulking and annoyed, and they'd had fun driving through the vast empty desert landscape that looked a bit like pictures he'd seen of the surface of the moon, lonely and vacant and odd.

"Was it like this the first time you were here?" Oliver asked Mimi as he peered out the dusty window.

"No. It's always different. I think it looks like this because you're with me. It uses things from your mind that you can process."

Oliver fiddled with the radio tuner on the dashboard, but the only music was Wagner.

"Figures," Mimi said. "Helda's a fan. You might as well rest a bit. We won't get there for a while."

"How long have we been down here?"

"Time isn't the same," Mimi explained. "Not like it is up there. In the underworld, there isn't a past or a future; there's only now. We get there when we get there. It's a test of endurance. We could drive in circles forever as a punishment."

"Good lord."

"Wrong guy." Mimi smirked. "But you're not dead, and I'm not human, so I think Helda's just playing with us."

"Who's this Helda you keep talking about?"

"She sort of runs the place. Named it after herself."

"Right."

Oliver took a series of naps, but since time was no longer a factor, it was difficult to tell how he was supposed to feel. Was he hungry? He'd had an enormous breakfast, but the transition from the glom had taken a lot out of him. Did they serve lunch in Hell? Should he have packed a snack? Why was he suddenly thinking about food? He felt tired and mixed up; it felt a little like jet lag, which he was still fighting. He hoped Mimi knew where she was going.

He had agreed to come with her. After graduation, when Mimi heard he had deferred his Harvard acceptance, she had offered him the position as her Conduit, and he had accepted. His parents had tried to talk him out of it, had wanted him to keep his position at the Repository, where he would be safe. But the clerks were only interested in storing and archiving, preparing for the eventual dissolution of the Coven. It was disheartening. He wasn't sure what would happen if the vampires went underground, and his parents didn't seem to know either. Joining Mimi seemed the more adventuresome task, and he wanted to be of service. He didn't want to spend hours doing inventory.

It was also becoming clear to Oliver that Mimi could not handle the Regency alone, and she would need Kingsley's firm hand alongside hers to guide the flailing Coven. Oliver took his duty as a vampire's Conduit seriously. He would not let the Coven fail, and he was determined to fulfill his duty to the Blue Bloods by ensuring that Mimi had what she needed to keep the Coven safe and whole, no matter what kind of sacrifice it would entail on his part.

Besides, he considered Mimi a friend. They had come to an understanding, and Oliver was surprised at how well they got along. He'd realized that underneath the princess act was an old and practical creature, and he respected her. When she'd invited him to come down to the underworld with her, he'd jumped at the chance, out of duty, curiosity, and a desire to make sure she was safe. She might be the fearsome Angel of Death, but even Mimi had a heart that could be broken, and Oliver didn't want her to be alone if she failed in rescuing Kingsley. She would need a friend. What did he have to lose? He'd already lost Schuyler.

Still, they drove for what seemed like hours. For miles and miles there was nothing on the radio but the "Ride of the Valkyries," which definitely got old after the *nth* go-round. Oliver could sense Mimi's growing frustration, and it was with relief that at last they reached a primitive-looking checkpoint—just a wooden sawhorse against the road—and beyond it a small gas station.

Two men—Oliver thought they looked like men, but on closer look they were not men at all—spoke to Mimi in a language he could not understand. They were almost nine feet tall, and their large bulky bodies were covered in matted brown fur, while their facial features were gnarled and twisted, with bulbous noses and beady yellow eyes. They wore painful-looking collars made of silver barbed wire.

Mimi made some strange noises that sounded like grunts. After a moment the men moved away to confer with their supervisor.

"What *are* they?" Oliver whispered.

"Trolls. They work here . . . for the demons."

"Ugly things." Oliver shuddered. "Those collars."

"The only thing keeping them from attacking us," Mimi said in a matter-of-fact tone.

The collars were wound tightly around the trolls' necks, and drew blood every time they moved. Oliver could not help but feel repulsion and pity for the creatures.

He looked around. "So this Helda you're meeting— she's a demon?"

"No." Mimi shook her head. "She's more like their . . . grandmother."

Oliver blanched, and Mimi continued to explain. "She's one of the goddesses. The old ones, before we came along, like the witch we visited in North Hampton."

"There's so much I don't know about the world," Oliver murmured.

The trolls returned and motioned to a gas station beyond the checkpoint. Mimi parked the car. "Wait here," she said.

"With them?" Oliver balked. He wished he'd thought to put the roof up, but now it was too late. The trolls sniffed him, one leaning forward so closely, Oliver could feel its hot breath on his cheek. "Human," it said to the other, in perfect English.

"Living." His friend nodded with a sly smile.

"He's mine, *beastia*! Touch him and you'll know the taste of Azrael's steel," Mimi snapped. The trolls backed away, but Oliver wasn't sure if he felt safer. They were still looking at him as if he were dinner.

"They're only teasing you. They don't eat meat," she assured him. Mimi neglected to add "only souls," but Oliver didn't have to know that, and he looked terrified enough already. "Stop being such a wuss. Trolls, leave him alone."

Mimi walked toward the small office located in the back of the gas station. She didn't want to tell Oliver, but the endless driving had bothered her. She'd worried that it was a sign that Helda would not allow her past the lower levels, and she would have to reach the seventh if she was going to find Kingsley. Another troll, a fierce female with a bronze mane, guarded the door to Helda's office. The she-troll was wearing a heavy iron sash loaded with bullets, and carrying what looked like an AK-47. She gave Mimi a pat-down to check for weapons. "What's this?" she asked, her hand on Mimi's back.

Amazing that the troll had found the needle Mimi kept pinned to her bra. "It's my sword."

"You'll have to leave it here. You can have it back when you finish with Helda."

Mimi complied and handed over her needle, pulling it out from underneath her shirt. "Can I go in now?"

The troll nodded and kicked the door open.

Helda did not look pleased to see her. The Queen of the Dead was an older woman dressed in severe black, her hair in a tight gray bun. Her face was wrinkled and drawn, and she had the thin, puckered lips of a lifelong smoker, as well as the hard beady eyes of a gambler who had spent her last dollar on a losing horse. She looked nothing like her niece in North Hampton. There was something cruel and ancient about her, as if she had seen the world at its worst and had merely shrugged. She sat behind a desk that was messy with ledgers, receipts, crumpled notes, and torn envelopes. It looked like the desk of a harried accountant, which, when Mimi thought about it, was what Helda was, since the Kingdom of the Dead was a little like a bureaucracy that collected souls instead of taxes. "You're back," she said flatly.

"Thanks to your niece," Mimi said.

"Which one?"

"Erda."

"How disappointing. Erda was always the smarter one. Freya, she would do it just to spite me." Helda regarded Mimi coolly. Mimi thought Helda was not unlike one of those rich women who ran the charity committees and took pleasure in excluding social climbers from the group. "So. What do you seek from my domain, Azrael?"

"You know what I want. The same thing I wanted last time. I've come to retrieve a soul from beyond the *subvertio.*"

"Back for Araquiel, are you? Shame. He's been an asset down here; a great help keeping the demons in line. There's no way I can dissuade you from your quest?"

Mimi shook her head. Did Helda expect her to believe that crap? Kingsley was suffering down here. Who knew what kind of tortures and agonies he'd endured. She didn't know what kind of game Helda was playing, but she decided to keep her mouth shut so the old bird would let her pass.

"You are prepared this time. You have your barter?" Helda asked.

"I do," Mimi said, motioning to the window.

Helda observed Oliver trying to lean as far away from the trolls as possible without looking like he was avoiding them. "I see," she sighed. "A human's a poor substitute for the soul you're taking from me. But very well. If you are able to convince Araquiel to return with you, you may have him."

NINE

Studio Session

The address that the gallery assistant had left on her answering machine brought Allegra to a warehouse near Market Street. She took a creaky factory elevator to a loft on the top floor.

Last night she had spent the remainder of the party reminiscing about high school with her old friends, many of whom were starting their lives in the world: newly minted investment bankers and law students, a scattering of television PA's and cub reporters, along with fashion assistants and the self-described ladies and gentlemen of leisure who had come into their inheritances and were whiling away their days on the social circuit—their lives a succession of parties and benefits and festivals; a jet-setting crowd who frequented Wimbledon, Art Basel, and the Venice Film Festival. Her friends had cooed over her new haircut and wanted to know why she had disappeared from their lives without an explanation. People like Allegra were not supposed to do such disagreeable things. Their kind kept in touch out of habit, forever recounting the glory days when one had been a scrapper at St. Paul's or Endicott. She had apologized profusely and promised to have them all over, in New York, once they were finished with the renovations on the town house on Fifth Avenue, where she and Charles were supposed to live after they were bonded.

The elevator opened right into Ben's studio. "Hello?"

"In here!" Ben called. She walked out to find him standing in front of a large painting, wiping his hands on a wet rag. "You're here," he said, as if he didn't quite believe it. He put the rag away and wiped his hands on his jeans. He was nervous, she was surprised to discover. He had none of the breezy nonchalance he'd displayed the night before.

"You invited me."

"I wasn't sure you would come," he admitted.

"Well, I'm here now." She gave him a tentative smile. She didn't know why he was acting so strange. Had she misread him? He had invited her to see the studio, and she had thought it was a sincere invitation—not one of those casual, polite things that people say to each other at dinner parties. Was this yet another mistake? She had woken up this morning excited at the prospect of seeing him again, and hoping that he would be alone. They stood facing each other for so long that Allegra finally felt he was being rude. "Well, are you going to show me your work?"

Ben blushed. "Sorry, seem to have forgotten my manners. Please, by all means."

Allegra walked around the room. The studio was a large white loft with floor-to-ceiling windows overlooking the bay. There were paint cans and paintbrushes everywhere, and plastic on the floor. The oily smell of gesso filled the air.

"Sorry it's a bit messy," he said.

She nodded, not quite sure what to say. The loft was filled with an assortment of canvases in all sizes, a few stretched eight feet high and ten feet across. There were smaller paintings propped on easels or tacked on the walls. Some were framed and encased in plastic. As Allegra looked around, she noticed a theme in all of his work. Every painting— from the mural that showed a girl lying dreamily in bed, like a modern odalisque, to the small ones, which were like the one she had purchased—each and every painting in the studio was a portrait of her.

She walked through the space, studying the paintings and drawings in complete silence and utter shock. Ben followed her wordlessly, waiting to hear her reaction. For now, she didn't have one. She was merely processing the information he was giving her. The paintings held the breadth of their short love story: Allegra on the bed, in her white camisole; Allegra in the woods, the night of her initiation into the Peithologians, "a secret society of poets and adventurers," which meant they got drunk in the forest after curfew; Allegra holding up a Latin textbook, laughing at how terrible she was at the language; Allegra nude, her back turned to the viewer. There was a small dark painting, all black except for the bright blond hair and ivory fangs. Allegra the vampire princess.

She understood now. The carefree artist and jocular heir-about-town from the night before was all an act. The familiar's kiss had marked him, had changed him, and in order to deal with her abandonment, he had created a shrine to her. This obsessive recollection of every moment of their relationship was his way of keeping her close to him. He painted her over and over so that he would never forget her. It was all there—his love and need for her. This was his true heart, open and exposed and bleeding.

Now she understood what his mother had tried to tell her when she had said, "You're the girl in the paintings." Decca Chase was worried about her boy, and had thought that maybe if she brought Allegra to him, he would find a way to be with her or get over her. Smart woman.

Ben shuffled his feet, his face slowly turning a brilliant shade of crimson. He gulped. "Well, what do you think?"

"I'm so sorry for leaving you," Allegra said slowly, not quite able to meet his eyes. "I'm so sorry I disappeared that night. You don't understand—I'm not free. . . . I don't have a choice about whom I can love. You have to forget about me. . . . It's better for everyone. For you."

Ben frowned. "No . . . no . . . you don't understand."

But Allegra was back in the elevator, and this time she would not return. She had made a mistake in seeking him out, in putting her entire future at risk, and she would not make it again.

Sometimes it was better to keep Pandora's box closed.

TEN

City of the Dead

*I*t was only after the Venators had relaxed their hostile stance that Schuyler noticed their surroundings. They were inside a small stone room, and she wasn't sure, but it looked as if the shelves were made from grave markers, and that two ornately carved tombstones formed a table. "Are we where I think we are?" she asked.

Sam nodded, apologized for the smell, and explained why they were living in a mausoleum, called the City of the Dead by the locals. They were in the eastern part of the city, in a necropolis that served as a home for people whose ancestors were buried in the basement catacombs, or for those who had been forced out of the crowded areas of Cairo, unable to afford apartments. There were anywhere from thirty thousand to a million people living among the dead, Sam explained. The cemeteries were equipped with a minimal sewage and water system, while electric wires connected to nearby mosques provided light and heat. Since the tombs had been built to accommodate the traditional mourning period, when people stayed at the cemetery with their dead for the requisite forty days and nights, living in them was a natural progression when there were no other options.

"We got a lead on a Nephilim hive in Tehran. We shut that down, did the same to one in Tripoli, then came here when we heard rumors that girls have been disappearing from the City of the Dead." He explained that the disappearances and kidnappings did not conform to typical Red Blood crimes. There was a systemic, even ritualized aspect to them that piqued the Venators' interest. "It's got Hellborn written all over it, so we've been bunking here to be close to the target."

"Last week we raided their nest and got them all—except for one that got away," Deming told them.

"You thought that was me," Schuyler said.

Deming nodded. "Yes." She did not apologize for the mistake. She recounted the events in New York, how she had caught the Nephilim who had been after the vampires.

"So it is as we suspected," Schuyler said, catching her breath at the news. "This has been going on for some time now." She told them what they had discovered in Florence, and confirmed what the Venators already knew about bloody work of the Petruvian priests, who hunted and killed the human women who had been taken by Croatan, along with their offspring. "The girl who'd been taken had a mark on her: three intertwining circles that contained Lucifer's sigil, a sheep, and the Blue Blood symbol for union."

"Paul—the Nephilim in New York—carried the same symbol on his arm," Deming said. "It looked like a birthmark instead of a tattoo. All the Nephilim carry it on their bodies."

"But they aren't born evil," Schuyler said. "These women and children are victims of a vicious crime; they're innocent."

"I don't know about innocent," Deming argued. "Paul Rayburn took two immortal lives. Who knows how many more vampires he's murdered over the years."

"So these Petruvians . . . these killing priests who believe they do God's work," Sam said. "I had never heard of them until Deming told us what that bastard said, and I'll bet no one in any Coven has either, which means they're not part of the official history. How can that be?" he asked his former commander.

"I don't know." Jack frowned. "I was not part of the Order of the Seven and not privy to decisions made at the time."

"Regardless, the Petruvians' cleansing goes against everything in the Code of the Vampires, which mandates the protection of human life," Schuyler maintained.

"The Nephilim are not human," Deming said. "I have the scars to prove it." She raised her sleeve to show the white marks she carried from battling their foes.

"Has anyone seen the Venator reports on this area?" Jack asked. "I tried to find the local conclave offices, but no one would tell me where they had relocated."

Sam shook his head. "The Coven here is barely hanging on. Many of their members have been brutally murdered, burned—not just young ones but Elders. There was an attack at the Cairo Tower last month, their headquarters. That's why you couldn't find them. They're ready to go underground. It's like that everywhere. Our kind is retreating—they went back into the shadows."

"What's the latest in New York?" Jack wanted to know.

Deming and Sam exchanged glances. "The Regent's disappeared and supposedly she took the Repository keys with her, to keep the Coven from disbanding. No one knows where she went. But without your sister, New York is not going to last very long," Deming said.

So. Mimi was Regent. Oliver had told the truth. Schuyler watched Jack process this information. She thought she knew what he was thinking—that he should have been with Mimi; that without the twins, the Coven had no one.

"We thought Azrael had come after you," Ted said to Jack. "For the blood trial, when you didn't return to New York."

"We haven't seen Mimi," Schuyler said. "Not yet, anyway."

"What are you doing in Cairo?"

Schuyler was careful not to reveal the exact reason for

their journey. "We're looking for someone. Catherine of Siena, a friend of my grandfather's. Jack heard of a holy woman named Zani, who we thought might be her. One of her disciples was supposed to meet us at the market and take us to her. You guys must have scared him off. Do you know where we can find her?"

"The name rings a bell—where have we heard it before?" Sam asked.

"It's name of a priestess at the temple of Anubis," Deming said. "Where the girls have been disappearing."

ELEVEN

White Wedding

"Where to next? Is there a map?" Oliver asked. When he saw the look on Mimi's face, he felt chastened. "Okay, I promise to stop asking stupid questions. I'm just making conversation."

"There'll be a second checkpoint or something," Mimi explained. They were still driving through the desert, but after a few miles, Oliver noticed the road was now along a seashore, and he could see the blue waves of an ocean, and a breeze blew. If they were descending deeper into Hell, it was getting nicer instead of worse. Mimi drove until they spotted an elegant hotel by the beach.

"Am I dreaming? It looks like Martha's Vineyard," Oliver said. He recognized the hotel. It was a famous one on the island. He half expected a group of inebriated teenagers to walk out wearing Black Dog T-shirts.

Mimi pulled into the driveway and looked around

expectantly. When no one came to park the car, she sighed. "In Hell there's no valet?" she asked, driving into the parking lot.

Oliver chuckled. "Isn't that just like the Vineyard? What is this place?"

"We'll find out soon enough," Mimi said. They got out of the car and walked toward the resort entrance. There was music playing from a string quartet, and a waitress in a crisp white shirt and black pants appeared carrying a tray of champagne. "The party is in the back. Come join us."

Oliver took a glass. The champagne smelled delicious— buttery and bubbly, with a hint of apple and strawberries, along with a musky undertow of something earthy and delightful. He was not surprised to find he was wearing a khaki suit and a pressed white shirt, while Mimi was now wearing a plain linen dress and sandals, and she had a flower in her hair. "If this is what life is like in the underworld, it doesn't seem too bad," he said, clinking Mimi's glass.

"That's what you'd think, of course," Mimi said, rolling her eyes. "But wait till you've seen Paradise."

"What's that like?"

"It's been so long I don't even remember anymore. It was just—different. Peaceful," she said wistfully.

"Boring."

"No. It wasn't like that. Of course people think it would be boring, but it's not. It's like the best day of your life, for the rest of your life," Mimi said. "Anyway, it looks like we're here for some sort of wedding." They'd followed the crowd to the back of the hotel, by the beach, where white wooden folding chairs had been set up, and a sandy aisle led to a flowered trellis. The guests were a ruddy-cheeked New England bunch—the men in seersucker, the women in modest day dresses. Children ran round blowing bubbles. It was beautiful and festive, and not too hot.

Yet there was something about the scene that felt familiar, that felt too close to something that Oliver did not want to acknowledge, and he never took a sip from his glass. "Whose wedding is this?" he said, gritting his teeth, as the string quartet began to play "All Things Bright and Beautiful," his favorite hymn.

"Ours, of course." A girl appeared by his side. She looked exactly like Schuyler. She had Schuyler's long dark hair and bright blue eyes, and she was wearing her bonding dress, the one made of the palest blue silk that hung off her shoulders. She had a spray of freckles on her cheeks that she always got during the summers, which they used to spend together right on this beach.

Oliver did not know what to do or where to look. His cheeks burned, and he felt as if his heart had been put on display only to be humiliated and broken.

"Ollie, what's wrong?" She looked and sounded exactly like Schuyler. What was this—*who* was this? A true mirage. What devilry had created this doppelganger, Oliver thought, trying to move away from her. Where was Mimi? He looked around wildly but could not find her. Not-Sky took his arm and linked it through hers, the way she used to, and rested her head against his shoulder.

"I missed you," she said.

"I did too," Oliver replied, without thinking.

"I'm so glad you're here," she whispered.

He took back his words. This was Hell. He knew exactly where he was now, and exactly what this was. This was his deepest desire, his deepest secret, which he had buried deep inside his heart so that he had been able to fully celebrate with his dearest friend on her special day. Now, to see his desire so cruelly made real, forced him to acknowledge that even if he was healed, even if he did not ache for her anymore, even if he was no longer her familiar nor her Conduit, and merely her friend, he still loved her, and would always love her.

How was it possible to feel love and desire but no pain? Freya, the witch he had met in the East Village, had healed his blood of the familiar's mark, but his heart would always remember and would always yearn. As long as he lived, he knew he would love Schuyler Van Alen.

"Don't hate me, but I don't think I can go through with it. I love Jack. I do. But seeing you today . . . Ollie . . . I'm so sorry." The girl who wasn't Schuyler looked deep into his eyes, and it took his breath away.

"About what?" he asked, and it was then that he realized they were replaying the same conversation they'd had the night before her bonding—but it was going a different way, and he knew exactly what she would say before she said it, because they were the words he had wanted her to say.

"Making the biggest mistake of my life," she said huskily, tightening her grip on his arm. He could smell her perfume. She had started wearing it only recently, she'd explained back then. A scent made for Catherine de Médicis that she'd bought from the convent of Santa Maria Novella.

"Don't," he said in a strangled voice, and he pulled at his collar, as he had found it suddenly hard to breathe. "Don't do this. You're not Sky. Leave me alone."

"No, you have to hear it," she said, and put her mouth right on his ear. He could feel her soft breath as she whispered the words he wished she'd said to him on that fair day in December, in Italy. "I should never have left. I love you. *I love you more.*"

Then she was kissing him, and it was Schuyler's lips, and she smelled just like Schuyler, and her hair was silky and soft like Schuyler's, and he knew that when her back was turned, he would see a mole right between her shoulder blades that was just like Schuyler's. She *was* Schuyler, and she returned his love, and Oliver did not see why he had to pretend he did not want this, did not want her, did not want exactly what was happening right now.

TWELVE

Blood Service

"Charles! You're back so soon," Allegra said, when she returned to the apartment. She hadn't expected to see him, and as she pulled off her coat and scarf, she hoped that he would not notice her hands were shaking.

"Everything finished up earlier than expected." His eyes lit up upon seeing her walk into the room. "Where've you been?"

"Looking at paintings," she said. Since they could read each other's thoughts—up to a certain point—it was easier to conceal lies with half-truths.

"Did you buy anything else?" He knew about the purchase she'd made the day before, but not who the artist was, or what the subject of the painting was.

"Not today."

"It's nice that you've taken an interest in art again," he said, smiling affectionately at her. Charles had come into his own the last few years, shooting up to his full height. He had finally lost the awkward formality and stiffness he'd had as a teenager. These days he moved with confidence and grace. At twenty-one he had gotten hold of the substantial Van Alen trusts that made up the bulk of their inheritance, and he talked about building a media company, making a difference in the world. Recently tapped as one of New York's most eligible bachelors in a popular society magazine, Charles Van Alen was handsome and striking, with his dark blue-black hair and strong Roman features. He did not have Bendix Chase's affable geniality, but instead displayed a kingly benevolence that had earned him respect and fear beyond the vampire community.

He patted the space on the couch next to him, and Allegra cuddled up beside him, his arm curled over her shoulder. They fit together—they always had—it had just taken her too long to see it in this lifetime. She began to relax, feeling the distress of the day's revelations beginning to fade in his presence. What happened with Ben had been a mistake from the beginning, a schoolgirl crush, unworthy of her attention. She felt bad for Ben, of course. A familiar's mark was hard to bear, but Ben would be all right. He had money and comfort, and in time he would forget about her. If only she hadn't walked into that gallery.

"Everything all right with the Elders?" she asked. "What did they want?"

A dark shadow passed over Charles's face, but it cleared

without Allegra noticing. "Just the usual Transformation issues. I don't even know why they wanted me here. They're just wasting my time."

"Mr. Van Alen? Your car is here," the butler said, noiselessly entering the room.

"You're going out?" Allegra asked, leaning away from him. Charles knew she had plans that evening with her old field hockey teammates, and it was only natural that he would make plans of his own. "Dede is it?"

Charles nodded. He had started taking familiars, and looked robust, flush with blood and life, power and invincibility. As leader of the Coven, he was allowed certain privileges, and kept a retinue of familiars in every city, a girl in every port. He was good to them, showering gifts, attention, and the occasional bauble from Cartier or Buccellati. Allegra had seen the bills; she was the one who paid them: a rose-gold watch with a diamond bezel, its heavy weight like a comfort; sparkling bracelets finely wrought with sapphires and emeralds; delicate petal earrings from Van Cleef.

"Did she like that watch you gave her for her birthday?" she asked, thinking that thirty thousand dollars bought a very generous gift. But then again, the Red Bloods gave them something much more precious.

Charles looked concerned at the sharpness of her tone. "You can't be jealous, Allegra." He sounded confused, as if she had changed the rules.

"I'm not," she said, giving him an easy smile and reaching

to ruffle his hair. This was the way it was. The way they had always lived. The Blue Blood way. There was the bond and then there were human familiars. One provided nourishment for the soul, the other fed the immortal blood.

Charles rested his warm hands on her face. "You look pale and you feel cold," he said, rubbing her cheeks. "You need a bite. And I don't mean dinner."

"I know." She hung her head. It was an unspoken disagreement between them. She knew Charles did not like that she had not taken a familiar since that first doomed disaster in high school. They never spoke of Ben, but she knew Charles would be relieved once she took a new familiar. She had been putting it off, hesitating, afraid of falling in love with the wrong person all over again—a ridiculous fear, surely. She had had thousands of human familiars in her multiple lifetimes and had only fallen that one time. There was another reason, of course—one she did not even want to admit to herself—but she didn't want to forget about Ben, and taking another's blood would wash away some of the memory of their joining.

Charles frowned. "If you don't want to go through the trouble, there is always the service. Let the Conduits take care of you. You'll feel much better."

Allegra nodded. Blue Bloods whose familiars were not available or had passed away had the option of using a blood service founded by the Conduits, wherein screened humans were offered to the vampires at their discretion. The service did not have the seedy undertone of the blood houses. They were clinical transactions, not unlike ordering a steak from room service. "I'll think about it," she promised.

Charles kissed her on the forehead. "I know you're still worried about what happened last time, but you need to move on."

There were no secrets between them. Not anymore. Charles knew she had been in love with Ben, that her relationship with her human familiar had almost jeopardized everything, including the bond that was the foundation of the Coven and tied them to the earth and to each other. That he forgave her, that he still loved her, was something Allegra had to live with every day.

She sank down on the couch, relieved that she had left Ben's studio as quickly as she had. There had been no temptation to stay. She was home and safe. She would meet her friends for a quick dinner and maybe dial up the service, as Charles had suggested. It was time.

"Good. Charge it to my account," Charles said. He had read her mind as usual.

When Allegra returned from a raucous night with her old teammates, she found a note on her bedside table. It was a business card with the name of the service and a phone number. The Conduits could be trusted to provide a good familiar, maybe someone they could send to New York with her afterward. She picked up the phone to dial, when there was a knock on the door and the butler appeared. "A letter arrived for you, Miss Van Alen."

Allegra opened the envelope. Inside was a note hastily scribbled on an embossed monogrammed card. *SBC.* Stephen Bendix Chase.

Meet me in the Redwood Room at the Clift. Please.
It's important.

—Ben

Thirteen

Cycle House

A few days after they met up with the Venators, Jack came back from a scouting trip with unsettling news. The human Conduit Alastair Robertson, who had told Jack about the holy woman who might be Catherine of Siena, had been found murdered in his home. Red Blood police were convinced the violence had been random, a home invasion that had gone awry. But with Nephilim about, and the Coven in shambles, Jack believed otherwise. He teamed up with the Lennox twins to track down a lead on Gezira, an island on the far side of the Nile, as mud found at the crime scene had telltale red clay from the northern riverbank.

With Jack away, Schuyler was the only one in their hotel room when Dehua Chen burst through the door. The Angel of Immortality looked uncharacteristically unhinged. A sleeve on her blouse was torn, and her face was covered with scratches.

"What happened?" Schuyler asked, jumping up immediately and reaching for her weapon.

"The Cairo cycle house is under attack—that Nephilim who got away came back with a few new friends," she huffed. "The boys won't be able to get back in time. Deming is fighting them, but she will be overpowered soon. I got here as fast as I could. Come. Help us."

Schuyler followed Dehua as they raced through the winding streets of Cairo, the two of them a blur of black silk and silver steel. The cycle house was located in the Citadel, an ancient complex built high on the cliffs towering over the eastern edge of the city. Built by Saladin to ward off the Crusaders, it was the most dominant place on the skyline. The cycle house was under attack! The Nephilim truly were bent on revenge if they were after the unborn Blue Blood spirits that were stored there. No more blood spirits meant no more births for this Coven.

Dehua led Schuyler through the footpaths that led to the hidden secret chambers. The Venator explained that they had received an all-points-distress signal from the Wardens at the Citadel. When Schuyler and Dehua arrived, the vampires working for the House of Records were already dead, and a fierce crew of Egyptian Venators was engaged in battle with a host of Nephilim. The demon-born were carrying torches burning with the Black Fire, but so far they had been unable to break into the sacristy, where the canisters holding the blood spirits were kept.

The heat was overpowering, and black smoke covered the hallway. Dehua pushed through into the antechamber. "Oh no," she cried, as she and Schuyler stepped over the fallen bodies of dead Venators, whose corpses had been hacked to pieces or beheaded, with their eyes gouged out or burned. The door to the sacristy had been blown open, and Schuyler feared they had come too late to save anyone, least of all themselves.

Deming was surrounded by a swarm of the human demons. She was fighting them off, but they were closing in one by one. She held a golden urn tucked under one arm, while she slashed at her enemies with her sword. "*NEXI INFIDELES!*" she screamed. *Death to the faithless! Death to the traitors!*

The Nephilim screamed, and their fury filled the smoky black room. There were ten, twenty, thirty of them, and they fell upon Deming in a rage, like cockroaches in a frenzy. Soon Schuyler could not see the brave Chinese Venator or her golden sword.

"Dear god, there's too many of them," Dehua cried, falling to her knees. "We're not going to make it! Deming!" she wailed.

Schuyler held her ground. "Pull yourself together!" she ordered the flailing Venator. She wished Jack were here, but since he wasn't, she had to be brave for all of them. Abbadon would never let the unborn spirits die. He would not give up the cycle house. He would die defending it, and so would she.

They didn't have much time, as smoke from the Black Fire was engulfing the room, and Schuyler had to squint to see, and try not to breathe. They had to get out of there as quickly as possible. She wasn't a trained fighter, but she was light and fast, and if she and Dehua worked together, they could surprise their enemies. "You go that way, I'll take the front."

The stricken Venator nodded, wiped her tears, and unsheathed her sword. They split up and crept toward their respective stations.

When they were ready, Schuyler raised Gabrielle's sword and took up the Venator's rally. *"DEATH! DEATH! DEATH TO THE FAITHLESS! DEATH TO THE INFIDELS!"*

Dehua joined Schuyler in screaming the Blue Blood battle cry. They were angels and warriors, and if they fell, they would die fighting. There was no other way. With a mighty swoop, they hacked their way through the dark, heaving crowd.

FOURTEEN

Doppelgangers

Mimi kicked off her sandals as she wandered through the party, liking the feel of sand on her bare feet. She didn't know where Oliver had disappeared to, and thought that she should start looking for him soon, in case he had gotten into some trouble. As far as she could tell, they had arrived at a perfectly pleasant and ordinary New England wedding. It was a strange venue for their quest, but when she noticed a certain dark-haired gentleman dressed in a beautifully tailored linen suit, making his way to her side, she suddenly understood what this was all about.

"Mimi," the man said, with a rougish smile she remembered so well.

For a moment her heart leapt with joy to see him—her love come back to her—but it was soon extinguished when she looked into his eyes. "I'm not a fool. I know what this is. You're not him," she said flatly. Her words were stronger than her conviction, however, for it was a good imitation. The boy standing next to her had Kingsley's swoop of dark hair and dark eyes with the mischievous sparkle. He even smelled like Kingsley—like cigarettes and whiskey, burnt sugar and coffee—and the combination made Mimi's heart beat a little faster. Seeing this double was painful. It only reminded her how long it had been since she had seen the real Kingsley. How long it had been since he had held her in his strong arms. How long it had been since he had teased and cajoled her into a smile.

"How do you know? You came down here to get me back. Well, here I am," he said with that familiar, flirtatious grin. "How are you?"

"I'm *from* here, remember? This isn't going to play with me."

"Speaking of play, I know how much you loved our little games," he said, taking her hand and rubbing her palm. When he touched her, she had a flash of memory—of a bathrobe falling to the floor, and his fangs on her neck . . . of his body, lean and hard against her.

She shook her head. "I didn't come down here for some doppelganger," she snarled.

Not-Kingsley winked at Mimi. "Suit yourself. But you're not going to be able to keep going downward without your friend. I'm pretty sure we've claimed him," he said, motioning to the terrace, where Oliver was kissing the girl who wasn't Schuyler.

"Oh, for goodness' sake! This has gone far enough!" Mimi tossed her champagne glass to the ground and stomped over to give her Conduit a piece of her mind.

"Oliver Hazard-Perry!" she yelled, feeling embarrassed for him. Oliver and the wraith were seated on a lounge chair, wrapped up in a tight embrace, and the heated action had almost reached the "get a room" stage. If Mimi didn't know better, she would have sworn the wraith was about to stick her fangs in Oliver's neck. "We need to move on, bud," she said, shaking him.

Oliver opened his eyes. He looked drugged and dazed, as if Mimi had woken him from a wonderful dream.

He shook his head slowly. "I can't leave. I'm getting married today."

"That girl isn't who you think she is. You know that. I know you do. You're not an idiot," Mimi snapped.

"She has no idea what she's talking about. She never did," Not-Schuyler said, with a contemptuous toss of her head. "Stay here and grow old with me, Ollie. Just like we always talked about."

"Let him go, siren," Mimi said.

"Don't listen to this bitch. I know you hate her. We've always hated her."

Oliver sighed heavily and pushed her away. "No. We didn't. We never hated Mimi. We might have been a bit afraid of her, or intimidated by her, and I know you pitied her at the last. But we never hated her." He turned to Mimi.

"We didn't hate you, Mimi. Schuyler doesn't hate you."

Mimi nodded as she helped him off the chaise. "I know. That's why I provoked it. I thought it would help if this thing said something Schuyler would never say. Come on."

The doppelganger glared at Oliver. "You dare defy the desires of a siren?"

"Yes," he said, finding his voice.

The siren screeched her disapproval and dug her claws into his arm.

"RELEASE HIM!" Mimi roared, as Oliver tried to pull away, blanching at the sight of his beloved's face morphing into a harridan's mask.

The siren shrieked in anger.

Mimi removed the needle from her bra so it turned into her sword, and she swung at the harpy. The blade glinted with silver sparks.

The siren hissed and spat acid, but recoiled at the weapon as Mimi thrust it forward. Mimi held the blade at the creature's throat, and finally it dropped its hold on Oliver, disappearing into silver flame. In a blink, the skies overhead turned black, and booming thunder roared in the distance. Lightning cracked, and rain began to fall in stinging shards. The illusion had been broken, melting into the shadows once again.

Oliver and Mimi walked quickly through the scattering crowd back to where the Mustang was parked by the entrance. Mimi rolled up the roof hurriedly before they were drenched.

"You all right? I know it's a hard one," Mimi said as she pulled out of the lot. This was only the first test, the first temptation. She knew the path would be difficult, and that Helda would not let go of Kingsley's soul so easily.

Oliver rubbed his arm where the creature's claws had dug into his skin. He was beginning to realize that he might have bitten off more than he could chew with this little adventure into the underworld. But it was with relief that he saw they were wearing their old clothes again. The hideous wedding mirage was truly over. "Where were you?"

"They tried to tempt me with some fake version of Kingsley."

"Why was it so easy for you to walk away from him while I couldn't?"

Mimi thought about it. "I was . . . born here. Angels of Darkness were made from the clay that made the underworld. So I knew it was just a fake. I know their tricks, which gave me an advantage." There were other signs, too, she thought. The real Kingsley was always unshaven, and the one at the wedding had skin that was smooth and soft to the touch. Too soft. Kingsley was a glittering knife with a diamond edge, and his skin was rough like sandpaper. Even so, resisting the siren had not been as easy as she made it seem, remembering that when she had first spotted the doppelganger under the trees, she had been convinced that her love had returned to her at last.

"I'm sorry," Oliver said thickly. "I didn't know where I

was for a moment. It won't happen again."

"Good, because you sure as hell don't want to get stuck down here. Besides, she's not worth it, you know. She left you," Mimi said. She hadn't meant it unkindly; she was only stating a fact. Truly, Schuyler and Jack deserved each other. They were both disloyal and worthless.

Oliver decided to ignore the dis, and changed the subject. "What would have happened?" he asked. "If I'd stayed with that . . . thing."

"I'm not sure, but it wouldn't have been pretty."

Oliver could imagine it. He would have married the siren under the belief that he was living a real life with Schuyler by his side. But little by little, the illusion would fade—not in one quick shot like today, but slowly, over time, the wraith would tire of the charade, and the mask would begin to slip. He would discover he was bound to a harpy, to a monster, that he had shackled himself to a soulless creature who would taunt him day and night, mock him for his doomed love. Thank god Mimi had interrupted when she did.

Besides, he did not want to think of Schuyler in that way. He did not want to admit that even if he had been cured of the familiar's kiss, he still loved her. He had loved her before she'd taken his blood, and so that love would always be part of him, whether he was her familiar or not. He strove to hold on to the memory of his happiness for his friend at her bonding, when he had felt strong and brave and generous. He had been able to be truly happy for her then, and the doppelganger had taken that feeling away from him. He wasn't proud of himself, and he hated himself for succumbing to his dark fantasies. He wasn't that guy. He had given Schuyler away, had shaken Jack's hand. Oliver felt as if he had betrayed everyone by giving in to his deepest and most secret desire. Worse, he had betrayed himself. He was better than that.

"You don't have to apologize or explain," Mimi said gently. "That test, what you just went through . . . it was cruel." She tried not to think too hard about it, especially since she planned to leave him down here, which meant he was doomed to live exactly that sort of misery for all eternity.

"It doesn't matter now," he said, shrugging. "Let's just find Kingsley and get out of here. Hell isn't as fun as I thought. Let's get this over with."

FIFTEEN

The Bendix Diamond

*T*he giant towering redwoods were a marvel, some of the most beautiful and majestic beings ever to grace the earth. Allegra remembered when they were planted, at the dawn of the universe, and once in every few cycles she strove to visit them, to smell the air that was the closest earth came to Paradise. Hence the Redwood Room was one of her favorite bars in San Francisco. She was happy to find it was still the same, still a soaring space with that long, enormous bar. Legend said that it was made from the trunk of one redwood tree. The bar had been through many different owners, but since it was now housed in the hip Clift hotel, it was considered young and trendy enough that Charles would never think to step inside. Her twin was a staunch traditionalist, and loathed such things as Louis Quatorze furniture rendered in plastic, which could be found at the Redwood Room in great abundance.

Allegra found Ben sitting at a back table, and she slipped into the banquette, feeling sheepish. Twice now she had run from him, and twice now she had returned. "I'm sorry about this morning. I didn't mean to leave so abruptly," she said.

"I seem to bring that out in you," Ben said, sounding amused. He appeared to have recovered from his earlier embarrassment. The preppie façade was back in place, along with his lopsided grin. "What are you having?" he asked.

"Martini."

"Old-school." He smiled and motioned to the waitress, then placed their orders.

They looked at each other across the table, a heavy silence hanging between them until Allegra could bear it no longer. "Ben . . ."

"Legs, hold on. Before you say anything, let me explain. I wanted you to see the paintings because they were of you. But I did those years ago, right when you left me." He leaned over and was about to say more, when a girl joined their table. It was the pretty brunette from the gallery.

"Hi sweetie," she said, kissing Ben on the lips. She smiled at Allegra.

"Allegra, this is Renny. Renny, you've met Allegra," Ben said, raising his eyebrows.

"Renny and Benny!" Renny giggled. "Nice to see you again. Ben said we were meeting you here. You should have told me you were his old friend when you bought the painting." The girl beamed at her and put a possessive hand on Ben's shoulder.

Allegra kept smiling and nodding, speechless for a moment, and she was relieved when Renny excused herself to chat with some friends she'd spotted across the room.

They watched her go, and Ben turned back to Allegra. "I didn't want to give you the wrong impression. Renny hasn't seen those other paintings of you. Mother wanted me to put them away years ago, but I wanted you to see them. I needed you to see them. But like I said, they were the work I did right after Endicott, after you disappeared."

"I'm so sorry."

"It's fine. . . ." He waved off her apology. "I know you changed me. I could feel it. Sometimes I would wake up and just . . . need you so much. But then I started painting, and it got better, little by little."

"And you're okay," she said brightly.

"Yes." He studied her. "I didn't want you to go back to New York worrying about me. I wanted you to know that I went through hell—but it's all right, I survived." He blushed. "Sorry to be so melodramatic, but it's why I invited you to the studio. I just wanted you to see them."

Allegra gave him a brilliant smile. "I'm so glad. She seems like a wonderful girl."

"She is. Smart. She keeps me grounded." Ben cleared his throat. "We're getting married in the spring."

Allegra nodded and took a sip from her martini glass,

forcing the cold liquid down her throat. She could not begrudge him a wedding, especially since she herself was getting bonded to Charles soon.

"I figured, why wait, right? When you've met the person you're going to spend the rest of your life with, why wait at all." Ben sighed. "Renny's good for me."

"And your family?" Allegra had to ask. *Do they like her? Does your mother wish it was me?*

Ben smirked. "Mother isn't terribly pleased. She thinks I should wait."

Allegra tried not to show that she agreed with Mrs. Chase. It did feel as if Ben was rushing into this—and what was the reason for it?

"But I don't want to."

"Good for you." Allegra finished the rest of her drink. "I'm so happy for you. I'm happy for you both."

Renny made her way back to the table and sat next to Ben. "What did I miss?"

"Congratulations. Ben told me the good news." Allegra smiled as Ben kissed his fiancée's hand. She could not help but notice the diamond the size of a meteor on the girl's finger. Renny laughed and waved her hand, sending waves of light across the room. "I know it's a bit much, isn't it?" she asked Allegra in a conspiratorial tone. "I told Ben I didn't need a ring, but he insisted. It's the Bendix diamond. It was designed for his great-grandmother by Alfred Van Cleef himself."

"It's beautiful." Allegra called to the cocktail waitress. "A bottle of your finest champagne, please. We're celebrating."

Ben looked pleased and abashed at the same time, while Renny beamed. The waitress set a magnum of champagne in a silver bucket in the center of the table, and Ben did the honors, popping the cork and pouring three glasses of the frothy, bubbly liquid. The champagne was perfect: bracingly cold, tart and smoky. Allegra did not know how she was able to keep a smile plastered on her face for the entire evening, but she managed, ordering up bottle after bottle of champagne, her vampire blood immune to the alcohol content. It gave her a small dark satisfaction to hear Renny complaining of room spin after a few rounds.

As the happy couple nuzzled at the table, Allegra decided she would call the service first thing tomorrow morning. Charles was right, as usual. She didn't know why it had taken her five years to figure it out, but it was time to move on. Ben had.

SIXTEEN

Holy Water

*T*he demon children had crimson eyes with silver pupils, and when they hissed they showed their forked tongues. They parted easily as Schuyler and Dehua charged through them, but only when Schuyler put a hand on Deming's wrist did she understand why.

Deming was a doppelganger, and she faded into the mist when Schuyler touched her. It was a trap. In seconds, Schuyler and Dehua were surrounded by the Nephilim. There was a scream from a far corner, and they saw the real Deming tied to a column, flames of Black Fire nipping her ankles.

"NO!" Dehua screamed as she moved to save her sister. But soon she too was lost under a fury of blows from their enemies.

Schuyler thrust forward with her blade, and her parry was met with the heavy steel of a demon axe. The Hell-born human laughed horribly and slashed, and Schuyler felt a cold and shooting pain as his weapon met its mark, cutting her deeply in the middle of her chest.

The Nephilim raised its axe again to finish her off, but suddenly a sword—shining with the pure light of heaven— appeared and cut the black axe deftly in half. Help at last! The new Venator made quick work of the demons surrounding them, and soon the room was filled with the smell of death and blood. The Nephilim broke ranks and fled. Dehua, bloodied and scratched, had survived, and she ran to untie Deming.

"How many lost?" their unknown hero asked the twins. He was tall and dark-haired, with a classically beautiful face—a cleft chin, and a dreamy gentleness in his deep-set eyes.

Deming shook her head. "They burned everything else. I was able to save just one canister," she said, removing a small golden urn from her pack.

"The Regent of Cairo is taking a felucca to the safe house in Luxor," the stranger said. "Take the back roads to the river and give this to him."

The Venators nodded and left to deliver the last of the blood spirits of the Egyptian Coven to its surviving leader.

From the floor, Schuyler groaned. The Nephilim's sword carried the Black Fire in its poisoned tip. It burned with a dull throbbing ache, as her blood gushed from the wound, pooling underneath her shirt.

"How bad?" the handsome Venator asked, kneeling next to her. "Your blood is red. You are the *Dimidium Cognatus*. Gabrielle's daughter." He said it matter-of-factly, without prejudice.

"Yes," she said.

"Where are you hurt?"

She lifted her shirt and showed him where she had been cut—right next to her heart, a deep, ugly wound.

"You are lucky," he said, pressing his fingers on the wound. "A few inches to the right and the poison would have entered your heart. You would not have survived. Still, we must work quickly."

He looked at her kindly. His hands were gentle, but Schuyler felt her eyes water from the pain as he ministered to her wound. He produced a small bottle, engraved with a golden cross.

"You're a healer," Schuyler coughed. The Venators were organized thus: investigator, healer, soldier, high command.

He nodded and poured a few drops. Schuyler had to bite her hand to stop from screaming. It burned like acid on the wound. But slowly it dissolved the wound and dissipated the poison until there was nothing left but a small scar.

"I'm afraid that's not going to heal all the way. You'll always carry that mark," the healer said. "But things could be worse." He gave her the bottle. "Here, drink some of it. It will clear out any of the poison left. It's holy water."

Schuyler took a gulp. "This isn't what they have in churches."

"No." He smiled. "Red Bloods . . ." He shrugged. "This is water from the fountain," he said. "From the gardens of Paradise, a long time ago."

The water was the purest, cleanest Schuyler had ever tasted. She felt renewed and revived, as if her body was beginning to knit itself together.

She pulled her shirt together and sat up. "Thank you."

The man nodded. "You're welcome. The Venators tell me that you came to Cairo looking for Catherine of Siena."

"Yes. What do you know of Catherine?"

"Unfortunately, I am looking for her as well." He held out his hand. "I seem to have forgotten my manners. I am known in this part of the world as Mahrus AbdelMassih. I live in Jordan now, but a long time ago I was a healer in Rome. Catherine of Siena is my sister."

Seventeen

The Demon of Avarice

*T*he rain did not stop, and they drove for hours under the dark and thunderous skies. The road was changing and they were no longer alone, as there was traffic in all directions. Oliver wondered where they were going. They were no longer in Not-Nantucket, nor anywhere that resembled the eastern coast of the United States, and still the rain continued to pour and flood the highways. But as suddenly as it began, the rain stopped abruptly, and the two-lane highway expanded to a roaring eight-lane freeway, with overpasses that swooped in every direction.

Mimi looked up at a blinking freeway sign. It read: TAKE THE NEXT EXIT. "I think that's for us," she said, accelerating into the right lane. The exit took her to a wide boulevard of skyscrapers, and a valet wearing a shiny red jacket waved her into the driveway of the tallest and shiniest building on the street. The valet line was filled with a row of expensive and rare European cars.

"Right in there," the valet directed, pointing toward the glass doors. "They're expecting you."

"You were wrong; they do have valets in Hell," Oliver joked. He noticed the valet was wearing a silver collar around his neck. So the trolls did run the place. They were the invisible hands that made sure the trains ran on time and dinner was never late. The slave labor of the underworld.

Oliver scratched his face, feeling a sudden five o'clock shadow on his chin. When he passed through the doors he noticed his reflection. He was wearing a flannel shirt, a beret, aviator sunglasses, baggy blue jeans, and expensive sneakers. "I look like a douche," he said.

"Stop complaining," Mimi said, puckering her lips at the glass. For this part of the journey she was dressed in a trendy outfit: tight jeans, high heels, a slouchy and comfortable black sweater. She had sunglasses on her head and an expensive handbag on her arm. She almost felt like herself again.

Through the glass doors was an expansive marble lobby. Mimi walked to the elevator and pressed UP. When the elevator doors opened to the top floor, they found themselves in yet another stark and beautiful lobby. Everything in the place had been designed to intimidate and disconcert, to make a person feel small and humble and not quite pretty enough.

Oliver followed Mimi to the reception desk, where three good-looking she-trolls in headsets fielded calls. The headsets were made of silver, and wrapped around their necks like dog collars. No blood, though. The nearest one smiled when they came closer. "Yes?"

"Mimi Force and uh . . . Oliver Hazard-Perry. We're expected," Mimi said.

"Of course. Have a seat and I'll let him know you're here."

They walked toward the uncomfortable but beautiful furniture. Another impossibly gorgeous girl troll in an improbably chic outfit approached them. Her silver collar was a choker, and Oliver could swear it glittered with diamonds. "Mimi? Oliver?" she asked. "Can I get you anything? Water? Coffee? Iced tea?"

Mimi shook her head. "I'm good."

"Nothing for me, thanks," Oliver said. When the assistant left, he turned to Mimi. "What's this all about? Where are we?"

"I think Helda's going to make me an offer," Mimi said. It was another temptation, another obstacle to keep her from what she truly wanted.

As soon as Mimi explained, it suddenly clicked, and Oliver understood why everything looked so familiar. Since Helda was making Mimi an offer, their environment had been designed to look and feel like a sleek Hollywood agency.

They waited for an hour; the assistants continued to

hover and brought drinks even though they hadn't ordered them. Oliver felt itchy in his jeans as the fabric scratched. "How long do we have to wait?" He hoped it wasn't as long as their drive through Limbo.

"Unpredictable," Mimi huffed.

Finally the assistant returned, and this time she didn't ask them what they wanted to drink. "Come on back," she said, with the pat smile of a stewardess or restaurant hostess.

"Wait here. Don't drink that," Mimi warned. Oliver spat out the coffee in his mouth, and Mimi followed the assistant into a large office with a spectacular view of rolling green hills dotted with Spanish-tiled rooftops.

The demon sitting at the desk was turned away from her, with his legs on the armrest of his chair. He twirled around and winked at her. "She's here in my office right now. Yes, I'll tell her. Sounds good. We'll do lunch. There's a new place that everyone is raving about. You can't get a reservation but I know the owner. All right. Good-bye. Talk later." He removed his headset and turned to Mimi with a crafty smile on his face. He had slicked-back hair and a shiny suit, and he was handsome in the way that powerful men are. He had an aura of confidence, wealth, and ruthlessness. His cuff links gleamed in the sunlight, a hard silver glow. "Azrael! Sexy! Been too long, babe," he said, getting up and giving her a bear hug.

"Mamon," she said. "I see you've redecorated."

"You like the ninja thing? It's very in now, or so my

overpriced designer tells me." His face broke into a broad grin. "So how's life been? I hear things aren't so great up there lately. Michael and Gabrielle are gone, Covens are heading underground, etcetera, etcetera."

"I didn't know you cared. I thought gossip was beneath you."

"I like to keep my ear to the ground, or in this case, the ceiling." He smiled. "So how's the trip so far?"

"Inconvenient."

"Good enough, good enough," he said, shuffling papers on his desk. "Well, you know you can't expect the red carpet."

Mimi fumed. "What do you want, demon? Why am I here? I need to get through to the seventh circle, and you're keeping me from what I want. I hate that."

"All right. Hold your horses. I called you here because Helda wants to make you an offer. And before you say no, hear me out."

Mimi raised an eyebrow. "Unless it's Kingsley back and safe, I'm not interested."

The Demon of Avarice wagged his finger. "Well, you know it can't be that. But we've got something better for you. Regis of the Coven."

"I'm already Regent," she said. "And they offered me the top job last year and I didn't take it." She crossed her legs in annoyance.

"Ah, but they haven't tapped you again, have they? Right

now you've taken them hostage by spiriting away the key. But if we make you Regis, your word alone will bind them together and you won't even need the Repository. The soul of the Coven will be in your hands."

Mimi shrugged.

"I know how you've felt over the years, Azrael. They've never trusted you, not since the Fall, not since you betrayed them. All those centuries toiling for the Uncorrupted, and for what? They still see you as one of us. But with Michael lost and Gabrielle who knows where—and you as Regis— you could have the respect and the power you've wanted all these years. You could lead the Fallen. You could be their queen. With you at the helm, no one will even remember Gabrielle. Gabrielle—who's that? Some slut who got pregnant too many times, that's who."

She did not want to show that she agreed with him, even if she did. She had to focus on what she had come down here for. This was merely a distraction. "What else have you got?"

Mamon frowned. "That's not enough?"

"Not by a mile."

The handsome devil looked at her shrewdly. "All right, then. How about this? Your brother dead at your hands."

"You can get me Jack?" Mimi asked, unable to hide the excitement creeping into her words.

"Abbadon? Sure. Piece of cake. Just say the word, sweetheart. You know we can. Send our best Hellhounds after him. They *fetch*." When he smiled, his teeth were dagger-sharp, like little knives in his mouth, glinting in the light. He jumped from his seat.

Mimi shuddered. The hounds' power and capacity for evil were mythical in dimension.

"Come, take a trip with me," he said, and reached for her hand.

When Mimi opened her eyes, she was standing by the altar alone. It was the day after what would have been their bonding, the day Jack had left her to go to Florence with Schuyler. Mimi was there to fulfill her duty, but he had left her. The old anger and hate bubbled to the surface. Jack was with his half-blood, his little Abomination, while she waited at the church alone. How funny that Schuyler did not hate her. But Mimi was not so generous. She hated Schuyler with every ounce of her immortal soul. She hated Schuyler for what she had done—she had made Abbadon forsake his bond and allowed him to forget the Code. Without either, then the vampires were nothing. No one was worth that. No love was worth that much. The blood of the angels was on Schuyler's hands. Allegra's daughter was said to be the Savior of the Fallen. Yeah, right.

"They laughed at you, you know," Mamon said into her ear. "When they heard that Abbadon ditched you at the altar. That you were jilted. They said to each other, of course he would leave her. Azrael—who could love her—didn't he always love Gabrielle—wasn't that Abbadon's weakness for the Light? They still laugh at you behind your back. They call you Azrael the Unwanted."

Mimi closed her eyes and could feel the tears and the rage behind them. She knew that every word the demon said was true. Of course, she was not the first to have been humiliated in such a manner—even the greatest angel of them all had been jilted at his bonding—but Mimi had not been in cycle then and did not see it. All she knew was what she had experienced. The cold nausea of shame and rejection.

"Helda could change all that."

When she opened her eyes again, Jack was lying on the ground in front of her. His sword lay broken in two, and he looked up at her with fear in his eyes. She loomed above him, holding her sword aloft; and without warning, she bore it down upon him, right in the middle of his chest, straight into his heart, so deep that it cut him in two, killing him. The heat from her sword set his body and his blood on fire.

Mimi felt her brother's blood on her face, felt the heat from the dark flames. Jack was no more. Her joy was dark and deep and triumphant.

"Mimi! Mimi! What are you doing?" Oliver was running toward her, his eyes wide with fright and worry. "Mimi! Stop this! Stop this at once! You don't want to do this!"

Mimi stood over the dead, broken body of Abbadon and howled. "Yes I do! He left me! Centuries we were bonded, made of darkness and bound to our duty! HE NEEDS TO DIE!"

She pointed her sword at Oliver. "Do not stop me!"

"You don't want this. You want Kingsley, remember? We're here for *Kingsley*."

"Make your choice, Azrael," the demon thundered. "Say the word and Abbadon is yours, and all you see before you will be made real."

Yes. Yes! Yes!

"Mimi—think of Kingsley."

Kingsley. If she took what Mamon was offering, she would never get to him. She would have her power and her revenge, but not her love. She would not have anything to live for once the blood dried from her face and her sword was wiped clean.

"Remember what we came for," Oliver pleaded. "Remember why we're here."

"Say the word and he is yours. His death will bring you glory," Mamon whispered.

Glory. Revenge. Blood. The laughter would stop. The humiliation would end. She would have her pride back and her name. She would see it through, and show Abbadon what happened to those who did not follow their bond.

Kingsley . . .

But when she thought of Kingsley she did not feel rage and heat. When she thought of Kingsley she thought of his smile and his words, and a softness came to her, a blanket of coolness that made the rage and heat go away. She thought of his sacrifice, of what he had done for her, for them, for the Coven. Of his words on her bonding day.

Come away with me, and live a new adventure.

She had gone to Hell for him. She would not leave the underworld without him by her side.

"No deal," she said, spitting out the words. "Get me out of here!"

As the words left her lips, the vision cleared, and it was as if heavy velvet curtains had parted on a stage, and they were through to the seventh circle.

They were standing on a hill, looking down upon a tall city.

Tartarus. The capital of Hell.

"How strange," Oliver said. "It looks exactly like New York."

Eighteen

Truths and Lies

*M*onths passed, and Allegra returned to her life in New York. The portrait arrived with a cheerful note from Renny. *Thanks again for the fun night. Hope to see you again soon!* Allegra tore the note in half and put the painting away in the attic before Charles could ask her about it. The fall social season was in full swing and there was a lot to do: charity work, overseeing the renovations on their town house on the Upper East Side, supervising the various committees that made up vampire society. The immortal routine, Allegra thought, finding so much of her work ornamental these days, and no different from the daily frivolity enjoyed by empty-headed Red Blood socialites who partied their way through life in the name of philanthropy. She tried to put Bendix out of her mind, and most of the time she succeeded. He was living as he should: he would marry, have children, and lead a happy, uneventful life. He didn't need her, he never did. She would only have brought him despair and madness. It was lucky that he had been strong enough to survive being chosen as her familiar in the first place.

On this brisk October day, Allegra was walking back home from visiting the Repository when she noticed a huge white van blocking the side entrance on 101st Street. It looked like an ambulance, but it did not carry the name of any hospital or clinic. While theirs was not a particularly busy street, it still needed both lanes for traffic to work properly, and a curious crowd of rubberneckers had gathered around the van, waiting to see if anyone would be wheeled out in a gurney. They smelled blood and disaster, and Allegra was a bit repulsed by their avid interest. She was also just beginning to worry. What if something had happened to Charles or Cordelia? She pushed her way through the crowd and let herself inside the front door, trepidation in her chest.

Nothing seemed amiss, however. Cordelia was discussing the dinner menu with the staff in the kitchen, and Charles was in his study, where he was in a deep discussion with Forsyth Llewellyn. Charles was trying to coerce Forsyth into moving to New York and joining the Conclave. Forsyth wasn't one of her favorite people, and Allegra wished Charles didn't depend on him so much. There was something about the way Forsyth looked at her that she found unnerving. It was as if he knew things about her—secret dark things that she herself did not. Charles had grown close to Forsyth in this cycle. She remembered their father had never liked him. Lawrence would not have been pleased.

They stopped speaking the moment she walked into the room.

"Charles, what's that van outside? Does it have something to do with us? It's blocking the whole street. There's a crowd gathered around it now."

"Forsyth, will you move it?" Charles asked.

"Of course," Forsyth said, jumping up from his chair. He looked nervous, Allegra thought. Why was he nervous?

"What's going on?" she asked Charles when Forsyth had left.

"There's been an incident," Charles said. "But nothing that you need to worry about, darling." He did not say anything more, and Allegra felt annoyed.

"You're doing it again, shutting me out. You know I hate that."

Charles looked wounded. "I don't mean to. It's just . . ."

Allegra bit the inside of her cheeks in frustration. She knew why Charles acted this way. It always came down to what had happened in Florence, during the Renaissance, when she'd made that horrible mistake that could have cost them everything. She would never overcome it. She would never forgive herself. It was a memory she would carry her entire immortal life. The worst thing about it was she didn't even know everything about what happened. She knew what she had done, of course, but there was more to the story, she was sure of it. Charles denied that he kept secrets—told her she knew everything she needed to know—and she had tried prying once in a while—tried to see if she could access the hidden corners of his memory—but she never found it. Either he was good at hiding his thoughts or he was telling her the truth. She didn't know what was worse.

Charles sighed. "Anyway, the situation is under control. But you asked, so I'll tell you. There's some sort of sickness infecting humans that has affected several young vampires in San Francisco. There's a human familiar in the ambulance that died from it. We're having the doctors analyze its blood."

Allegra raised an eyebrow. "You know as well as I do that there's no human disease that can affect the vampires."

"Not one that we know of." Charles frowned.

"Charles, even you know it's impossible. Don't be obtuse." She crossed her arms. "Tell me what's really in the van."

He looked her directly in the eyes. "Are you accusing me of lying?" His voice was calm but tight, and Allegra could see the hurt flash in his dark gray eyes.

Her shoulders slumped. "No . . . I'm not. You know I don't doubt you," she said, backing down. "It's just strange."

"I agree, which is why we're keeping a close eye on it."

He cleared his throat. "What's really bothering you? You've been irritable since we took that trip out to California. Did something happen? I didn't want to pry. I figured you would tell me if it was important."

Allegra shook her head. She had wanted to tell him, but she didn't want to cause a scene, and without even meaning to, she realized she had distanced herself from him again. "I saw Ben," she finally admitted, steeling herself for Charles's disapproval. "It's not what you think . . . nothing happened . . . he's getting married." She exhaled. "But that's not the reason why. I mean . . . you know what I mean."

Charles took the information in stride with a thoughtful nod. "I'm sorry you're upset. I know you cared for him."

Allegra felt as if a huge burden had just been lifted from her soul. She sat down next to her twin and leaned her head on his arm. "Are you all right?" he asked softly.

"Yes. It just . . . scared me. Seeing him again. After what happened last time, you know?" She had forgotten how close they were. Charles was her best friend, the person she told all her secrets to, the person she trusted the most, the one who knew her intimately. They were two sides of the same coin. They shared an immortal life: countless memories reaching back all the way to the beginning, when they were first blood bound to each other. She had nothing to hide from him.

He pulled her close to him. "Don't be frightened."

Forsyth returned, twirling his keys. "All clear. Found a great parking space on Riverside."

Charles reluctantly disentangled from his embrace with Allegra. "Darling, would you mind leaving us alone for a bit? Forsyth and I have some business to attend to."

Allegra shut the door behind her. She felt better after confessing to Charles, and what he'd said was true: he had never lied to her. But lies of omission were sins just the same. She couldn't help but feel that there was more to this story, and that there was something Charles was keeping from her, something important, and she had to find out what it was.

In all their history she had never heard of such a thing as a human disease that could affect vampire physiology. Nothing could affect vampires. Oh, they caught ordinary colds and flus like everyone else. They were made of the same basic material as the Red Bloods, with one crucial difference, of course, but on the whole they were immune to serious disease. When the cycles were over and it was time to rest, "death" was just a deep sleep until the *sangre azul* was woken again in a new shell. There was no such thing as cancer or heart problems in the Fallen.

Would Charles lie to her? It made her sad that she was even entertaining the possibility. It just showed how estranged they had become. She didn't trust him anymore, not completely, and it wasn't even his fault.

Allegra put on her running gear. She liked to run in the

park to clear her head. "I'm going out," she called, so no one would worry.

She jogged down the hill, planning to run down to the loop by the river, which took her all the way to the boat basin. There were a few other runners on the trail, some Rollerbladers and bicyclists, moms jogging with their fancy strollers. She kept an easy speed, her sneakers pounding the pavement in a staccato rhythm. On the way back to the house, she passed the van, which Forysth had parked on Riverside and 99th. She hesitated for a moment, but her curiosity and skepticism won, and she moved toward it. There was no one else on the street, and it was easy enough to pop the lock. She pulled open the back door and crept inside.

There was a body bag on the floor. It contained a human body, Charles had said. A familiar who carried a disease.

She had a flash memory of being a Venator in Florence, when she'd been called Tomasia. With her team she'd spent her nights skipping over rooftops, hunting the renegade Silver Bloods who were trapped on this side of the gates. As Venators they had caught and killed all the remaining Croatan on earth—or so they had believed. Like Charles, she'd been certain that they were finally safe from harm, but then there was that incident at Roanoke. They'd lost an entire colony. Cordelia and Lawrence had always believed that the Silver Bloods had never been defeated, that the Coven had been compromised, corrupted somehow. Charles thought it was ridiculous, of course. He put his faith in the gates. But what if Lawrence and Cordelia were right and Charles was wrong?

Who—or more likely *what*—was in the body bag?

Allegra unzipped the bag, her heart beating. Not sure what she was looking for, or what she expected to find. She had seen lifeless bodies of vampires who had been taken to Full Consumption before; had listened to Silver Bloods who spoke in the voices of her fallen friends, her dead comrades who had been sucked into becoming part of a monster, their immortal spirit trapped forever, chained to the devil spirit. But nothing had happened since Roanoke, and Charles had been convinced that perhaps the lost colony had simply decided to go underground, even with that message on the tree that said otherwise. The Silver Bloods were eradicated from their history books. Charles did not want old fears to plague their new lives in the New World.

What was in the bag?

Could it be?

She didn't even want to voice her fear.

Finally, she pulled apart the opening to see.

There was a girl in the bag. A human girl, her skin already gray. There were two small scars, almost unnoticeable, on her neck, which indicated she had been a vampire's familiar.

What disease did she carry, Allegra wondered. To die this way, so young and so alone. It was such a pity. The Red

Bloods had short enough lives as it was.

Allegra zipped the bag back up. She couldn't admit it to herself, but part of her had almost expected to find a dead vampire in there, as impossible as that sounded, and she was relieved to discover that Charles had been telling her the truth after all.

NINETEEN

The Last Venator

It was late in the evening when Jack returned from Gezira, and the first thing he did was check on Schuyler's wound, unpeeling the bandages around her torso and studying Mahrus's handiwork. The skin was still nubby but no longer red, and while the scar was noticeable, it was not ugly. "A battle wound," he said. "I am proud of you. You were brave to fight the way you did."

Schuyler buttoned her blouse and sat cross-legged on their hotel bed. The small room had begun to feel like home even though the clerk at the reception desk still cast suspicious glances their way. "I didn't have a choice," she said. "I knew you would have done the same."

"I should have been there with you," he said. He had listened to her story without interruption, and had kept a stoic front, but now the full brunt of it—what he could have lost—was slowly hitting him, and Schuyler could see how hard it was for him to keep his emotions in check.

"Don't worry, my love." Schuyler smiled and put a hand on his cheek. "I felt your strength was with me. I couldn't have done it without you. What about you . . . did you find what you were looking for across the Nile?"

Jack shook his head angrily. "When we arrived at the safe house, the Nephilim were long gone. I think they meant to lead us astray. The Lennox brothers visited the temple, but they say there's no priestess named Zani, that they'd heard wrong."

"Maybe Mahrus will have some news that can help us in that arena," Schuyler said.

"If he's been working this area for as long as he has, I'm hoping he does." Jack nodded. They planned to meet with the Venator after Jack had returned, so they could trade information and discuss their future strategy. The Lennox twins had gone after Deming and Dehua, who were still trying to track down the remaining members of the Eygptian Coven, to hand over the blood spirits.

The coffee shop was crowded with students, old men trading war stories, families having their late dinner, as Franco-Arabic music tinkled over the speakers. Jack and Schuyler took a table in the back, where they could see all the entrances. So far, the Nephilim did not strike in Red Blood areas—they seemed to confine their attacks and violence on the vampire strongholds—but it was better to be prepared and on guard.

Mahrus arrived promptly at the designated hour. He was so beautiful that many in the shop turned to stare at him.

Jack rose from his seat to greet him, and pumped his hand. "I owe you her life. Thank you, healer. I know I can never repay you, but my sword is yours whenever you need it, you have my word."

Mahrus bowed. "The honor is mine, Abbadon."

The waitress arrived with cups of steaming Turkish coffee, and for a few minutes the three sat and enjoyed the early evening air, drinking the strong dark blend. Schuyler felt better with some caffeine in her system. The coffee made her senses feel more alert. Since she did not take the blood anymore, she had to rely on other sources for a spike of energy.

"I have not heard of priestess named Zani," Mahrus said. "If she is a famous holy woman, then the Wardens would know. I will ask."

"We think she might be Catherine," Schuyler said.

"Interesting," he said. "Could be. I thought I would find my sister at the Cairo Museum. She was fond of Egyptian history, and an art lover. But she was not there." Mahrus told them about his life in Jordan. After leaving Rome during Caligula's reign, he had traveled to the eastern front, finding a home in an outpost of the former Ottoman Empire.

"We were a peaceful Coven," he said. "For centuries we lived in harmony, until . . ."

"Go on."

Mahrus's eyes clouded. "It happened so slowly and insidiously that we did not even notice at first. We were blind to the threat—the Coven did not warn us. There was nothing from New York; no one informed us of what happened in Rio or Paris. If only we had known, we might have been able to prepare," he said bitterly. "As it was, we were sitting ducks."

Schuyler gripped Jack's hand under the table as they listened to Mahrus's story.

"It started with the humans first, the missing girls. It was a Red Blood problem, we thought, but we kept an eye on it. Then we discovered a nest of Nephilim, but as my Venators were fighting them, the hidden Croatan in our conclave took the opportunity to strike as well."

He looked at them with great sorrow. "Everyone from my Coven is dead." He closed his eyes. "I am the only one left. The last Venator standing." He sighed. "It is only thanks to my fellow Venators that I am alive."

"Deming and Dehua, you mean? And Sam and Ted?"

"Yes. They were fighting the Nephilim—they were the only help we received from outside. They were headed to Cairo, on the trail of a new hive of demon-born. I came with them as well, since I knew that Catherine was here, and I had to warn her about what was happening. There is something more important here than even the Coven."

"You knew she was part of the Order of the Seven."

"Yes." He nodded. "I was there when we built the gate

in Lutetia. I knew what she had been called to do."

"You think the Nephilim are here for the gate?" Schuyler asked.

"I am sure of it. In every city, the pattern is the same. They strike first at the young, then the Elders, then the unborn. The Nephilim knew exactly where to hit the cycle house. They are vicious and strong, but they do not know our hidden workings. They need a hand to guide their evil. This was the work of a Croatan. One of Lucifer's mightiest allies, who harbored the Dark Prince and kept his spirit alive on earth. My guess is it is the same one who has systematically destroyed all the Covens, beginning in New York."

TWENTY

Nightclub at the End of the Universe

*O*liver was wrong. As they walked around the crowded streets, he changed his mind. Tartarus was not like New York City at all, not at all like the city he called his home. New York was dynamic, alive: it breathed with ambition and fire, its energy infectious. It was elegantly structured, laid out on a grid from river to river, aside from the one charming exception of the former cows' footpaths that made up the West Village. New York had an order and a logic to its existence. You always knew where you were. At least, Oliver did. Growing up, he had explored its many corners and hideaways. He knew Manhattan like the back of his hand, and he was proud of that. He loved New York. Like many residents, he couldn't imagine living anywhere else.

Tartarus, in comparison, was dead, rotting from the inside and filled with maggots. It was not just the capital of the dead, but a corpse of a city laid out on a mortuary slab. There was no sun, but it was hot and sticky, and everyone crowded together. The bodies on the sidewalks moved listlessly; everyone looked exhausted, beaten. There were no children. Oliver thought he had never been any-where so devoid of hope. It was a terrible place, ugly and overwhelming. It smelled like garbage, and there were flies everywhere—the largest flies he'd ever seen: they moved quickly, little carriers of disease.

Looking down at the twisted streets, he thought that one could easily get lost forever in its serpentine alleyways. As Mimi had said, in Hell there is no past, no future; only now. And so Tartarus was a jumble, a hodgepodge, an ugly patchwork of buildings that had no rhyme or reason to be standing next to each other. Everything clashed, colors, styles, zoning—there was no order, there was no aesthetic design. Parts of it looked like a strip mall on steroids: all blinking lights and tiny little shop fronts with peeling paint and antiquated video posters. Otherwise, there were dozens of abandoned empty lots, and almost everything—the walls, the sidewalks, the streets—were covered in grime and soot.

"Come on, this is only the outer ring. We need to get downtown," Mimi said, leading him toward what looked like a subway station.

The train that roared into the station was covered with graffiti inside and out. Every seat had been vandalized—windows scratched. When the announcement crackled, it was all static; no one could understand what had been said. They hopped on. Mimi seemed to know where she was going, and Oliver trusted her to lead the way. She drew some stares with her platinum hair—the brightest thing in the dark city—but other than that they were left alone. No one threatened Oliver. The only palatable emotion he could sense was massive indifference. No one cared. Their indifference was a physical entity. Oliver could almost *feel* them not caring; not at all interested or curious about their presence. It was an active, hostile disinterest, the likes of which he had never experienced. It gave him the creeps.

The subway lurched forward, and they rode it for a few stops.

Finally they reached their destination. "This is it, let's get out," Mimi said.

Oliver noticed a sign right above the exit from the subway: ABANDON HOPE, ALL YE ENTER HERE.

Not for the first time did he wonder what he was doing down here. This was no place for a human being, let alone one who was alive.

Back outside, downtown was even uglier than midtown, or wherever they had been. The streets were even more tightly packed, the air smelled like ash and cinder, and it was becoming more and more difficult to breathe. Oliver saw the trolls chained with their painful silver collars. They worked as cab drivers and waiters and swept the streets, which looked impossible to clean. He recognized the demons with their slightly red faces and small protruding horns above their foreheads; their ugly scowls. But the very worst were the creatures with faces that were so beautiful they were hard to look at. Their eyes were flat and cold; their indifference was the strongest of all.

"Croatan," Mimi whispered.

Oliver shivered. The demons were rough-looking and beastly, but the Silver Bloods, who had been angels once, had a corrupted beauty, like paintings that were smeared in excrement.

"They won't bother us down here," Mimi said. "Even if we saw the Dark Prince himself, he wouldn't care."

"Is this why they want earth?" Oliver asked.

"Yes. Hell is dead. Nothing grows here," Mimi told him. "It wasn't always this way, but that was how the world was divided in the beginning. All the light at the top, and darkness below."

"Where *is* Lucifer?" Oliver asked.

"Probably past the ninth."

"What's that?"

"The core," Mimi said. "The center of the underworld. Where the Dark Angels were made. No one is allowed there. We barely got permission to get here, in the seventh." She explained the hierarchy of Hell. On top were the Croatan, Lucifer, and his Silver Bloods. And right below them were the demons of ice and fire, who lived in the underworld. Then there were the lost souls, humans who'd been judged upon entering the Kingdom of the Dead and were consigned to the underlayer for all eternity. Then there were the shackled trolls, who were neither angel nor demon nor human, but another creature entirely—no one knew for sure, except that they carried out the demons' wishes. They were the lowest of the low, the underclass, the lowest caste, the untouchables. "There are Hellhounds too, of course," she told him. "But they're very rare—probably down in the ninth with Lucifer. After they rebelled and stood with us in Rome, he brought them to heel. Gabrielle held out hope that she could bring them back to our side one day, but who knows if that will ever happen."

Oliver regained his bearings. If Tartarus were New York, it looked as if they were now on the Lower East Side, before the hipsters and trendy wine bars and fancy hotels had moved in, but without the cozy Italian delis with the made men in velour sweats playing cards by the front doors.

In the middle of the neighborhood was a dark building with a large crowd standing in front of it. Music—droning, tuneless music, but music nonetheless—boomed from the doors. Oliver noticed that the crowd waited anxiously, and that a beautiful demon, her horns filed into sharp sexy little points, was sitting on a lifeguard's chair, looking down disdainfully at the crowd. Once in a while she would motion with her tail, and the burly trolls—bouncers—would push through to help the chosen few make their way to the front of the velvet rope.

Oliver was all too familiar with the practice. They called

it "face control" or "working the door," and it trafficked in rejection and humiliation, doling out both in spades, along with low self-esteem. It was Hell, and Oliver thought he should really stop thinking that. It was getting a bit clichéd. Next thing he knew he would be trapped in an elevator with strangers.

Mimi was making her way toward the teeming, anxious crowd. "Well, are you coming?" she asked, turning around when she noticed he was dawdling behind, hesitant.

"Yeah," he said, resigned. Maybe with Mimi he wouldn't have to stand in the crowd forever.

"This looks like as good a place to start as any. God knows Kingsley loved a nightclub," she said. "Just need to get that devil bitch to notice me." Mimi stuck two fingers into her mouth and let out a huge, piercing whistle.

Everyone turned to look at them, including the stuck-up demon, who looked them both up and down for what seemed like an eternity. For a moment, Oliver felt small and unworthy and fourteen years old again, trying to sneak into Moomba and failing. But in the end, the she-demon flicked her tail in their direction.

Mimi preened. The crowd parted like the Red Sea, the bouncers collected them, and just like that, they were delivered inside.

TWENTY-ONE

Dream House

*I*n the spring of the next year, Charles bought a media company and planned his takeover of the airwaves, which would include a competitor to the current twenty-four hour cable news channel, a fifth network, and multiple radio and newspaper holdings. He aimed to direct the global conversation, and influence Red Blood culture through its most insidious mechanism for communications. He was buying himself a pulpit.

The Fifth Avenue town house was almost ready, and Allegra spent most of her time with decorators, debating wall colors, window treatments, and furniture. They planned to keep a few of their things from the mansion on Riverside. Cordelia had promised them the chesterfield and the silver as bonding gifts, but Allegra was looking forward to a fresh start. There were those who believed that buying furniture was a bourgeois practice. In certain circles, only inherited furniture was deemed appropriate, but Allegra disagreed. While tradition was well and good, she wanted everything in the new house to be light and new, with nothing that hinted of the heavy baggage, or held too many memories of the past.

There were some traditions she did keep, however. Since Egypt, when they had ruled as Menes and Meni, their union was sealed by the bride moving her possessions to her new home. The movers would take care of the heavy stuff, but Allegra planned to bring a few items on her own: her jewelry box, the little crystal vase of oil, a cup of rice, and a flagon of water, to bring luck to their new home.

That afternoon, Allegra stood in the soon-to-be finished living room.

Charles walked in. "I didn't know you were here."

"I just wanted to check on the wallpaper. I was worried it might be too bright for the room, but I think it's fine."

"It looks lovely," he said.

"You like it?"

"Very much." He nodded.

"Good," she said.

Charles smiled at her. "I'm glad to see you happy."

"I am happy," Allegra said.

If she said it enough, maybe she would believe it.

TWENTY-TWO

Blood Sick

"**Y**ou've been quiet all evening," Jack said, when they returned to their room after their lengthy conversation with the Venator from Amman.

Schuyler nodded and sat at the edge of the bed, kicking off her shoes and taking off her earrings. She was still digesting everything Mahrus had told them about the systemic extinction of the Covens. Rio, Paris, Kiev, Shanghai, Amman, and Cairo were no more, or had gone underground. New York was barely hanging on—one of the few remaining safe havens left—and who knew how long it would continue to survive. They had to find Catherine and secure the gate before the rest of the Silver Bloods were able to burst through from the other side.

Jack saw her distress and put a hand on her shoulder. "Don't give up hope. It is a bleak time in our history, but I have faith that we will find a way to stop this evil and that we will survive."

Schuyler nodded. She had to think of a way to reach Catherine. Where was she hiding? She was in the city, Schuyler knew; even Mahrus had agreed that her theory was solid. The Nephilim activity was strongest here. This was the place. Schuyler had to find a way to draw her out.

"Don't you think it's strange?" she asked Jack suddenly. "If it's easier to keep the demons out of this world by obliterating the paths entirely, like Kingsley did when he released the *subvertio*, why did Michael create the gates instead?"

"He must have had a good reason. The law of Creation mandates that that which was made by the Almighty should not be unmade. The Gates of Hell have kept this world safe for centuries. Michael put his strength into their foundation. They have been weakened because he has been weakened," Jack said thoughtfully.

"Do you think Mahrus is right? About the Silver Blood who's behind this being from New York?" Schuyler asked. It was where the killings had begun, after all, where the first deaths from Full Consumption had occurred. In Italy, Oliver had told them about how Forsyth Llewellyn had disappeared, and how Mimi and the Venators had fingered him as the traitor. Bliss had confirmed as much—that her cycle father, Forsyth, the most trusted of Charles's associates, was actually the hidden Croatan in their midst, who had been keeping the spirit of Lucifer alive in his daughter. "Do you think Forsyth is here?" she asked, shuddering. "That he's the one who's planned all this?"

"We'll find out," Jack said. "And when we do, we will destroy him," he promised. "We have nothing to be frightened of, least of all that traitor."

Schuyler huddled next to him, and Jack rested his head against her neck. She put a hand on his cheek, feeling the stubble. She turned toward him, and they slowly fell onto the bed. Soon she felt his fangs puncture her skin and begin to draw blood.

Schuyler felt the same drowsy happiness she always did after they performed the Sacred Kiss. She felt Jack release her, rolling over so he could turn off the light. She was about to surrender to sleep when she felt a sharp pain in her stomach, and she sat up, doubling over, clutching her middle.

"What's wrong?" Jack asked, alarmed. "Did I hurt you? Schuyler . . . talk to me."

She shook her head. She couldn't speak: it was too painful. She felt as if she were being split in two. She felt dizzy and disoriented, nauseated, and she took a few gulps of air.

"I'm all right . . . I'm all right . . ." she said, right before she vomited her dinner all over the floor.

"Schuyler!" Jack yelled, feeling helpless.

She clutched the nightstand, her shoulders heaving, ignoring Jack for a moment. The wave of nausea passed, and she took the moment to breathe. Then another wave crashed—harder this time—and this time it was more frightening. . . . Blood and bile, a dark viscous puddle.

Jack quickly cleaned up the mess with a towel from the bathroom. He looked up at her. "Lie down."

"I can't. It feels better to stand."

He tossed the towel into a corner and walked to her side. "Lean on me, then."

She clutched him, shaking. She'd felt off since they'd arrived in Cairo, but now she felt sicker than she ever had in her life. This was worse than the Transformation; worse than the time she had been away from the Coven and her blood had thinned. She felt as if she were dying. But the feeling passed, and her stomach settled. She felt much better. "I'm all right," she said, still holding him. "Probably just some sort of virus. Maybe Cairo Belly finally caught up with me."

"Are you sure?"

"Yes. I'm okay. Just a bit of nausea. I've had it before." She gave him a reassuring smile.

Jack did not hide his concern. He had not noticed that she had been feeling sick, and they shared everything. He was appalled at the depth of his ignorance, but there had to be a reason. Then he knew. "How long has this been going on?" he asked quietly. "Tell me, my love."

Schuyler shrugged. A few weeks, maybe a month at the most. He was right. She had hidden it from him, which was why he had not known. "I didn't want you to worry, what with everything that's going on. I'm all right, I promise."

Jack did not answer, but continued to hold her, the two of them silent. They each had secrets they were keeping from the other; secrets they were keeping out of love. But slowly, and surely, both would soon come to light.

TWENTY-THREE

In the Limelight

Only when they were inside did Oliver notice that the nightclub was housed in a space that looked like an old cathedral; a deconsecrated church that had been turned into a haven of sin. The music was deafening and the club smelled like smoke and body odor. They could barely move, the crowds were pressed so tightly. It was pure misery. Oliver was afraid to look down to see what he was wearing, but he needn't have worried: he was dressed as he had been that morning, in a safari vest and jeans. His regular clothes. Maybe in Tartarus they didn't care about illusions, or perhaps the underworld's stylist was off today? He wanted to ask Mimi, but she was intent on pressing forward. She swiveled her head every which way, looking for Kingsley. She seemed to know her way around the club, and led them up a staircase, where the VIP rooms were.

The private back rooms were built like Russian matryoshka dolls, in that each new space led to another. Oliver had the feeling that one could spend eternity wandering through a succession of ever-smaller, ever-darker, ever-hotter rooms, while the droning sound of a monotone techno beat—*bumf, bumf, bumf*—resounded in the brain until one went as insane as the demons that surrounded the place. Each back room was guarded by a door bitch and a bouncer, but Mimi glided through like she owned the place.

She finally stopped, and Oliver almost bumped into her back. She had come to the end of the VIP rooms. There were no more doors at the other end. This was it.

She took a seat at a table and motioned for Oliver to do the same. They settled into the thick red velvet banquette. No sooner had they sat down than the manager, a bulldog in an ugly shiny suit, came up to the two of them. "Fallen," he said, pointing at Mimi. "You're not one of us. Get out!" he growled. "No service for your type here."

Mimi sat up, affronted, and began to argue. "Helda gave me permission to—"

"Helda's up there," the demon answered, pointing with his thumb. "I don't care what Helda said. No Fallen in my club. Unless your blood is silver, no dice, baby. Makes everyone uncomfortable." He gestured to two ugly trolls who were stationed at the doors—who'd just let them in, in fact—and they pulled Mimi and Oliver from their seats.

"Let me go!" Mimi demanded. "You can't do this! Do you know who I am?"

"What about him?" one of the trolls asked their boss, nodding at Oliver.

"What about him?" the demon snarled.

"He's alive," the troll said hungrily. "Can we have him?"

"Yeah, I don't care."

The trolls grunted their approval and began to drool.

Mimi struggled, but the trolls were too strong. They began to march them out of the VIP room when a low, smooth voice cut through the drone.

"Let them go, Beelzebub." The voice was familiar, and Mimi froze. She couldn't breathe for a moment—scarcely believing that after all the hardship in her journey, she would be rewarded at last. She slowly turned around to see a handsome man standing to the side, his face hidden in shadow.

Nothing happened. The demon growled.

"I said, let them go. Or am I not making myself clear?"

"Down, boys," the demon said, and the trolls released their hold.

Oliver squinted at the dark figure who'd saved them. He was pretty sure he knew who was talking, but for a moment he didn't know whether to feel relieved or to remain frightened. He decided anything was better than having those trolls salivating over him.

"But boss, they're stinking up the place," the demon whined, looking cowed and frightened.

"You're only smelling yourself," the handsome fellow said, with an amused grin at his delectable insult. "Go on, now, and find other guests to harass; but leave my friends alone."

He stepped into the light and held out his hand. "Force," Kingsley Martin said, looking just as smooth and debonair as ever. There was something new and different about him, but it wasn't his looks: he was still the same sexy beast with the same saucy forelock, the same sparkling dark eyes. Kingsley always looked ready for fun, but now he also looked relaxed and at ease, perfectly comfortable in his new surroundings. He looked neither miserable nor tortured, and Mimi had to stop herself from running to his arms, as something she saw in his face made her hold her emotions in check.

Kingsley did not look surprised to see her. Or shocked, or excited, or any of the emotions she had thought he would show when they were finally reunited. He looked as if something of minor interest had wandered in. "How nice to see you here. You need a drink?"

Mimi wondered what kind of game he was playing. Did he not want to show her how he felt about her in front of the trolls and demons who surrounded them? This from the boy with the quick fingers and insatiable lust? She remembered how fast he could get her undressed when he wanted her—and he'd wanted her very much and very often back then. This from the boy who'd sacrificed himself so she could live? Well, she could match his light tone. She was Mimi Force, after all, and if Kingsley was going to play that game, if he wanted a chase, then she would give him one.

"Sure. What are you pouring?" she asked, flipping her hair over her shoulder and settling back into their corner table.

Kingsley snapped his fingers and a beautiful virago appeared. The Amazon was almost six feet tall and dressed in a tiny silver dress that showed off her bountiful assets. "Siren, make sure my friends get everything and anything they wish," he drawled.

"Sure thing, boss." The cocktail waitress placed two leather-bound drink menus on the table. "What'll you have? Everything's on the house."

Mimi opened the book to choose a libation, and when she looked up, Kingsley had disappeared. She turned to Oliver questioningly, but he only shrugged.

"You're friends of Araquiel's? You're so lucky," their waitress whispered.

"Why? Does he own the club?" Oliver asked.

"Better. He's the consigliere," the waitress said.

"He's a mobster?" Oliver looked confused.

"Sort of. He's Helda's right-hand man. How about that," Mimi said, leaning back in the booth and taking a moment to assess the situation. No wonder the underworld had put up such a tough fight during their journey. Helda would not want to lose her closest adviser just because Mimi wanted her boyfriend back.

"Huh. Well, it's good to have friends in high places, right?" Oliver asked, with a nervous smile.

Mimi did not answer. She had found Kingsley, but it appeared that Helda had been telling the truth. Kingsley was far from lost, and had no ambition to be found.

TWENTY-FOUR

The Bride Wore Orange

"You look beautiful," Charles said, finding Allegra standing before her dressing room mirror, getting ready for the evening.

She turned around and smiled as she finished putting on her earrings. "You remember these?" she asked. "You gave them to me in Rome."

"I do." He nodded. "They were from Greek artisans; they cost me a fortune."

"Thank goodness Cordelia didn't auction them off. I was worried I wouldn't find anything after she did her spring-cleaning." Allegra carefully removed a necklace from her jewelry box. It was a Carnelian necklace, from Egypt. "Help me with this one?"

Charles carefully laid it on her neck and clicked the lock into place. He kissed the back of her neck tenderly.

"Now, go on with you. Isn't it bad luck to see the bride

before the wedding?" Allegra smiled, even though she was far from superstitious, as this was only one of innumerable bondings they had shared since the beginning of time, after all. She felt lighter—and for the first time since Florence, she did not doubt herself. She looked forward to moving on with her life, to their life together, as well as to the party that would immediately follow the ceremony.

The Coven was gathered at the Temple of Dendur, and soon she would make her way to the altar and say the words that would bind her to her twin in this lifetime.

She had dressed in a way to remind everyone of their storied history, with the Roman earrings, the Egyptian neck-lace, a dress made of silk and linen cut close to the body. Hattie had woven lavender into her hair so that Allegra wore it just as she had at their bonding in Rome. She did not wear a white dress, but donned a gown of a ravishing orange hue, just as she had on the Nile. Bright and happy and festive. Then there was the veil, a curtain of silk that would cover her head.

As was the custom, Charles would travel to the bonding on his own, with his attendants, and Allegra would arrive a few minutes after. They would meet in front of the temple steps at sunset.

She was almost ready when there was a knock on her bedroom door. "There's someone downstairs for you. Says he's an old friend of yours," Hattie said, sounding a bit skeptical.

"Who is it?"

"He wouldn't say. I told Julius not to let him in. I don't want you to be late."

"This really isn't a good time," Allegra said. "Can't you get rid of him?"

"We've tried, but he won't budge. Maybe it's best if you do the shooing."

Allegra walked carefully down the stairs in her jeweled slippers and walked out the front door to find Ben Chase idling by the stoop, with Julius, their driver, keeping a watchful eye on him.

"Hey," she said, tapping him on the shoulder. "What are you doing here?"

"Hey. Sorry is this a bad time . . . ?" He looked at her dress and veil. "Costume party?"

"No, it's . . ." She could not tell him what she was wearing. Of course he didn't know. It was her bonding gown, but Red Bloods wore white to their weddings. "What are you doing here?"

He stuck his hands in his coat pocket and cocked his head to the park. "Wanna take a walk with me?"

"Right now?" Allegra looked at her watch. She was supposed to be en route to the Met right now.

Julius looked at her curiously. "We'll be late, miss." But what bride was ever on time for her bonding?

And if there was ever a time to hear what Ben needed to say, it was now. After tonight it would be too late. "Sure."

She kicked off her high heels and changed into a pair of flip-flops she kept in the foyer.

They walked a few blocks down to Riverside Park, and walked by the water. The leaves were starting to turn. It would be winter soon, cold. Their shoes crunched in the leaves. Her dress made a rustling noise in the grass. In an hour, she would be bonded to Charles.

Allegra spoke first. "What are you doing here?"

"I didn't get married," he said.

"Hmm," she said, not knowing quite what to think, and somehow not surprised. When she saw him at the stoop, her heart had taken a grand leap, and she knew instantly that this was what he was going to say. Somehow, even though she believed this part of her life was over and the danger had passed, it was as if someone kept opening the book to the same page—someone was insisting that she and Ben see each other again. Who was that someone? Was it her? Was it him? Why was it suddenly so easy to forget about the carefully orchestrated plans for her bonding day? She was supposed to get in the car now. In a few minutes she was supposed to be standing in the temple.

Charles would be standing at the altar in his tuxedo. Their guests would be arranged around them, holding candles. They would say the words to each other. She had already moved her belongings to the town house that morning—a careful ritual they still practiced from the ancient Egyptian world, back when a bonding was signified by the wife bringing her things to her husband's home and there was no need for ceremony. How sensible they'd been then, truly.

And yet, in a whisper, in a flash, she had tossed the plans to the wind, had agreed to take a walk with Ben. Perhaps they should have been superstitious after all. Perhaps it had been bad luck this morning—for Charles to see her.

Or maybe it was good luck—since why on earth was Ben here, now, at such an inopportune time? If he had come tomorrow, she would not have recognized him. Or if he *had* come yesterday, she might have had more time to think it over before acting—time to come to reason and gather her wits. But the time was now. There was no time to waste, no time to think. There was only the drumbeat of her heart. She was in her bonding dress. She had lavender twined into her hair.

Ben found a bench and motioned for her to sit with him. "I couldn't tell you back then because I didn't think it mattered. But it matters now. Renny was pregnant. Or she thought she was."

"What happened?"

"I don't know. I'm not really sure. It sounds like she was never pregnant in the first place. She only believed she was. Mother thinks that she was trying to marry the boss's son. Mother always thinks that of every girl I date." Ben sighed. "I was going to go through with the wedding anyway. What did it matter if she was pregnant or not. . . . I loved her."

Allegra nodded. It was hard to hear him declare his love

for another girl, but she had seen it herself that evening at the Redwood bar—his gentle way with Renny, the obvious affection between them.

His leaned back against the bench and pulled off his scarf, twisting it in his hands. "In the end . . . I couldn't do it. I called it off. I realized I had to follow my own happiness, which is why I'm here now." He turned to her, and his eyes were the brightest and clearest blue she had ever seen.

"Ben . . . don't say anything you don't mean," she warned. "You've just gone through a crisis. It's not an easy thing to break up with someone you were going to marry." She should know, she thought. "You don't know what you're saying."

"That's just the thing, though," he said. "I know what I want now. And it's what I always wanted. I just didn't think I could get it."

Allegra began to panic. This was not what she wanted—she was wearing the oils, the swords had been blessed, the rings collected from the safe. "You're making things complicated, and I want us to be friends. You don't know what you're doing."

"Hear me out, please, Legs," he said.

She nodded, her heart pounding. She should leave right now—she could not stay here and listen to this—it would only complicate things. But instead of thinking of the guests at the temple, or the orderly procession of events that were now slowly going haywire, she wanted, so badly, to hear what Bendix had to say.

"That night when you walked back into my life . . . I could never forget you. It stirred up so much in me. . . ." he said, his hands making circling motions above his chest.

"Ben. I can't. I told you . . ." Allegra's voice rose, strangled by emotion. "I told you I can't."

"I know what you are, and I love you. I want you. I don't care that you're . . . not human." He could not bring himself to say the word.

She shook her head. "It's more than that. It's so much more than that." She bowed her head. "There's something you need to know."

She told him the vision she had seen the first time they had been together, the first time she drank his blood. She told him about their baby, and then seeing herself comatose on the bed, and her certainty that if they were together it meant that he would die, that her love for him would mean his death, that being together would mean the end of him somehow.

Ben remained silent for a while. Finally he spoke. "So if we stay together, I'll die?"

"I don't know." Allegra kept her face hard and resolute. "I think so."

"Hey." Ben smiled, and it was like the sun shining through the clouds. He chucked her chin. "Listen, Legs, I'm going to die anyway. I'm human. And I don't know about you, but I don't believe in visions of the future. I believe we choose our own destiny. You didn't give me a choice last time. You just left. But I'm here now. And I love you. Stay with me. Don't fear the future; we'll face it together."

He brushed away her tears. His hands were warm and soft.

TWENTY-FIVE

Temple Maidens

For a week, the team combed Cairo for any trace of the Nephilim, hunting down every lead they could find, but it was as if the demon-born had vanished into the air. As each avenue proved fruitless, and the days went by with no resolution or progress, Schuyler decided it meant they were going about it the wrong way. She still felt sick to her stomach and nauseated in the mornings, and the smell of meat could make her vomit. But her head was clear. She had a feeling she knew what her sickness was, but she kept her hopes to herself. She did not want to tell Jack until she was sure. In the meantime, they had a job to do.

If they could not find the Nephilim, they would have to find a way to make the enemy come to them. She remembered something that Sam had told them when they'd first met—that they had tracked the Nephilim to the City of the Dead because they were working on a hunch that the girls who had been disappearing from the necropolis were being taken to the underworld.

The girls who were kidnapped were followers of the temple of Anubis, the ancient Egyptian god of the dead. While modern Egypt had moved on from the old ways, the people of the cemeteries had never forgotten, and a crew of temple maidens still kept the sacred flames alive. Schuyler formulated a plan and shared it with the team, and they spent an evening hashing out all the details. When they were satisfied, everyone went home.

"I don't like this," Jack said, the next morning. "It's too dangerous. You're putting yourself at too much risk."

"There's no other way to find the gate unless they take me there," she reminded him. "I'll be fine." There was no more time to question or wait. They had to act now, before the hidden Silver Blood broke down the barrier.

"But you're still sick," Jack argued. "It's not safe."

"It comes and goes," she said with a smile. "I'll be okay. I'll have Deming and Dehua with me. They're a match for any demon." She put on the white robes of the temple maidens and hid her face behind a veil. "Besides, you're going to be right behind us. Once they bring us to the gate, you and the rest of the team will be able to take them down."

Schuyler had asked the priest who manned the temple not to send any other girls that day, as she and the two Venators planned to perform all the duties. They'd learned that the girls were usually abducted at night, when they walked from the temple to the outskirts of the southern cemetery, where they gathered firewood for the next morning.

The temple was located in a busy part of the cemetery, next to shops and cafés. It was a simple square structure, with a forecourt where the public gathered, and an inner sanctum where only the priests and maidens were allowed. In ancient Egypt, only the pharaohs and ordained priests could offer gifts to the jackal-headed god, but in the nineteenth century, the rules had changed so that girls as young as fourteen were called into service to perform many of the rituals of cleansing and prayer, as it was believed that only the prayers of the pure and virginal would be answered by the god of the tombs.

When Schuyler and the Venators arrived, they dipped their hands and feet into the shallow pool at the base of the temple, a cleansing practice that was mostly metaphorical in nature (in the past, the pool was deep and the priests bathed in it before entering the temple). Schuyler washed as quickly as she could and followed Deming and Dehua into a massive hallway lined with great stone columns. The temple dated from the Ptolemy era, and was painstakingly preserved by the people of the cemeteries.

Since Schuyler and the girls were pretending to be disciples, they had to do everything ordinary temple maidens would have done so that in the event that the Nephilim were watching, they would not suspect anything was awry. The first order of business was to light the candles and cleanse the air, and the three of them proceeded into the inner chambers with their candles lit, chanting softly as they made their way to the chapel that housed the statue of Anubis. They placed their candles in the holders and waited a few moments before beginning to clean the statue.

Anubis had the body of a man and the head of a beast, and Schuyler felt a little uneasy as they began to wipe and oil down the stone. Deming brought the folded linen from the back room and dressed the statue, while Dehua was in charge of rubbing rouge on his cheeks and applying sacred oil on his forehead.

Schuyler brought in the gifts of food and drink—baskets of bread and a few bottles of wine that that been left at the temple as offerings—and placed them in front of the statue.

"What now?" Dehua asked, inspecting their handiwork. The statue shone in the dim light.

"The faithful are waiting," Schuyler said. "Let's get to work."

They spent the whole day in the forecourt, leading prayers, keeping the fire lit, anointing worshippers with holy oil. Schuyler had asked the priest to tell his flock not to schedule a funeral or memorial on this day, as she did not feel right about leading the incantations and prayers for true believers.

"Hot in here," she said, when the three were alone in the inner chamber. She was sweaty underneath her layers.

But the twins only shrugged, since, as vampires, they were able to regulate their body temperature.

Schuyler began to feel a bit woozy and light-headed, and wondered if Jack was right in worrying about her on this undertaking. She'd convinced herself she had no choice. While Deming and Dehua were trained fighters, she was the one who had to carry out her grandfather's legacy. She could not let them find the gate without her.

How's it going in there? Jack sent.

Quiet, she replied. *You guys see anything?*

Not a thing.

The Venators were edgy, regarding each worshipper with suspicion. But the day passed uneventfully, and then it was sunset, and they had to set off to collect the firewood. Jack and the Lennox brothers would follow a few steps behind.

The girls walked slowly through the dark uninhabited streets. Most people lived in the northern part of the necropolis, and it was not a good idea to walk the southern area at night, which was said to be the home of drug dealers and thieves. There were no streetlamps, and there was a hushed quiet that was unnerving. The girls did not whisper to each other, and Schuyler felt the hairs on the back of her neck rise. But they arrived at the woodpile undisturbed, gathered what they needed for kindling, and returned to the temple unharmed.

"What now?" Dehua asked, setting her bundle of wood by the grate.

Schuyler shrugged. Were they doing something wrong? Did the Nephilim suspect something was different?

They're not taking the bait, Jack sent. He and the boys were back to guarding the temple from a rooftop across the way.

No, they will come for us, I can feel it, Schuyler sent. She closed her eyes and listened to the wind. She could sense something in the air, expectation maybe, like the quiet before a battle; everyone tense until the first shot was fired.

Deming exchanged a skeptical look with her sister. "Maybe they've gone. They've destroyed the blood spirits and the Coven's gone underground. What more do they want? We should move on. Mahrus thinks they're out to target Jerusalem next."

Schuyler was about to protest when a strong wind blew out all the candles in the temple, plunging the room into darkness. *This is it,* she sent. *Don't fight,* she reminded the girls. *Don't move. Let them take us. Remember, for this purpose we are human and weak.*

A group of men surrounded them—appearing out of the mist. Schuyler was surprised to find that their captors were human and did not have the forked tongues and glowing crimson eyes of the Hell-born. Rough hands held her on both sides. She screamed in terror, as did the Chinese twins. It was a good performance. The room rang with their panicked cries.

Schuyler did not have to try to pretend very hard, as a cold fear gripped her soul—but she trusted the Venators and her beloved to find them.

"The Zaniyat will have her kindred!" their leader

announced, and the group cheered lustily. Their laughter had a sickening, crazed quality, like that of hyenas howling at a carcass, and Schuyler shivered.

She noticed the men had tattoos on their arms—the triglyph symbol she had seen on MariElena. The mark of Lucifer along with the Blue Blood symbol for humankind, to symbolize the unholy union of the two races.

"Let us go!" she cried. "Leave us alone!"

Deming and Dehua pretended to resist as well, struggling against their attackers.

The men ignored them, and the leader cackled as he struck his spear into the fireplace and the floor of the temple fell away. Schuyler gave out a real scream this time, as they all disappeared into a hole in the ground, and tumbled straight through the living glom into the underworld.

Jack! Can you hear me! They're here! she sent, but she knew it was useless. They were out of sight and out of reach.

She could fight, and she *would* fight, she thought. Maybe there was still away to use their weakness to an advantage. The Nephilim servants believed they had kidnapped three help-less human girls. It was always good to be underestimated.

TWENTY-SIX

The Only Girl in the World

"So it's okay to drink these?" Oliver asked, motioning to the cocktails set in front of them. One of them looked like it was made from hot lava: it was a deep scarlet hue, and it bubbled and smoked over a silver chalice. The second was a brilliant shade of green, and set off minty sparks that fizzled. He had never seen the likes of either, and while a deep-seated fear of everything in the place was still rooted in him, he was curious to find out what they tasted like. They had not drunk nor eaten anything since their arrival, and he was still light-headed and hungry.

"I don't know. I don't really care," Mimi snapped, whipping her head around the nightclub to look for Kingsley.

Oliver took a tentative sip. The lavalike concoction was warm and buttery, delicious, but almost too sweet. The green cocktail tasted like a honeydew melon, except again, there was a sense that the melons were too ripe, and almost—but not quite—rotten. It was a pattern that he was starting to notice in Tartarus, that even if something was nice, it wasn't quite right. The club was either too hot or too cold—one could never get comfortable. It was as if the ideal temperature, the ideal state of anything, really, didn't exist. It was always just a hair off, one way or the other. It could drive a person insane, he thought, if everything one ate was either too tasty or too bland, too salty or too sweet, too crunchy or too mushy, and nothing was ever just right. Well, where did he think he was . . . right? Oliver chided himself for making jokes, but he couldn't help amusing himself. It was all he had, at this point.

He wasn't sure what to make of Kingsley. He hadn't known him all that well when they were at Duchesne together, but the cool-kid act didn't surprise him. Oliver didn't know if Kingsley was pretending not to care, of if he had been in the underworld so long he truly didn't feel the same about Mimi anymore. Poor girl. She wasn't expecting this. She looked a little lost, a little forlorn, as she looked around the club. Her face sagged; her brittle armor was cracking, and Oliver felt for her. She didn't deserve this after all the hard work she had put in to getting here. He wished he could cheer her up, offer some sort of consolation. When the DJ played something new, something that wasn't such an earworm or designed to annoy, a song that actually had a beat and a melody, Oliver saw an opportunity.

"Come on," he said. "Let's dance."

Mimi could not resist a twirl on the dance floor, and if at first she had been inclined to say no to Oliver, she swallowed her frustration and annoyance. If Kingsley wanted to play this silly game, one where he pretended not to feel what he felt for her, then there was nothing she could do about it. She had begun to doubt her memories of his so-called love. What did they have between them anyway? They'd hooked up a few times, and sure, he'd come back to New York to convince her to forsake her bond; and sure, he'd sacrificed himself to save her—to save all of them—but Kingsley never promised anything; never even told her how he felt about her. What if she'd been wrong? What was she doing here? Mimi took a few deep breaths. She didn't want to think about what it meant, so instead she took Oliver's hand and they stepped onto the dance floor, in the middle of the writhing bodies. She would give these demons something to remember her by.

Oliver was a good dance partner. Unlike a lot of guys, he didn't look like he had no idea what he was doing. He had rhythm, and they moved elegantly together—Mimi shimmying up next to him while he put his hands lightly on her waist.

She twisted and turned, feeling the music in her veins, feeling the liberation that came with moving to the sound of the beat, slowly becoming one with the music. Her face flushed, her breasts heaved, she began to glow with an inner light, and for the first time during their journey to the under-world, her face relaxed and she smiled. Oliver grinned and clapped his hands.

This was fun, Mimi thought. It had been a very long time since she had done something just for the pure enjoy-ment of it, and for a moment she was a teenager again, without a care in the world. When she closed her eyes she could pretend she was back in the city. There had been a nightclub just like this one once. Funny how the New York landscape changed like that. While the buildings themselves remained the same, nineteenth-century synagogues turned into hot fashion-show venues. Banks and cathedrals now housed cocktail bars and discos.

The dancing grew more frenetic, and the crowd pressed tightly so that Mimi was pushed back against Oliver, jos-tling him. As she turned around to apologize, she caught a glimpse of him back at their banquette, sipping his devil cocktail. (She probably should have warned him about them, but it was too late now.) He shrugged his shoulders as if he had no idea how that happened.

So whose hands were on her waist, then? Who was press-ing his body against hers with a possessive, familiar weight? She turned around slowly, although she already knew the answer.

Kingsley smiled his wicked grin, and she could feel his body responding to hers as they swiveled and ground to the beat of the music. He leaned over and rested his chin on the base of her neck. She could feel his slick-warm sweat on her skin. His hands wandered, dropping from her waist to her hips, pulling her closer to him. She could feel her heart thudding with the music but also in rhythm with his—as if they were alone together, the heat of the dance floor and the darkness a cocoon that surrounded them.

"Nice moves, Force," he murmured.

She pulled away, not willing to give in so easily. He twirled her expertly around, spinning and dipping her so far backward that his nose was practically in her cleavage. Damn, he was smooth. But then what did she expect? She realized that in the time they had been apart she'd constructed an ideal image of him; had only remembered the shining parts of his personality, and the way he had looked at her that last time, before he'd disappeared into the White Darkness. That was all she had set her hopes and heart upon, that one last look. She had forgotten what he was really like. Unpredictable. Cocky. Sly. He'd never said he loved her, after all. She'd just assumed. . . .

But now he was pulling her toward him again, and they were facing each other, her head resting on his shoulder, and his hand was on her back. The music was something she recognized. Marvin Gaye's "Let's Get It On." Too many of her human familiars liked to play it before the *Caerimonia*. The classic makeout song, almost as clichéd as Van Morrison's "Moondance." Kingsley sang softly in her ear, and his voice had that low, smoky quality she'd liked so much from the beginning. "'Giving yourself to me can never be wrong if the love is true . . .'"

Mimi tried not to laugh. He really was a piece of work, this guy. Was he freaking serious? Did he only think of one thing and one thing only? Was that all it was? Did he really believe she had come all the way to the underworld so they could hook up? She tried not to feel too insulted.

The music stopped, and she moved away from his embrace. Taking her cue, Kingsley slouched away as well. He was still smirking. He didn't need to say it: she knew he was thinking that she was being silly to pretend they weren't going to end up in bed sooner or later.

Am I wrong? His voice was loud and clear in her head, and she could hear the confidence behind it.

But Mimi ignored it for now. She didn't want to fall back to their old ways—pretending that they didn't care about each other; pretending it was all just Venators-with-benefits; that he hadn't sacrificed so much for her, or that she was in the underworld for any other reason than to get him out of there. All the events of the day—Oliver's fake wedding, Mamon's offer, the journey to Tartarus, and actually seeing Kingsley again—were suddenly overwhelming. She felt a bit dizzy and as if she were going to burst into tears. It was too much, and she felt her knees begin to buckle underneath her. She was going to faint.

"Hey," Kingsley said, looking concerned. He slung a friendly arm around her shoulder and pulled her toward him. "C'mon now. I was just kidding around. You all right?"

She nodded. "I just need some air. It's hot in here."

"No kidding." Kingsley walked her back to her table. "Where are you staying in town?"

Mimi shrugged. "I don't know." She hadn't thought that far ahead.

"Go see my man at the Duke's Arms. He'll give you guys a nice room. Make sure Hazard-Perry over there doesn't get targeted by the trolls—or worse, by the Hellhounds," Kingsley said, writing an address on the back of a calling card and handing it to her.

"What'd he say?" Oliver asked, when Kingsley left.

"To stay in a hotel," Mimi said, again feeling the absurdity of the current situation. She'd risked everything for him, and now . . .

"So what do we do, boss?" Oliver asked.

Mimi fingered the card. Her head ached. She had journeyed all the way down. She wasn't about to give up now. She had to find out how Kingsley felt about her. If he wanted her the way she wanted him—and not just for a one-night stand or a meaningless, loveless affair. The real thing. The love that had eluded her all her immortal life in her years with Jack.

If Kingsley didn't want her around, he wouldn't have asked her to stay, would he? Boys. Even in the underworld it was hard to decipher their intentions. She thought of the way they had moved together, what it felt like. There had to be more than just physical attraction between them. It had to mean something, didn't it? She thought of how she had laughed at girls who thought just because a guy slept with them it meant that he loved them. Now she was one of those needy, clingy girls. How ridiculous to find that her heart was so much more vulnerable than she had ever imagined it could be. How the hell had she allowed herself to fall in love with someone like Kingsley Martin? It was infuriating. He was like a shooting star you tried to catch with your hands. She would only get burned.

But she was made of sterner stuff than that. Mimi would play the game. She would stay until he told her she had to leave. Until he told her the truth of what was in his heart.

She noted the address and put the card in her purse. "I guess we should get settled. Looks like we'll be here for a while."

TWENTY-SEVEN

The Dovecote

Allegra's favorite time of the day was just before sunset. That summer in Napa, almost a year since she'd left New York, the days were so long that it would be nine o'clock by the time darkness descended on the valley. The heat of the day would dissipate in the late afternoon, and a rustling breeze would blow through the trees. The rolling hills were covered in a warm russet glow, in an ephemeral, timeless beauty. The vineyard's tasting rooms and cellars would be joyously empty. The tourists and wine lovers had gone, along with the field hands and vintners who'd become their friends and colleagues, and it was just the two of them. Ben would shuffle in from his studio, and Allegra would open a bottle of their newest Chardonnay, and they would eat their dinner under the trees, watching the hummingbirds flit from flower to flower. Life could not be sweeter.

"Aren't we lucky your family bought this place," Allegra said, dipping a piece of crusty French bread into their homemade olive oil. "It's like a dream."

They had moved to the vineyard ostensibly to help prepare for the fall harvest, when the grapes would be plump and bursting with juice. Ben's father had bought the whole spread on a whim one afternoon a few years ago, when he'd stopped by for a drink at his favorite *enoteca* only to discover that his usual glass of Syrah was no longer available, as the vineyard was closing due to bankruptcy. It was something his parents did often, Ben explained—they bought things that they enjoyed in order to keep them in existence. Their hobbies and interests had led them to assume ownership of a Greek diner in New York that still served egg creams, and a whole French cosmetics line. They were preservationists and traditionalists. One of the great benefits of being so privileged was their ability to keep the beautiful things in the world they loved from going extinct and disappearing forever.

The question of where Allegra and Ben would live was answered when Allegra happened to mention that she had some knowledge of winemaking. Right then it was decided that they would not settle in the Bay Area, but instead would move up north to help run the winery.

Allegra had left her life that afternoon when she had taken a walk in Riverside Park, and had never returned. She had not left a note of explanation, and had cut off the telepathic communication she shared with Charles, even going so far as to cloak her glom signature. She had taken the extreme precaution to make sure he would never find her. She was certain that Charles could send an army of investigators and Venators after her and never even come close to finding her true location. He would never forgive her for this—for walking out on him on their bonding day—and she did not want to think of the pain she was causing. All she knew was that something inside her could no longer stomach the life she had been living; and even though every fiber in her blood and her immortal being told her she was making a huge mistake, her heart was steadfast in its resolution.

It had been madness, really, to walk out of her life with nothing. She was still in her bonding dress when she jumped into a taxicab with Ben. She brought nothing with her: not a toothbrush or a change of clothes, not even enough money for a bus ticket.

No matter. Money was no object, as Ben had arranged it all. They had left the city that evening, and she was whisked away on his jet—the family plane—directly to Napa. Now they were both hiding in the dovecote, Allegra thought. Two lovebirds.

During the day, Ben painted in a small cottage on the property. The room had good light, and from the picture windows he could see vines growing on the hillside. Allegra ran the shop: she had an instinctive feeling for the vintner's trade, and enjoyed every part of it—from pruning and nurturing the vines to designing the labels; from testing the barrels to see how they were fermenting to selling the vintages in the little tasting room. She had gotten a dark tan from working in the fields, and she was known in the small farm community for her cheese and bread. She had invited children from the neighborhood for the annual crush at the end of the season, as theirs was one of the last vineyards to keep to the tradition of stomping the grapes after harvest. Their vintner, a world-renowned winemaker, had named their latest Chardonnay after her. GOLDEN GIRL, it read on the label.

The sun finally set that evening, and they brought in their plates and empty bottles. After cleaning up, Ben said he wanted to work a little more, and Allegra joined him in his studio.

She curled up on the rickety couch covered in canvas and watched him paint. He was working on a more abstract series these days, and she knew it was good. He was going to be famous, and not only because of his family, but because of his talent. Ben turned around and cleaned his brushes into the turpentine.

"How do you feel about another portrait?" he said.

"Do you think it's wise?" she teased, flirting a little. "Might bring back old memories."

"Precisely." He grinned.

He was so beautiful, she thought, towheaded and tan, with his generous laugh. She loved the way he made her feel: light-headed, joyful. The way they were together: easy, laughing. She felt human with him. She did not think of the future or what was in store for them. She had walked away from all of that. Here, in the heart of the sleepy Napa valley, she was not Gabrielle the Uncorrupted, no vampire queen, but merely Allegra Van Alen, a former New York girl who had moved to the country to make wine.

She moved to the sheet on the platform and slowly peeled off her clothing. The overalls she unhooked and let fall to the ground, the old T-shirt that she wore on the days she worked in the fields and not in the store. She twisted her torso and asked, "Is this good?"

Ben nodded slowly.

Allegra held her pose. She closed her eyes and breathed deeply. She could feel him watching her, memorizing every line, every curve of her body for his work.

There was no sound for the remainder of the hour but that of the quiet taps and soft strokes of a paintbrush on canvas.

"Good," he said, meaning she could release the pose.

She wrapped herself in a robe and walked over to look at his painting. "Best one yet."

Ben put away his brushes and pulled her onto his lap. "I'm so glad you're here."

"Me too," she said, sinking into his arms. She traced the veins on his neck. Then sank her fangs deep into his skin and began to drink deeply.

Ben leaned back, and soon the robe fell away and they were together.

It was the happiest she had ever felt.

Allegra could almost convince herself that they would be able to live here together for the rest of their lives.

TWENTY-EIGHT

The Brides of Lucifer

*T*hey were deep underground, on a path beneath
the necropolis leading to a subterranean stairway.
Schuyler stumbled on a rock and cut her ankle. It was hard
to keep balance as the men alternately pulled and carried her
to their destination. Their attackers had blindfolded them
after they'd fallen through the void, and while she knew they
were in the underworld, she wasn't sure how far down they
had taken her. Were they through the gate already? Had her
plan worked? But if they had breached the Gate of Promise,
where was its keeper?

And what did they do now that Jack and the rest of the
team had no idea where they had gone? Did they fight? Did
they wait? Schuyler decided to wait. Finally the marching
stopped, and her blindfold was removed. Schuyler looked
around. She was in some sort of waiting room, and she did
not see Deming or Dehua anywhere. She was alone with her

captors, two swarthy men who looked at her appraisingly. The Red Blood by her side slobbered over her. "Our masters will reward us. You're a pretty one."

Schuyler's stomach tightened, and she comforted herself with the knowledge that she had Gabrielle's sword hidden in her robe. When the time was right, she would be able to fight her way out of here.

The door opened, and a female demon entered. Schuyler had never seen one before. Jack had told her about the different creatures of the underworld, of the demons that lived in Helheim, who'd been made from the darkness and breathed the Black Fire.

"What did you bring in?" she asked. "We got twins in the other room. Nice one. Lads will like that. What've we got here?"

Schuyler's attackers pushed her forward. "Worth the top bride price, this one is."

"Take off your *hijab*," the demon barked. "I want to see what we're buying. Go on, now."

Schuyler slipped the garment over her head, pocketing Gabrielle's sword, which had collapsed into a small knife in her fist. She stood in her slip and crossed her arms before her chest.

The demon leaned forward and sniffed her. "What have you got in your hand, missy?"

Before Schuyler could react, the demon's hand clamped down on her wrist and squeezed tightly.

Schuyler's knees buckled from the pain, and she had no choice but to open her hand and give up her weapon.

The demon picked it up, and the knife transformed into a long gleaming saber. "Just as I thought. This is a sword of the Fallen. Have Baal take a look at it. And warn the others—they might be just like her." She put her meaty hands on her thighs and smiled. "Thanks, boys, you did well. The bosses will find some angels in their beds tonight." She smiled. "Go on now, out with you. The trolls will pay you at the till."

The men shuffled out, and the demon studied Schuyler. "This is an interesting proposition. You're not exactly what we asked for, but I think we'll find someone who'll like you just the way you are." She left the room, banging the door behind her.

Once Schuyler was alone, she paced the entire length of it, trying to find an exit, as the door was locked with an invisible spell and the walls were made of solid rock. She tried everything, but no incantation even moved the rock an inch. She tried to quell the panic that threatened to wash over her, and forced herself to think. She'd lost her sword, but surely she could find something else to defend herself with before it was too late. Yet before she could form even the bare bones of an escape plan, the demon returned, and this time she was not alone.

It was a Croatan, a silver-haired angel—beautiful but with hard, flat crimson eyes, and scars on his face that marked him as one of Lucifer's own. The Corrupted leered at her, and Schuyler could smell its lust as a physical assault, as he sent her images that she could not escape from. She could not close her eyes, as the thoughts had penetrated her mind, and she saw exactly what was in store for her if she did not get away. She felt her courage begin to wane. She was trapped here—disarmed, vulnerable—but she raised her chin and her eyes flashed with rage. She would fight with every ounce of her body and soul.

"She'll do," the Croatan said. His voice was low and melodious but frosted with malice. "Get her ready." He held her by the chin with his hand. "The boys were right. You are a pretty one. But I'm not paying the bride price for her. The Fallen won't be able to bear me the children I need."

"But look at that hair, those eyes—she's the spitting image of Gabrielle," the demon protested. "Surely—"

"No negotiation. You're lucky I'm taking her off your hands," he said, and stroked Schuyler's cheek one last time before leaving.

"Well, you heard the fool. Let's go," the demon grumbled. "Come on, let's get you to Zani's house."

"Zani?" Schuyler asked. "You mean the priestess of the temple of Anubis?" She felt her heart beat faster at the prospect of finding the woman who might be Catherine of Siena.

"What are you talking about, child?" The demon clucked

her tongue. "Down here, the Zaniyat Babel is what we call a cathouse. The Whores of Babylon. Lucifer's brides. 'Course, not everyone gets chosen by the Dark Prince. You'll be wed to Danel, for instance. Lucky you, he's quite the looker, don't you think?"

Schuyler swallowed her shock to digest the information. "Zani" was no priestess. It was a code word for this operation—taking human brides for demons.

No. The Zaniyat Babel was no holy woman. She would not find Catherine of Siena here. "Zaniyat" was an ancient name, all right. There had been many names for the women who had been taken by the Croatan over the centuries: Deming had told her the Nephilim had called his mother "The Mistress." Satan's mistresses. Whores of Babylon. It was all the same. The Mistress of Florence must have been the first to birth a human-demon hybrid, but since then, there had been many to take her place, and now Schuyler would be one of them.

The demon led her down another underground passageway, and when they emerged out of it they were standing in the middle of a small-town bazaar, ringed by dusty buildings that did not look very different from the marketplaces of Cairo. Schuyler's captor rapped on the door of one of the buildings, and after a few minutes they were ushered inside.

A group of scantily clad heavily made-up human matrons greeted them in the entryway. Schuyler thought the presence of the Red Bloods meant that they must be in Limbo, the first circle of Hell, just beyond the living glom. Humans could not survive too long much deeper in the underworld.

"Danel wants her ready for the bonding in a few hours," the demon told them. "And he doesn't want her drugged."

The matrons nodded, and two of them led Schuyler to a small boudoir with a dressing room. They pushed her down on the cushioned stool in front of a vanity mirror.

"Let's see what we got here," the fatter, older, and darker lady said, jangling her gold bracelets.

"Too thin," her companion said. "We'll have to use the cutlets."

"Danel always picks the young ones."

Schuyler sat on the stool and glared at them. "Let me go," she ordered, but either the powers of compulsion were diffused in the underworld, or the humans had learned how to protect their minds from it. It was useless. The ladies merely laughed.

She couldn't believe how casual they were about what they were doing. "You give your daughters to these demons," she said to them. "You should be ashamed of yourselves."

The Red Blood madam slapped her across the face. "Speak to me like that again and you will lose your tongue."

"Stop!" her companion warned. "You're going to give her a fat lip. The boss doesn't like it when they're beaten up. Remember, we've got to make her look pretty."

Twenty-nine

River Palace

he Duke's Arms turned out not to be a hotel. Instead it was a palace, a veritable castle in the sky, a lavish fourplex penthouse in a grand skyscraper located at the far edge of town near the river Styx. The building was gaudy and gilded and frightfully ugly and tacky, with soaring pink columns, golden cherubim, leering gargoyles, decorated in nouveau riche flamboyance, Mimi thought. A real expensive eyesore. She didn't think it was Kingsley's fault: the place probably always looked like this no matter who was installed as consigliere. She noticed it was in a better part of town, though; the air along the river wasn't as gray or smoggy.

The doorman told them they were expected, and ushered them into the elevator.

When the doors opened, Mimi and Oliver found themselves standing in the foyer of a magnificent apartment with a curved, three-story staircase. A group of troll servants dressed in uniform stood in a row: butlers and footmen in livery, the maids and cooks in black dresses with starched aprons. All of them were wearing silver chokers with the sigil of the house engraved on the front.

"Welcome," the head butler said. "We have been expecting you, Lady Azrael."

Mimi gave him a queenly nod.

Now, this was more like it, Oliver thought.

"Shall you require supper, or shall I show you to your rooms?"

Mimi raised an eyebrow to her traveling companion. Oliver yawned. "I'm starved, but I think I'd rather sleep first."

"Our rooms, then."

"This way, please," a maid said, curtsying. They followed her down the hallway to another elevator, which brought them to a suite of rooms facing the river's eastern shore.

"This is where Helda stays when she visits," the maid whispered as she opened the double doors to a luxurious room with a grand view of the river. Mimi nodded. Kingsley meant it as an honor, surely, and while she was grateful to be so well taken care of, she was also just a little disappointed that he had left her side so quickly. She would have appreciated a shack alone with him rather than all these froufrou accoutrements. She said good night to Oliver and prepared for bed.

Oliver turned in as well. His bedroom suite was lavish and well appointed, but as he expected, the pillows were too soft, the bed too big, the air-conditioning turned up too high. Still, he didn't complain. He was just glad to have a place to rest at last, even if it was in an ersatz Trump Tower with a creepy troglodyte domestic staff. When his head hit the pillow, he didn't care that it was too soft; he slept immediately, like the dead, never moving from one spot.

For her part, Mimi sat up in bed for hours. She had found a selection of silk, sheer nightgowns in the walk-in closet, and after a long soak in the marble tub, she had changed into the sexiest one, slipped under the covers, and waited. Finally, after what seemed like hours, she could hear the elevator doors open—and recognized Kingsley's rolling step. She waited for him to sneak into her room and have his way with her.

She would tell him to stop, of course, and demand that he explain his feelings for her before they went any further. But afterward, after he pledged his devotion and begged for forgiveness for that casual, ambivalent greeting at the club, she would let him do whatever he wanted—and she had to admit she could not wait to be ravished. She squirmed with anticipation, remembering the way they had danced together—the feel of his strong arms circling her waist, and the way his body had moved with hers—and she arranged herself on the pillows to look as sleepy and innocent as possible.

But the steps grew farther away instead of getting closer, and then there was silence. Mimi cocked an eye open in annoyance. She fluffed her hair and the pillows again, made sure her nightgown fell on her body in an attractive, sultry angle, and resumed her position. Maybe this was part of the game? Teasing her again? But the minutes ticked by and still there was nothing. Mimi practically slept with one eye open the entire evening, but Kingsley did not visit her bedroom. Not that first night, and not for the nights after. In fact, she did not see him at all for the next couple of days.

Well played, Martin, Mimi thought. Well played. She determined not to inquire about his whereabouts or give any indication that she was waiting for him to make the first move. He had invited her to his house, so obviously he wanted her there. She thought she knew why he was making her wait. He wanted her to crumble and surrender so his victory over her heart would be complete. Mimi had a little more pride than that. A week after they had been installed at the Duke's Arms—so named, Mimi learned, because it was traditionally the seat of the Duke of Hell—a week after their awkward reunion, Mimi bumped into Kingsley in the breakfast room, and was able to match his polite tone.

"My trolls taking good care of you?" Kingsley asked, sitting down at the grand dining table with his bowl of fruit and cereal.

"Yes, very well, thanks." Mimi nodded.

He inquired about the comfort of the rooms and urged

her to make herself at home, and to order the staff to do whatever her heart desired. Kingsley was the consummate host. It was totally depressing.

"How do you find the view?" he asked.

Mimi looked up from her granola (which Oliver would describe as too dry and not enough raisins) and shrugged. "It's all right."

"I know it's not Central Park."

"I didn't expect it to be." She looked down at her plate, unsure of how to broach the topic of their relationship. It was as if there were an impenetrable wall around him. They had not seen each other since that first night, and still he had not asked the reason for her presence, had not spoken to her in any real way. He was the Duke of Hell and she was merely an honored guest. She didn't know how long he planned to carry out this charade.

He picked out a piece of fruit from his bowl and began to eat. "I know it's all a mirage, and that I'm not really eating this apple. But it helps, doesn't it? To have the daily rituals, to have some sort of order to the day. It never gets dark here, or light. No sun, of course. Only the light of the Black Fire, which never goes out. Ever burning but never sets," he murmured.

"Mmm," Mimi said.

"Enjoy your time here," he said. Then he was gone, and Mimi was left to eat her slightly sour yogurt alone.

* * *

For his part, Oliver spent most of his days swimming in the saltwater plunge pool on the top floor. After the initial excitement of living in a palace—not that it was all that different from the way he lived on the Upper East Side, really—he had started to feel lethargic and sluggish. As if his muscles had atrophied from not needing to go anywhere or do anything or use his mind for any reason other than to ask the trolls for his slippers. There were no art galleries, no music halls, no opera, no theater, no libraries, no literary or artistic amusements of any kind in Tartarus. Worse, there was nothing to read. There were only nightclubs and flesh bars, gladiator matches and sporting events. The television showed reruns of the most pandering type of programming: unfunny sitcoms, gross reality shows; and on the Internet there was only pornography. It was fun at first, but then vice is so boring when there's no virtue to balance it out. When there is nothing but sinful indulgence, sinful indulgence becomes a chore.

Oliver thought he would die from boredom. So he did laps in the Olympic-size pool—anything to make his muscles ache. He wished that Kingsley would just get back together with Mimi already. Well, what was he waiting for? Was he just stringing her along? Sure, Mimi was sort of . . . well, *annoying* was the word he was looking for, but she wasn't all that bad, and obviously Kingsley was attracted to her. A guy could do much worse than Mimi Force.

Not that it had never crossed Oliver's mind—he was a guy, after all, and Mimi was a beautiful girl—but the thought of the two of them as a couple was so alien and laughable, he couldn't see their friendship developing into anything more. And that's all they were, friends. Oliver liked Mimi, but he did not find her attractive in that way (she would tell him the feeling was mutual, of course). That's just the way it was.

Still, Kingsley was such a lucky devil. After all, Mimi had dropped everything in her life to be with him. She was here now. Their story was sure to have a happy ending if only Kingsley would stop being, well, Kingsley. Whereas he, Oliver, would never get what he wanted; not in this lifetime or any other. Not for the first time did Oliver wonder if nice guys really did finish last.

Mimi decided the reason Kingsley was acting so uninterested was that perhaps he no longer found her irresistible. When one night after another came and went, and she waited up for him to slip through her door and get under her covers, she began to think that maybe it never was going to happen. Maybe she had taken her duties to the Coven too much to heart and had neglected the full-time job it took to keep her looking like the Most Beautiful Girl in New York.

Well, then. That was easily remedied. She wore down the staff with her requests for egg-and-honey conditioner for her hair, orange rinds for her face, milk-and-almond baths to make her skin soft and supple. She burned kohl pencils at the tip with candle flame and drew in eyeliner, and wore lipstick made of crushed rose petals. She noted that Kingsley usually stopped at home for a drink before going out to his supper club or wherever he went that he didn't invite her, and she planned to swan down the grand staircase one evening in a smashing dress. The troll seamstresses promised that the silk was woven from the clouds of Elysium, that the Dark Prince himself had never worn a suit of such fine fabric. The dress was cut almost to the navel, and Mimi wore her hair in waves—ringlets—the way she had in Rome, when Kingsley had first laid eyes on her.

As if on cue, Kingsley was having a snifter of brandy at the bottom of the stairs when Mimi made her stunning entrance. His eyes flashed with appreciation. At last, a reaction, Mimi thought, and a smug smile played at her lips. Now this is more like it.

"Oh, hi," she said, as if she had not planned this all week, and she'd merely wandered in looking exquisite, like a goddess who had deigned to grace him with her presence.

"Going somewhere tonight?" he asked mildly.

"Yes. I thought I'd check out that new place Mamon's been raving about," she hinted. "You?"

"Well, enjoy," he said, yawning. "I've had a big day. I'm going to turn in. You have fun, though. Don't get into too much trouble, Force," he said, wagging his finger.

Mimi watched him disappear down the hallway to his personal apartments. Now she was all dressed up with nowhere to go. *Jackass*, she thought. The dagger he'd thrust into her heart twisted a little deeper. What on earth had made her think he was worth the trip?

THIRTY

Bitter Queen

ll fairy tales end at some point, and Allegra's world came crashing down one ordinary late fall day when she was tallying up receipts. The annual crush the past Saturday had been a rousing success, with hundreds of people at the vineyard dancing and stomping grapes. Allegra had laughed and danced with them, and had spent the evening in the close, warm company of friends. The following Tuesday, the vineyard was closed for business. Ben was in town fetching supplies for the week, and Allegra had just opened the ledger when the darkness fell.

They were a blur—too fast for the human eye to see— and yet to Allegra they appeared as if in slow motion. She could see each of their stoic faces clearly, as well as the weapons they carried, torches of Black Fire. This was an ambush, a sneak attack that she herself had once designed in order to subdue a demon. She was their queen and they had come for her as if she were no more than a Hell-born beast.

Allegra bolted for the door, sending a row of bottles crashing into tables. There was nothing in the world she could use to defend herself against the Black Fire. Her only chance for freedom was to make a quick escape.

"Tut tut," Kingsley Martin said, meeting her at the back door. He was holding a sword lackadaisically at his side. To his credit, he did not point it at her. "I don't think that's a good idea, do you?" he asked.

"What is the meaning of this?" she hissed, as she was caught by the Venator team, her wrists placed in silver handcuffs.

"You know why we're here, Allegra," Kingsley replied. "Just following orders."

Allegra scanned the impassive faces. Kingsley Martin, the reformed Silver Blood; Forsyth Llewellyn. Of course he would be roped into this mess. He looked like he was enjoying it a little too much; Nan Cutler, who had never liked her since Florence. Well, the feeling was mutual. They surrounded her with their swords and did not speak to her, did not listen to her pleas, or show her an ounce of sympathy.

"After you," Kingsley said, pointing the team down the stairs to the wine cellar.

They put her in a small room where the Syrah and pinot noir were stored, and handcuffed her to a chair. They worked quickly and systematically, creating wards around the area, making sure that no one would be able to get inside the room. Allegra noticed the Venators knew exactly where everything was, which meant they had been watching her for some time. They knew when Ben was going into town for supplies. They knew the vineyard wasn't open on Tuesdays. They knew she would be alone.

"What's going to happen to Ben?" she asked.

Kingsley shook her head. "You know I can't talk about the operation."

"Please." Allegra felt a panic grip her throat. She had once commanded missions just like this one—and while she knew the Venator's training would not allow for sympathy or failure—that she was now in the same position as all the criminals she had hunted in the past—she tried to appeal to Kingsley's better nature for the sake of her love. She knew this was punishment and retribution. She had left her own bonding to be with her human familiar, and now she would pay the price. No one was above the Code of the Vampires.

Kingsley checked her restraints and nodded, satisfied that they would hold. Then the Venators left, locking the door behind them, and Allegra waited for her brother alone in the dark.

Night came, but Charles did not appear, nor did the Venators bother her again. She did not worry for herself—but she could not rest thinking of Ben. Where was he? Was he safe? They wouldn't harm him . . . would they? He had gone into town—was he looking for her now? Why were they keeping her in the cellar? Had they already taken him somewhere else?

What have I done, Allegra thought. What have I failed to do.

The next morning—Allegra guessed it was after sunrise—Kingsley returned with a cup of water and bread. Wordlessly, he put them next to her chair. There was olive oil with the bread, and Allegra thought bitterly of the last time she had eaten such a meal: in the veranda, with Ben at her side, the two of them as innocent as children. She should never have brought him into this. This world of secrets and blood and darkness and immortality. He was like the sun while she was a meteor, debris, a falling star.

She had just finished her meal when the door opened with a bang and Charles strode into the room. His black hair was already streaked with gray and he was not even a quarter-century old. He walked in like he owned the place. Allegra was surprised at how commanding he had become. He had grown into his power and relished it. He enjoyed showing her how easily he had tracked her down. How had they found her? Even with all of her careful preparations? What mistake had she made? Or was the mistake in thinking that she would ever be free of him? That he would ever leave her alone? They were tied to each other. Their bond might fray but it would never break; she was learning that now. There was no hiding from her twin.

"Unshackle her," he ordered Kingsley, who quickly removed her cuffs.

Allegra massaged her wrists angrily.

"I'll make this easy for you," Charles said.

"How?"

"I have your familiar."

Allegra felt a stab in her heart. So they did have Ben. Of course. There was no doubt that it was part of the plan. Ben was human. . . . He had no defenses against the vampires. He was no match for them. Allegra could not believe Charles would stoop so low as to threaten a Red Blood. This was against every law they had made. This was unworthy of his power.

"No you don't," Allegra said hotly. "You would never."

"It's up to you, really, what happens to him," Charles said, his face emotionless. "I don't care one way or the other."

"You would never harm a human being. It is against the Code. The Code that you wrote with your own blood, Michael."

Charles bowed his head. When he looked up at her, there were tears in his eyes. He addressed her as she had him, with the names they had been given when the earth and the heavens were made, and they themselves were born into the beauty of the Light. "Gabrielle, this farce has gone on long enough. I know you want to hurt me, and you have. But please. This infatuation is a childish nuisance. *End it.*"

She saw what he was seeing: the bitter ruins of their bonding day: Cordelia waiting at the steps of the museum, then Charles, his face white and his hair turning gray in an instant. The hurt was so deep, a devastating blow. The guests horrified and confused—the Coven at arms. Allegra had disappeared—had she been taken? The fear . . . and then . . . the shocked understanding of what she had done. She had left him. She had left them. She had turned her back on the Coven.

"I love him, Michael," she said. "I would never have left—I could never have done what I did—if I did not. I love him with all of my heart and soul and blood."

"You cannot," Charles said flatly. "You do not know of what you speak. He is beneath you. You have a duty to your bond and your Coven." You have a duty to me, he thought but did not say.

"I love him," Allegra said. "I love him more than I ever loved you." Forget the bond, forget the Coven. Allegra was tired of being a queen; she just wanted to be a girl again.

Charles was impassive. "Love him all you want, Gabrielle. I still love you. I will always love you, and that is all that matters. I will forgive you anything, and I will forgive you this."

Allegra felt her stomach twist. She knew he was telling the truth, and she could see how much this was hurting him. She put a hand on his arm. "If you love me, tell me what happened in Florence—what really happened. Why don't I remember? I know what I did, but there are parts of my memory that are hidden from me, and I can feel you in them, Michael. I can feel your magic inside me. You are hiding my memories from me. You have no right."

Charles did not answer. Instead, as he walked out of the room and locked the door, Allegra heard him say softly, "I have every right."

It was then that she knew she would never find out the truth of her own history. And while she still believed that under no circumstances would Michael, Pure of Heart— the greatest angel who ever lived—harm a mere human, Allegra was suddenly very, very afraid.

THIRTY-ONE

Gatekeeper

chuyler flinched as the ladies-in-waiting did their worst. They rouged her cheeks and lips, slicked her hair with hippopotamus oil (a beauty secret that Nefertiti was said to have popularized), then curled it in ringlets and soaked her skin in greasy perfume. They told her to strip down to her underwear and forced her into a lacy white dress with a corset that nipped her waist and had a dangerously low neckline. As threatened, they padded her bustline with a pair of breast-shaped foam cutlets.

"Work with what we can," the older woman sneered, tightening the stays until Schuyler felt she couldn't breathe.

The younger one brought high-heeled slippers for her to wear. "Remember, it's better not to fight," she said kindly. "There's no getting out of it, so you might as well try to enjoy it."

Schuyler did not reply. When they left her alone, she

walked to the mirror, appalled at her reflection. She looked like a perversion of a bride: the dress bordered on indecent, with a slit up the leg that reached her thigh, and the fabric was almost see-through. She'd never worn anything this revealing in her life, not even at the beach.

She wondered how Deming and Dehua were faring, and hoped they would be able to take care of themselves. Had she led them into the worst danger of all? She thought of what was about to happen, and tried not to panic. She would find a way out of this, she told herself, with a hand on her stomach. She would survive whatever injury was awaiting her. She would be strong so she could live. She tried not to think of Danel's hard, cruel gaze, and the images he had sent to her mind. Whatever happened, she would fight him. And if she could not, then she would concentrate on living beyond it. She would not give in to fear and despair.

The door opened, and Schuyler inhaled sharply, wondering if her time was up. She whispered a prayer to her mother to help her stay strong.

Another of the ladies-in-waiting, a white-haired woman wearing gauzy silk robes and jangly bracelets, entered the room. However, she had not come to fix Schuyler's hair or check that she was adequately perfumed. "Come quickly," she said. "We have a little time before the Croatan arrive. We must free the others."

Schuyler followed her savior through the maze of hallways. "Who are you?" she asked.

The woman smiled. She had a serenity and grace about her that Schuyler found familiar. "I think you already know."

"You're Catherine of Siena," Schuyler whispered, a little awed that, in the end, her plan had worked. "The gate-keeper." Catherine reminded Schuyler of her own mother. Allegra had the same graceful sense of purpose, gave the same impression that she was floating far above the problems of the world.

"I'm sorry I couldn't come sooner," Catherine said. "But when they took away your sword I knew I had to wait until they handed you over to the ladies. I had a better chance of getting you out then."

"I came with two friends—"

"Yes. They're being kept down here," Catherine said, running a few steps that led to another long hallway. She tested a few doors in a row and finally found the right one. They burst into the room to find Dehua dressed in similar fashion. Her wedding dress was even more indecent—a jeweled bikini top and a low-slung skirt. She ripped off a gem-encrusted lace veil as soon as she saw her rescuers, and leapt to her feet.

"You are unharmed?" Catherine asked.

"Just let them try to touch me," Dehua said with contempt. "We need our swords back."

"I have them," Catherine said. "They were in the armory. I was able to retrieve them before the greedy demons took them," she said, handing the girls their weapons.

Dehua stuck her blade into her garter and nodded to Schuyler. "They found out you were Fallen as well?"

"Yes."

"Where is my sister?" she asked Schuyler.

"I thought she was with you," Catherine said, interrupting. "I thought they kept the two of you together. I heard that they were selling you both as one unit."

"No. They separated us when they handed us over to the devil's handmaidens. I heard them say something about taking her to the 'Castle Styx.' I think Deming fought them—I heard a scuffle—and that was her punishment. She never waits. I wish she hadn't shown her hand so early."

Catherine shook her head. "That's too far. The castle is beyond Limbo and right at the border of the Kingdom of the Dead. We can't make it there and back out of the gate in time."

"We are not leaving her!" Dehua cried.

Schuyler agreed. "We can't leave her here. I brought them here. I need to make sure they get out," she said to the gatekeeper.

"If you go after her, I cannot guarantee your safety," Catherine said. It was too late to argue, however, for as they turned a corner, they had to quickly back away, finding the next passage filled with trolls. Their disappearance had not escaped notice for long. Schuyler had never seen creatures like this before. They were wild and feral, and they sniffed the air, looking for clues.

"Too late—we've got to go now," Catherine said. "We'll take the underground path toward the gate. Once we reach past it, they won't be able to follow."

The trolls rounded the next corner and made guttural noises to each other; then one of them let out a long and powerful ear-shattering scream.

"That's the alarm. In a second we'll have demons here too, and Croatan," Catherine said, pushing them down toward an underground path. "We need to get through the gate. Now."

Schuyler and Dehua had no choice but to follow, and their speed took them quickly through the narrow passage until they reached an opening. They ran toward what looked like a huge fortress that blocked the whole sky. It looked as if it was made of sheer rock, impenetrable; less than a gate and more like a mountain made of granite.

"Where's the gate?" Schuyler panted.

"That is it," Catherine said. "It only stops the demon-blooded. We'll be able to pass." She shoved the girls toward it. Schuyler thought she would hit the firmament, but instead she passed through what felt like a field of cobwebs, a fluffy cotton gauze. Then she was through and standing on a hard stone floor, with a transparent wall behind her. She could hear their voices.

"NO!" Dehua said. "I'm not leaving here without my sister!"

The trolls were a breath away, their grunting language

ugly and harsh. Beyond them was a piercing scream, the sound of a woman dying. Schuyler felt her blood run cold. That was Deming's voice, and soon Dehua was screaming as well—a shriek that shook the heavens. "My sister!"

"Schuyler—help me!" Catherine called, and through the wall, Schuyler saw the gatekeeper push the Venator through the gate. She reached for Dehua on the other side, and together they were able to pull the screaming twin to safety, the three of them falling on the floor as the trolls thumped against the gate and a demon howled.

But the gate held. The strength of the angels kept the creatures on the other side for now. The trolls crashed against it, but it was no use. Dehua fell to the ground, weeping. Schuyler wanted to weep as well. She tried to comfort the girl and put her arms around her, but Dehua pushed her away roughly.

Catherine pressed her hands against the wall and muttered an incantation. The vision of the trolls disappeared and the wall turned solid, as the Gate of Promise closed.

Now that she was out of the glom, Schuyler looked at her surroundings. They were in a small stone room and the ceiling was pointed. She recognized the shape of the space even from the inside as one of the Giza pyramids. It was just as she'd thought; the Gate of Promise couldn't have been in a more prominent or popular area of Cairo. It had been right in front of her all along.

THIRTY-TWO

The Duke of Hell

*A*ccording to Mimi's internal clock, it had been almost a month since they had arrived in the underworld, and since then nothing had changed, nothing had happened. She did not understand what Kingsley wanted from her—it looked like the answer was nothing, and her ego was suffering a terrible beating. Oliver was increasingly restless, and if they stayed any longer they would never find their way back to the surface. They would get used to the air down here; their souls would begin to mesh with the fabric of the place. It was time to go.

Mimi swallowed her pride and made an appointment with the consigliere's office so she could have time alone with Kingsley. She lived in his home but he was never there, and he never sought her company. She was tired of being a neglected houseguest. If he didn't want to talk about it, then she would. She could not play the waiting game any longer.

There was the Coven to think about; she had responsibilities to the larger community and not only to the indulgences of her heart. She did not know what to expect anymore, and if Kingsley did not feel the same about her, well then—she would just have to deal.

Kingsley sat behind a long ebony table. He looked amused to see her when she entered. "How formal of you, Force. I've got to admit when I saw your name on the calendar I was taken aback. If you'd wanted to talk to me, I am down the hall," he said as he rested his long legs on the edge of the desk and put his hands behind his head. He rocked back in his chair, infuriatingly casual as usual.

"Right," Mimi said, sitting rigidly across from him. "Except you're never home."

"Hell's a big place. I'm busy," he said. "What's on your mind?"

Now that she had his attention, she faltered. She'd rehearsed her lines that morning, determined to lay the truth on the table; but "I love you" seemed too forward to open with, while "How do you feel about me?" too weak. She couldn't tell him what she felt, not with him smirking at her like that. It was just too humiliating, and even though she had sworn to herself not to let her conceit or his insouciance get in the way of declaring her love, she abruptly decided that he was simply not worth it. This was a joke. All this time she'd imagined that he had suffered greatly, that he had missed her, and that he would greet her arrival with the open arms that liberated citizens showered upon conquering heroes. Nothing could have been further from reality. She stood up from her chair. "You know what, you're right. This is ridiculous. I'm wasting your time."

Kingsley leaned forward, almost falling off his chair and losing that cocky demeanor for a moment. He righted himself, but kept his feet planted on the ground instead of swinging them onto his desk again. "Hold on, now. Before you go, I've got a question."

She remained standing, waiting for him to speak.

"What are you doing here, really?" he asked. "In the underworld, I mean."

Mimi scoffed. She glared at him. "What kind of a question is that? What do you mean what am I doing here? What does it look like? What did you think? Of course I came for *you*."

He looked confused. "For me? How so?" He tapped a finger on his cheek.

She loathed him. Did he really mean to humiliate her like this? He had always been aloof, but never cruel. He had a wicked sense of humor, but he was never mean. Fine. If he wanted her to spell it out, she would give him the satisfaction. At least it meant he would have to listen to what she had to say. "I mean . . . I missed you. I wanted to see you again. I came here for you. You know, so we could . . ." She hesitated, as a lump had formed in her throat and tears had sprung to her eyes—mostly because he was looking at her with so much hostility she couldn't bear it. "It doesn't matter now. I mean, it's obvious you don't . . ." She could not continue and made abruptly for the door.

Kingsley jumped from his seat and put a hand on her arm to keep her from escaping. His eyes were narrowed to slits, and his face was angry. "Hold on a sec. I thought you were here for the Coven. I know what's happening up there; thought maybe you needed something from the dead's kingdom. But you want me to believe you're not here for any reason other than . . . What d'you mean, all this . . . was for me?"

Mimi wanted to die of embarrassment. Kingsley was staring at her as if he'd never heard of something so stupid. There were so many things unsaid in their relationship—if you could call it that—and it was glaringly obvious that while she considered him the love of her life, in his view she was merely some chick he'd hooked up with a couple of times. The discrepancy was so large it was painful to learn she had lived under a misguided illusion all along. She'd spent the last year trying to get him back, and now this. "Yes. It was all for you. Happy?"

"But why?" he asked, still mystified.

"To *rescue* you."

To his credit, he didn't laugh at her. His forehead furrowed. "It's no small task to travel beyond the seventh. Surely you've got a more substantial reason for your journey. Why not be honest about your agenda? You always have a trick or two up your sleeve. What is it? What do you really want from the underworld? Maybe I can help."

Mimi shook her head. She'd told him everything and he didn't believe her. For a moment she was too shocked to reply. Finally she said, "I don't know what I can say that will make you believe that I'm here for you and only you." Her lower lip began to tremble. She didn't know what was worse, that she had told him the truth, or that he did not believe her.

Kingsley sighed and raked a hand through his dark hair. "I thought our former friendship would mean you'd be honest with me."

"I am being honest."

"So the great Azrael travels to the Kingdom of the Dead for love? Is that it?" His lips curled into a sneer. "That's why you were going to bond with Abbadon, right? Because of your great love for me?"

Mimi slapped him hard in the face. "You bastard. I came here for you. You know what, I don't care anymore. Rot in Hell."

Kingsley smiled and wiped his mouth with his shirt cuff. "Now, that's the Azrael I remember."

THIRTY-THREE

Plea Bargain

*T*hey starved her.

There was no more water. No more bread. No more olive oil. Kingsley Martin had ceased to perform his small acts of kindness. Charles had not returned to visit her either. She did not know how long she had been left in this room, but Allegra felt the change begin inside her. Since she had started to take the blood regularly, the deep-seated hunger had begun. She needed to drink. To perform the *Caerimonia Osculor* and take the living blood into her body.

It looked as if the Venators knew that too, as the next morning brought a knock on the door. "I was told to bring you this," Nan Cutler said, as she shoved a Red Blood male into the room. "Drink from him. You have gone without for too long." She thrust the specimen under Allegra's nose.

The human boy was gorgeous and looked exactly like

Ben: tall and blond and handsome. He had been drugged and he looked at her groggily.

"No," Allegra said, feeling disgusted and excited at the same time. She could smell his blood underneath his skin, thick and viscous and so alive—and here she was, so dizzy and thirsty and weak. She could rip his throat and take him, drain him until he was almost at the brink of death. But she held back.

If she took another familiar, then Ben would cease to be special to her anymore. She knew that was what Charles wanted. The familiar's bond was strong, but it was diluted by every other Red Blood a vampire took. Charles wanted her to forget about Ben, or at least have someone else in her system. He wanted to say to her, *This is all he is to you: a vessel for blood. Nothing more.*

"Do it!" Nan said. She pushed Allegra onto the boy, who had fallen to the floor.

Dear god, she wanted it so much; she wanted to taste him—maybe just a little? Was that so wrong?

What was she thinking—no. No. She did not want this. This was pure torture. She straddled the boy's chest and bent down, putting her mouth on his neck, her fangs out and salivating. She was so very hungry.

But finally she pushed herself away and staggered against the opposite wall, half delirious and her face white as a sheet.

Charles wanted to turn her into a monster. Wanted to

show her that her love was false. That it was a mistake and an illusion. He wanted to show her what they were: fallen angels, cursed by the Lord, feeding on blood to survive. How far they had fallen. How low she had become.

She would not do this.

"NO!" she said, more clearly now, as she stood up and crossed her arms. "Take him away from me."

"Fine," Nan said, shrugging. "If you don't want it, I'll have him." The vampire dragged the boy to a far corner and kissed him with her fangs. Soon the loud slurping noise filled the room.

Allegra felt sick. She'd been in the room for what felt like forty days and forty nights. She had no idea what had happened to Ben, or what Charles was planning, but for now she was certain that Ben was still alive. She knew she would feel it if he were dead.

He was alive for now, but she did not know how long. Did she trust Charles enough to keep him alive? Or would the pain of her love for Ben be too much for Charles to bear? After all, it was only too easy to break Ben's neck or drain him to death, or even make it seem like an accident so that she would never know for sure.

She thought of everything she and Charles had been through together, and wondered how it was that they had come to this. She had left him at the altar, she had humiliated him in front of the Coven—and even now she refused to return to him, as he held all the cards and she had no choices left.

Why did she resist anyway? What part of her heart believed that she would be able to make her own destiny? She was not meant to be with Ben, she could see that now.

She was only hurting everyone—her twin, her love, herself, her Coven—by refusing to acknowledge the truth: that she could not have this. There was no escape from an immortal destiny, and this, whatever this was, those golden months in the green valley living as a vintner as if she were nothing but an ordinary girl, was just as false as pretending she did not feel any vestigial love for her immortal mate. She loved Charles, but she could not deny that the love she felt for Ben was much stronger, and deeper to the core of who she was. It was as simple as that.

But alas, Allegra Van Alen was not an ordinary girl. She had to accept that, or Ben would die. She was sure of it now. There was nothing that mattered to Charles as much as keeping the Coven whole. He would sacrifice anything for it, including the Code of the Vampires. There was no way he would let Ben live; for as long as he was alive, Charles knew Allegra would pine for him and she would never give herself to him fully.

She made her decision.

"I want to speak to my brother," she told the guard.

Kingsley Martin saluted. "I'll get him right away." Allegra felt grateful that it was Kingsley who guarded her prison and not any of the others. They had been friends once. In Rome she had helped him with the Corruption in his soul. Few trusted the reformed Silver Blood, but Allegra had always been fond of him. She remembered him as a young boy, Gemellus, the weakling.

When Charles entered the room, Allegra threw herself at his feet and bowed her forehead so low it touched the edge of his wingtips, and her tears drenched his shoelaces.

"I'm sorry. I'm so sorry," she sobbed.

"Allegra, don't do this, you don't need to. Get up, please. I can't bear to see you this way," Charles said, kneeling down to her level and trying to remove her arms from his legs. "Please don't." His face was full of anguish, and she did not know who found this harder to bear—him or her. They shared this pain together, as they had shared everything else. He felt everything she did—of course he did. He was her twin, and her anguish was his own.

He was hurting to see her demean herself this way. But it was her love that was on the line, and she had no shame or pride anymore. "Don't kill him. Don't kill him, Charlie. Please. I'll go with you. I'll say the words and we'll be bonded. Just. Don't hurt him. Please."

THIRTY-FOUR

A Righteous War

*J*ack noticed that something had gone wrong right away when he saw the lights go out at the temple. "Something's happening. Let's move," he told the group. But the temple was empty when they got there, and there was no trace of the girls—or of any kind of scuffle. Even the candles were lit, and the place was quiet and peaceful. There was only the foreboding stare of the jackal god, looking down, as if mocking them.

"Where'd they go?" Sam said, raking his hair. "I can't feel them in the glom." The telepathic connections had been severed the moment the lights went out. Not a good sign.

"There's got to be a hidden path somewhere in the temple. If we didn't see them leave, then they had to go under," Jack said. He knelt on the floor and began tapping it, but there was only a dull sound that meant it was solid rock. If there was a passageway underground, it must only open to a certain incantation or spell. He tried several, unsuccessfully.

Ted had walked the perimeter, but reported that there was nothing out there either—there was no sign in the cemetery that anyone had even come to the temple. They'd been watching the place for hours, and still the girls had slipped through, disappearing into thin air. No. They knew exactly where they had been taken: to the underworld, to become demons' brides.

Jack steadied his breathing. He consoled himself with the knowledge that the three girls were dangerous as well: two were trained Venators, the deadliest of their kind, and armed. Schuyler would fight, he knew, and he tried not to feel angry and helpless. He had to think. If the passage went underground, then it meant the gate couldn't be too far away, which meant Schuyler was right: it was in the city somewhere. Probably just under his feet.

Not a minute had passed when he suddenly saw it: the spark went live, and in his mind's eye he saw Schuyler bursting through a wall, into a room inside a pyramid, followed by Dehua and an older woman.

"They're in Giza," he told the team.

When Jack and the Lennox brothers arrived at the tomb, Schuyler and Catherine were talking in hushed voices. Jack did not remark on the way they were dressed—they all knew the reason why the Nephilim were taking girls—but to see the grotesque parodies of white wedding dresses was too much. Jack didn't think there had been enough time for this elaborate preparation, but he remembered that time moved differently in the underworld. The girls had probably been down there for hours. He would kill every demon in Hell if one of them had as much as touched a hair on Schuyler's head.

"Where's Deming?" Sam asked immediately.

"We had to leave her," Schuyler explained. "It was my fault. The demons disarmed us before we could move. I'm sorry. I didn't think we would lose you guys."

"We'll get her back," Dehua said, her voice raspy and her eyes red and dry. "Don't worry, Sam. Deming can take care of herself."

"I trusted you," Sam said, his voice tight, looking directly at Schuyler. "From now on, we do things my way."

"I'm sorry," Schuyler said. "I'm so sorry. I didn't think this was going to happen."

"I don't need an apology. I need to find a way back down to the underworld. The gate is here, right? Let's go." He nodded to his twin and to Dehua. "Show us the way," he said, noticing the gatekeeper for the first time. "This is your gig, isn't it?"

Catherine said, "If you go now, you will only bring harm to yourselves, and will have little chance of getting her back, as every demon in Limbo is looking for these two right now." She motioned to Schuyler and Dehua. "The Castle Styx is in the borderland. If she's been taken there, it means she's been selected as the bride for the Harvest Bonding, and we have some time, as that's not until Lammas. She'll be left alone until then. No one will touch her, and you can rescue her during the Virgin Night right before, when the castle will be empty, as the demons will be feasting in Tartarus."

They watched Sam process this information. Finally he exhaled. "Fine. We'll wait till then. But I'm going to run this mission. No more mistakes."

Jack put his coat around Schuyler's shoulders to help her cover up, and the Venators left to confer on their own. The group seemed to have split, and once again the Lennox twins were wary of Jack and Schuyler, making it clear they preferred to keep their own counsel. Dehua refused to look at them as they left.

"You all right?" Jack asked. He had refrained from showing any emotion until now.

"Thanks to Catherine." Schuyler squeezed his hand, silently thanking him for the jacket. "I just need to get out of this wretched costume."

"So you're Halcyon," Jack said, turning to the gate-keeper. "I don't know if you remember me."

"It would be difficult to forget Abbadon of the under-world." Catherine smiled as she shook Jack's hand. "I'm sorry we are meeting under such circumstances, but I suppose it can't be helped. Come, let's find a better place to talk."

* * *

Catherine lived in an apartment in the Giza suburbs. The building was one that had been built in the nineteenth century, and divided into living spaces to house professors at the university and young families. It was small but comfortable, and it looked as if the gatekeeper had lived there for a long time. There were *Life* magazines from the 1930s on the coffee table, and an eight-track tape player and rotary telephone.

Catherine put on a kettle of water to boil. "As you can see, the gate is in terrible danger now that the Silver Bloods have found its location on earth," she said. "It's a pity we never found the Croatan who had infiltrated our Covens until it was too late."

"But Michael said all the Croatan were destroyed during the crisis in Rome," Jack said, knowing how weak that sounded.

"Michael said a lot of things," Catherine said with a wry smile. "Not all of them were true. He did not want the Coven to fear the enemy. Which is why he created the Order of the Seven. When the gates were created, there were Silver Bloods who were trapped on our side, and Michael and Gabrielle formed a team to hunt them down. It was our first duty as gatekeepers."

Schuyler watched Jack's face fall as he learned this information—to know that he had been kept in the dark for centuries. "It is true, then, what Mimi always said. The Uncorrupted never trusted us—which is why we were never told of any of this," Jack said. "They still see us as traitors.

Lucifer's generals, even though we tried to change the course of the war."

"Your sister always was observant," Catherine agreed. She brought out napkins and plates. "It's only a matter of time before they will be able to bring it down. The hounds slip through with regularity; now even a demon or two can manage it," she said. "They were never able to do that before. I did what I could through the years to throw them off the scent."

"The decoy in Florence," Schuyler said.

"Yes. It kept our enemies off balance for a while."

"And the Petruvians—was that part of it? Part of the plan?" Schuyler asked, feeling a little frantic. "Are you aware that they kill innocent women and their children in the name of the Blessed?"

"Like I said, I did what I could. I trained the Petruvians myself." Catherine poured steaming water into a fat porcelain teapot. "And here I do the same. I try to break out the girls before they're bonded to the Croatan."

"But what if they've already been seduced?" Schuyler wanted to know. *If they are already pregnant with the Nephilim child? What do you do then, gatekeeper?*

Catherine set the table, removing biscuits from a tin and arranging them on plates with the fleur-de-lis design. "I slit their throats," she said, without a trace of guilt or shame. "Come, eat," she said, taking a seat at the table and motioning for them to do the same.

"And the babies?" Schuyler's voice shook.

"The same," Catherine replied.

Schuyler went pale and could not breathe. She saw in a flash the long and bloody history of Catherine and the Petruvian priests: the babies spiked on bayonets, the girls with their bellies slashed from hip to hip, the blood and the burnings, the bitter war waged in secret.

"It has to be a mistake," Schuyler said, looking at Jack, who only bowed his head. *I did not know. There is no excuse for that kind of brutality, not even for the vampires' survival.*

The gatekeeper dipped a biscuit in her milky tea and took a bite before answering. "There is no mistake. The Petruvian Order was founded by Michael himself. I was charged to maintain its existence."

THIRTY-FIVE

The Living and the Dead

"We're leaving?" Oliver asked with palpable relief after Mimi had outlined the plan. She had stormed into his room looking murderous, and he had been worried for his safety for a moment. Thankfully, all she'd done was kick the pillows that had fallen on the floor, and after that she'd simply sunk into the couch next to him, a deflated little red balloon with all the fight seeped out of her.

"I bribed one of the demons with a vial of my blood. God knows what he wants it for." Mimi shuddered. "He said if we want to get out of here, all we need is to catch some train that will take us straight to Limbo."

"What about Kingsley?" he asked.

"What *about* Kingsley?" There was that murderous look again.

Oliver turned off the television. The show he'd been watching—about an alien who was part of the family and played by a puppet—was just about the height of inanity, and he was glad to find a reason to stop watching. He approached Mimi gingerly. "He's not coming back with us?"

"No," Mimi said, and she kicked the coffee table. "Ouch!" she yelped, holding her foot. "I don't want to talk about it, okay?"

Oliver nodded. "Okay."

Mimi went back to her room. She wanted to be alone. Her heart was broken, shattered to pieces, but she felt nothing. Just numb. She had been hanging on to this love—this hope—that she would find happiness one day. That she would have a happy ending. But instead there was nothing for her here. It was clear that there never was. She had read it all wrong. Kingsley had never loved her. He didn't feel the same way about her anymore, and possibly never had.

Her journey was over, and she had failed. She would return to the Coven, where hopefully she would be able to piece her life back together, and piece the vampires back together as well. She didn't know what to do next. Look for her brother? Find revenge? She felt too exhausted to think of revenge at the moment. She needed a good long cry, but she did not want to give Kingsley the satisfaction of hearing her sob. She hoped she'd hurt him when she'd hit him. His cheek had turned a deep scarlet, but the shocked look on his face was even better.

There was a quiet knock on the door.

"Go away," Mimi growled. "Oliver, I said I don't want to talk about it!"

The door opened anyway. "It's not Oliver. It's me." Kingsley hovered at the doorway, looking tired and nervous. His left cheek, Mimi noticed, was slightly pink.

"What do you want?" she asked.

"I came to apologize," he said, slouching against the wall. "It was rude of me to belittle your efforts. I didn't mean to make fun."

"Whatever."

Kingsley looked at her kindly. "I'm truly sorry to disappoint you. I'm . . . quite flattered that you cared so much to come all this way."

"So you didn't miss me . . . not at all?" she said, daring to ask one of the questions she had wanted to ask since they were reunited. Had she misunderstood everything? The way he'd looked at her before he disappeared—and the fact that he had asked her to break her bond and steal away with him—was it all a dream? All that time she had grieved for him, mourned for him, dreamed of him, schemed for a way to get him back . . . and it was all for nothing? He'd never felt the same for her? How could she have been so stupid?

"I'm so sorry," he said, patting her on the back as if she were a child.

Good god, if he'd meant to console her, he was going about it exactly the wrong way. He was making her feel like a silly schoolgirl who'd had a crush on her teacher. "Right."

Mimi nodded. She just wanted him out of her room and out of her life. She never wanted to see him again. If there was one thing she hated more than Kingsley's indifference, it was his pity. "I think you should go now."

But Kingsley stubbornly refused to leave. "Listen, come take a ride with me. I want to show you something. It might explain better than I can."

Mimi heaved a sigh. "Do I have to?"

"I promise I'll stop bothering you if you do."

"Fine."

He drove them out of the city, beyond the borders of the seventh, to the endless swaths of nothing that surrounded Tartarus. The dark incalculable void where nothing grew and nothing lived, and there was only the dead and those that kept the dead. They drove into the vacant barren land, to the black irradiated earth, the devastated valleys where the Black Fire had raged from the beginning of time. In middle of the infinite darkness he stopped the car and got out, motioning for Mimi to follow him.

He knelt by the side of the road and asked her to do the same. She crouched down next to him.

"See that?" he asked, pointing to a small red flower that was sprouting from the ashy black desert. "Remember what it was like before? Nothing could grow here. But it's different now. It's changing. The underworld is changing, and I'm part of the reason why."

It was just a weed, but Mimi did not want to take away Kingsley's fierce pride in its existence.

"It's going to take a long time, and maybe it will never be as beautiful as earth, but who knows." He touched the petal of the flower with the tip of his finger. "There's nothing for me up there, you know," he said quietly. "It's peaceful down here. I belong here."

She could read between the lines: this was the reason he would never return with her back to earth. To return to his former existence would only bring him pain. In mid-world, Kingsley Martin was a pariah, neither angel or demon but a Silver Blood, a vampire who was shunned and distrusted by his own people.

Maybe he'd loved her once, or maybe he hadn't, but it was all irrelevant now. Whatever love he had was gone. Perhaps it had never been real. Only his pride in this small growing flower—that was real.

Mimi finally saw what she had been denying from the moment she'd laid eyes on him again. Kingsley looked different because he was different. Down here, he was whole, he was himself. He was not plagued by the screams of the thousands in his soul. While he was Croatan, he was also free.

Now she understood why Helda had said, *If you can get him to leave with you, you can have him.*

Kingsley would never leave the underworld. He had everything here: adventures, new experiences; as the Angel

Araquiel he would bring life back to this dead land. She did not want to take that away from him. If she loved him the way she said she did, she wanted him whole. Maybe this was what love meant after all: sacrifice and selflessness. It did not mean hearts and flowers and a happy ending, but the knowledge that another's well-being is more important than one's own. It was so awful to grow up and realize you couldn't have everything you wanted, Mimi thought.

"I'm glad you're happy," she said finally, as they made their way back to the car.

"No one's happy here, you know that. But I am content, and maybe that's enough for me."

They drove back to Tartarus in silence. Mimi was afraid of saying something she would regret, and Kingsley was lost in thought. When they arrived back at the palace, the trolls seemed to sense their mood and kept out of their way. There was nary a servant in sight, when usually they were constantly hovering, offering cakes or champagne or hookers and hot tubs.

Kingsley walked Mimi to her room. "So I understand this is good-bye, then?"

"Yeah, well."

He lingered at the doorway. "It was good of you to come. It was nice seeing you again, Force. Come see me again sometime if you're ever in the neighborhood."

Smart aleck. He knew they would never see each other

again. She had come to Hell chasing a dream, and now it was time to wake up. Her Coven needed her; she had wasted enough time. Mimi knew this was good-bye, but she did not know how to say it—did not know if she had it in her not to break down if it went on too long. So she just gave him a little shrug and began to turn away. Then she remembered. "Oh, I might as well return this." She reached into her pocket and brought out a small rabbit's foot key chain. She had found it among his possessions and had held on to it, remembering the way he used to twirl it around; the way he would toss it in the air and catch it.

"I lost this in New York," he said. It had been special to him: it had brought him luck again and again, he'd told her once. He'd held a certain perverse affection for the ugly thing.

"I know. I found it."

"You kept this? All this time?"

"It reminded me of you." She shrugged. She'd kept it thinking it might be a sign that she would see him again.

He was still looking at it with wonderment, and all Mimi wanted to do was disappear into her room as quickly as possible. This whole ordeal had been agonizing.

"Wait," he said hoarsely, and reached for her hand.

She laced her fingers through his and gave it a good shake to let him know there were no hard feelings. They were friends. That's all she ever seemed to have. Friends. She had enough of those.

His hand was still gripping hers. She tried to pull away, but he just tightened his hold on her, and it was then that she felt the first flower of hope bloom in her heart. But she did not want to go down that road again. That road led to nowhere.

And still Kingsley did not let go.

It was as if they were rooted to that spot, frozen in time.

Finally, Mimi dared to look up.

When she did, she saw that there were tears running down his beautiful face. And when their eyes met, it was as if his whole spirit crumbled; as if seeing the worn rabbit's foot had reminded him of something—their time together in New York, perhaps—or maybe it had finally convinced him that she *had* come down to Hell for him after all. But whatever it was, the arrogant façade broke, and he surrendered to the love that he had been feeling all this time; the love that he had been hiding behind an arrogant, indifferent veneer.

But instead of feeling triumphant that Kingsley had told her the truth at last, and was showing her the true nature of his heart now that they were saying good-bye forever—instead of feeling justified and victorious, Mimi just felt tenderness for him, and protective.

"Of course I missed you," he whispered. "How could I forget . . ."

"Kingsley," she said, but he had already pulled her toward him, and this time she did not push him away.

THIRTY-SIX

The Prisoner

*A*llegra felt dizzy. She had no idea how long it had been since she had seen sunlight, how long since the Venators had stormed the place, how long since she had been imprisoned in the wine cellar. What was happening to Ben? Where had they taken him? What was going on with the vineyard, she wondered. The staff would worry, wouldn't they? Surely Ben's family was looking for them? Red Bloods were not completely devoid of resources.

She did not understand why Charles had not accepted her offer. She had groveled at his feet and begged for Ben's life, but her twin had merely knelt down and gently removed her hands from his ankles. He had placed her back on the chair and then left.

Allegra was exhausted. She did not know what would happen next, and she let Charles back into her mind so she could send him hopeless, anxious messages through the glom, begging and pleading with him, telling him she would do whatever he wanted. But Charles did not answer this time.

She would not be forgiven, she thought. She had pushed him too far, he would never return to her, it was too late. He was bent on revenge. Who knew what he would do to her, or to Ben.

Finally, sometime after she had begged Charles for Ben's life, the door to the wine cellar opened with a creak. But it wasn't Charles or any of his Venators who strode inside.

"Oh hey, didn't see you there," Ben said, looking surprised as he took a bottle of wine off a lower shelf.

Allegra blinked her eyes, not quite sure this was real. "Ben? Is it really you? You're all right?"

He smiled. "You missed me that much? I just got back from the store."

No one had taken him. No one had threatened him. He didn't even know that any time had passed. Allegra realized with a shock that everything that had happened to her was in the glom, in the twilight world where time did not act in the same fashion. While it seemed as if months had passed, it was only a few hours in the real world.

Ben was wearing the same clothes from the last time she'd seen him: a red flannel shirt, dirty jeans, and work boots. "Henderson's wants to place an order for another wheel of your cheese. If we're not careful, we won't have a vineyard anymore but a cheese cave," he said as he pulled another bottle. "Thought it might be time to try the eighty-eight Syrah." He looked up at her with a smile, but his expression changed when he saw her haunted face. "Legs . . . is something wrong? You're looking at me funny."

She shook her head and patted his arm. "No, I think I'm claustrophobic. I couldn't find the bottle I was looking for, and I panicked from being down here too long. I'll be all right." They walked up the stairs, back to the tasting room together.

Ben kissed Allegra on the forehead and returned to his studio to paint. She couldn't quite accept that she was truly free, and was shocked to find that he had never been in any danger, that she had been wrong. Of course Charles would never do such a thing as harm a Red Blood. The pretty oak-paneled room was almost empty, save for one customer sitting on a far stool: Kingsley Martin. He was nonchalantly reading a newspaper. He looked like any local, just another resident who'd come by to taste the new reds. Allegra approached him hesitantly. "What's going on?"

"Isn't it obvious?" Kingsley smiled that crooked smile of his. "You're free to go. I just thought I'd have a drink before I left; see if the cabernet lives up to the hype."

"Why?" she asked. She wasn't talking about the wine.

"Charles's orders."

"Where is Charles?"

Kingsley shrugged. "Didn't say. Probably back in New York." Everything had happened in the glom, and Charles had never even set foot in California.

"So what happens now?" Allegra asked.

The Venator laid down his newspaper. "The way I see it, nothing. I mean, I don't think you have anything to worry about anymore. As for the bond—that's up to you and Charles. But between you and me, I think he's done."

Kingsley swirled the wine in his glass and took a long sip. He tasted it for a moment, letting it cover his tongue. "Alas, taste buds never do come back once you have Croatan blood. I can't even smell it. Is it good?"

"We've had no complaints," Allegra said.

"I'm sure. Hope you don't think too badly of us. We didn't have a choice, you know. We only do what the Regis wants us to."

Allegra nodded and began to wipe down the counter. Kingsley read the paper and drank his wine. A thought occurred to her, and she asked suddenly, "Did you guys ever find out what happened with those diseased familiars?"

"What familiars?"

"Charles mentioned that the Red Bloods were dying of some new affliction and that a few of the Wardens were concerned since the disease looked like it was affecting new Committee members."

Kingsley shook his head. "I haven't seen anything about it in any of my reports."

"Forsyth knows."

"Probably his operation, then." Kingsley nodded.

Allegra found it curious that Charles had not told his lead Venator. Perhaps the threat of the disease had proven to be inconsequential, just as she had thought. She slumped against the counter, holding her head in her hands. She could feel the emotional exhaustion of the ordeal begin to take its toll. She felt as if she had just gotten off a roller coaster, and was drained and relieved in equal measure.

"Oh, before I forget, Charles wanted you to have this." Kingsley slid over an envelope.

She tore it open. There was a ring inside. It was a bonding ring. The ring she presented him with in every lifetime. He was returning it to her.

It appears I am not the one this is meant for, Charles had written.

Allegra felt her stomach fall at the pain behind those words. She would keep the ring, she thought, but she would not give it to Ben. She would fashion a new one to mark her fidelity. But she would hold on to the ring as a memento of her former love, her former life.

"Thank you," Allegra said. *Thank you, Charles.*

In the end, Charles could not bring himself to kill his rival. He couldn't kill Ben, and he had never threatened him. There was never any real danger. Ben had no idea. Allegra felt profoundly grateful. The return of the ring meant she would be free of her bond, free to be with the boy she loved.

There would be no blood trial, she was sure of it. Charles would never call one against her. The return of the ring said as much.

She slipped it into her pocket. "What else can I get you, Kingsley? On the house."

THIRTY-SEVEN

An Impossible Choice

*I*t was a difficult thing to lie to your beloved, Jack thought. He did not want her to see how deeply he had been affected by the events that had transpired that evening. It was only through luck that Schuyler had emerged from the underworld unharmed. There was no way he was going to let her out of his sight again, as much as he could help it.

"I'm okay, don't worry about me," Schuyler told him, walking out of the bathroom dressed in a baggy T-shirt and jeans. Catherine had offered to lend her some clothes, and Schuyler had taken the opportunity to wash up as well, scrubbing her face free of makeup so that her face shone. "I would never let anything happen," she said, and with a small, shy smile, she patted her belly. She had yet to tell him, but she'd told him everything in that smile.

It was as Jack had feared. Dear god, she thinks she carries

my child. His heart broke a little at this, and as they walked to the table together he wanted to tell her right then that this was not a possibility—not for him, not for the two of them. It was never in their future. It could not be. It would never be. The angels were not given the gift of creating new life. Schuyler was not pregnant. She was sick. The bond was destroying her, eating her inside and out. The vomiting, the bile, and the blood: it was the sign of the Wasting Disease.

Allegra had fallen into a coma a few years after she'd broken her bond, and before she'd lost consciousness she'd displayed the signs of this same disease. Jack had seen her files, had read the symptoms—they were the same as the ones Schuyler displayed: nausea, vomiting, blood. He'd believed the bond would destroy him, would weaken him, but this was so much worse. The bond was destroying his beloved, just as it had claimed Allegra. The Bond Would Claim Its Own.

But Jack kept his feelings to himself. This was his problem, his darkness that he had brought to her life, and he would take care of it. He had already asked for so much in asking her to love him.

"Does anyone want more tea?" Catherine asked. After disclosing the truth about the Petruvians, conversation had dropped, although the gatekeeper did not seem perturbed by their reactions. In her mind, she was carrying out the work of her Regis, orders of the Archangel, and was far from at fault. But Jack had other things on his mind than the Nephilim.

"Tea?" Catherine asked again.

"Yes," he said quickly.

"I'll get it," Schuyler offered, standing up and walking to the kitchen.

Jack was glad for the opportunity to have a word alone with Catherine. But the gatekeeper spoke first.

"You know, your sister was here. I saw her descend into Helda's kingdom," Catherine said with a conspiratorial smile.

"When?"

Catherine named a date, and it was roughly the same time they had arrived in Cairo, Jack thought. "I want to speak to you about Azrael," he said.

Catherine nodded. She looked pointedly at the bonding ring he wore on his finger. It was not one worn by the Fallen. It was man-made, a human ring, ordinary. "Of course. You seek to break your bond. To free your love from Gabrielle's fate, I imagine?"

"Yes." He looked tired and sad, but there was a flash of hope in his eyes. "You were there when the bond was made. You know what I am up against. Can you help me? Tell me, is there any other way?"

Catherine wiped her mouth with a napkin and did not answer.

Jack continued to press his case. "Because I do not want to kill my sister. It is the only way to stop her. The blood trial will mean only one of us is left standing. But I cannot bring her harm. I will not have her death on my hands. But I don't want her to kill me or my . . . my wife." At the mention of his mate, his face softened with love.

Catherine sighed. "The only way to end a bond is to serve a task of allegiance to the one who consecrated it. He alone can unmake what was made. Who sealed your fate?" From Jack's troubled face, Catherine knew the answer. "Your former master. Well then, you know what you have to do. Find Lucifer and offer him your services in return for an Unmaking."

"Is that my only choice? Serve Lucifer or kill Azrael?"

She nodded. "I'm afraid so."

"Then it must be," he said, and his face was full of sorrow; for even though he did not love her anymore, Azrael was part of him. But if he had to destroy her to keep Schuyler alive, he would do what he had to do.

THIRTY-EIGHT

Angel Heart

She melted into his arms, but it was Kingsley who kissed her first; and when their lips met, Mimi closed her eyes, every sense in her body tingling. It was as if she had never been kissed, as if they were kissing each other for the first time. His lips were soft against hers, and when she opened her mouth to him, they fell on each other hungrily, and pressed against each other with a passion that eclipsed every prior emotion, along with every kiss that had come before. If Mimi ever doubted his love, she was sure of it now. She folded her legs around him as his strong arms carried her into her room, and he kicked the door closed behind them.

He slammed her against the wall, putting his entire weight on her body, crushing her. She was breathless with desire, but she was still Mimi Force, and so when he moved to kiss her neck, she pulled at the roots of his hair so that she could bring her mouth to his ear. "Took you long enough," she snarled.

"I didn't want . . ." He tried to finish his sentence but inhaled sharply instead.

It was all right. She held him close, gently petting the fine hair at the back of his neck. Kingsley was afraid. He was so very afraid that his entire body was trembling.

Mimi soothed him and held him tightly. "I was only teasing."

Kingsley closed his eyes and pressed his forehead against hers. "I never thought to dream that you would come for me. I never expected to see you again. When I saw you at the club, I couldn't believe it. I still don't believe you're really here." He gritted his teeth. "I didn't think you were here for me. I thought you had to be here for something else. I didn't realize . . ."

Mimi almost laughed. All this time they had been playing a game of their own making. Kingsley was just like her—he'd harbored the same doubts she had—because when he'd done the rough mathematics of their relationship, he too had noticed that they had never once told each other what they felt. If he had never said the words, had never revealed the true passionate nature of his heart, then neither had she.

She cupped his face with her hands and looked deep into his eyes. Gone was the arrogant heartthrob, the smooth crime boss, the ageless Venator, the immovable Duke of

Hell. There was only Kingsley Martin: just a boy in love with a girl. In love with her.

"I love you," he said, over and over, as he kissed her face, her eyes, her nose, her mouth, her neck, her shoulders. "I love you, I love you, I love you."

Mimi said the same: their voices blending together in a chorus. "I love you, I love you, I love you," as if making up for all those times it had gone unsaid, when they had kept it from the other.

They were still kissing when his hands slipped under her shirt, and she smiled to think that even as vulnerable as he was now, he was still Kingsley. "Can I help you with that?" she asked. She moved to let him pull it over her head, and then she was the one frantically helping him undress, removing his jacket and unbuttoning his shirt, because now she wanted to feel him—his skin on her skin—so much that it was almost a panic. She needed him and wanted him now.

Kingsley carried her to the bed, laid her on the covers, and they helped each other remove the rest of their clothing, smiling shyly at each other, and then he was lying on top of her and kissing her again.

"You are so beautiful," he said.

"Even among all the virago and sirens you have here? Don't tell me you've been faithful. Not Kingsley Martin," she teased, nipping at his neck.

"It was easy. None of them were you."

She placed her hands on his flat stomach, tracing his fine

abdominal muscles and shivering at the scars on his skin. He looked as if he had been flayed: there were great ridges of seared, scarred flesh crisscrossing his torso and back.

"What happened?" she asked, feeling tears come to her eyes at the damage and pain he had sustained.

"It's what happens when you get too close to a *subvertio*."

"They're like glass shards," she said, tracing them gently. "Are they painful?"

"Yes."

Now she was the one who couldn't stop crying for him and for everything he had weathered. She kissed every scar, wanting to heal each one with her love.

"Don't," he said. "I can't stand to see you sad."

She closed her eyes tightly and nodded. "I just . . . I love you so much."

He cried out as he entered her, and Mimi gasped and held him even tighter. They rocked against each other, and his tears fell on her face. When they kissed, it tasted like salt and sacrifice, and she lost herself to the exquisite pleasure of his body and his love—carried aloft to an ecstasy that was beyond anything she had felt before.

Lying together in bed, her head resting in the crook of his shoulder, Mimi felt at peace. Kingsley was soundly asleep next to her. Boys. She nuzzled his neck and he gave her a sleepy kiss. Lucky rabbit's foot, Mimi thought.

Mimi could not remember ever feeling so happy. The

happiness was deep and sustaining, and she realized now that after innumerable years on earth, she had never felt this way. That no one had ever loved her this way, so completely and so thoroughly. She had never shared a moment like this with anyone, and the love she felt for Kingsley was a precious gift—a delicate, wonderful bubble that covered the two of them but grew to expand to the whole world and the entire universe, past the Kingdom of the Dead and the Garden of Eden, encompassing everything and everybody around it.

She loved and she was loved, and that was all that mattered. How simple, really. But wasn't that the reason she had traveled to the underworld in the first place? Her soul was at peace. She was happy and satisfied with life. Everything would work out. She had gotten what she wanted. Ask and ye shall receive. She had received it in spades.

There was something else, something unexpected: that darkness in her soul, that corrosive hate and anger, bitterness and humiliation that she had been living with for the better part of a year—it was gone. It had disappeared.

Mimi had another thought: one so new and surprising that she could not believe she was thinking it. But it was there all the same.

She would let Jack live.

She loved Kingsley so much that she had enough love in her heart for her wayward twin as well. There was no need to spend her energy looking for Jack and plotting to kill him.

She would release him from his bond. There would be no blood trial. There was no need.

"What are you thinking about, Force?" Kingsley asked. "You look so serious."

She turned to him and gave him another kiss—one of many they would share in an immortal lifetime. "I was thinking we should do that again."

So they did.

THIRTY-NINE

Twilight in the Garden

*L*eaving the Coven was no small matter, and even if Allegra had no doubts that she was doing the right thing, there would be moments when she would catch herself wondering how Charles was doing. She hoped that somehow he would find a way to recover and find some peace. She'd thought being free of the bond would lighten her load, but instead her heart was heavy. While she would have her love, she had lost everything else that was precious to her, including a storied, celebrated history that was an indelible part of her identity.

Ben loved her and thought he knew her, but there was so much that he could never know, never understand, which was why she loved him in the first place. She loved him for seeing the part of her that no one ever noticed—the human part, the vulnerable girl behind the vampire shell.

One morning, not too long after her imprisonment, a

telegram arrived at the vineyard. It was a summons. *I am at the Fairmont. I will wait for you in the tea room at four o'clock.*

"Who sends telegrams these days?" Ben asked, watching Allegra read the small typewritten note.

"My mother," Allegra said, tearing the note in half and tossing it into the garbage. She had not spoken to her mother since leaving New York, and Cordelia had never attempted to contact her before now.

"When am I going to meet her?" Ben asked.

"Not anytime soon," she said. "I'm sorry, it's just . . . she's not really the best person for you to meet right now."

Ben nodded, but he looked hurt, and they did not talk about it for the rest of the day.

When Allegra arrived at the hotel's grand lobby, her mother was seated on a divan, rigid, correct, and implacable as always. Allegra bent down to kiss Cordelia's cheek, and found it papery and thin, smelling of talcum powder and Chanel No. 5. But other than a few fine lines around her bird-blue eyes, Cordelia looked exactly the same. Allegra had a flash for a moment of Cordelia looking a little older and speaking to a girl who was just a few years younger than Allegra was. The girl regarded Cordelia in the same manner that Allegra had, with a little bit of fear and love. Who was that girl? Allegra wondered. Was it the daughter she would bear to Ben? The baby she had seen in that vision? Why was the girl with Cordelia? But of course—Allegra remembered now—because she would not be able to raise the child herself, remembering the image of herself lying comatose on that hospital bed. Was there anything she could do to change it? To change the future? Ben had told her not to fear—but he had no idea what they were up against.

"Scone?" Cordelia asked, breaking Allegra's reverie.

"No thanks."

"Pity. They're quite good."

Allegra watched her mother eat with precise, small movements, and, as if in retaliation, took a big noisy gulp from her water glass. "I know why you're here," she said finally.

"Oh?" Cordelia put down her teacup. "I suppose I'm not surprised."

Allegra nodded. "You're not going to convince me to change my mind. Charles and I have . . . ended it. He let me go," she said, even though she herself did not quite believe it.

"Yes. I know. The whole Coven knows, Allegra." Cordelia's tone became cold. "You know I have not always agreed with Charles on his decisions over the centuries, and so I will grant you the same courtesy. I will not talk about the choice you have made. You of all people know what you have given up for this . . . relationship you continue to pursue with your human familiar. And I suppose since you already know why I am here, but you have not acted, then perhaps this is a waste of both our afternoons."

"Yes," Allegra said. "I'm sorry to waste your time, Mother."

Cordelia sighed. "I thought more of you. I thought you would care. I did not expect you to be so heartless, Allegra. That was never like you."

"I care for Charles—I always will," Allegra pleaded. "But I can't do it anymore. He understands that. I love someone else. I don't know how it happened, but I do."

"Charles is dying," Cordelia snapped.

Allegra reared her head back. "What?"

"I thought you said you knew why I was here."

"Because I thought you were here to bring me back to New York."

"I am."

"I meant . . . to renew my bond. . . ." Allegra said. This was a trick, a way to get her to return. Cordelia was lying. "We're immortal. He'll come back in another cycle."

"You don't understand. If you don't renew your bond, he will weaken. He becomes half a person. The immortal blood—the *sangre azul*—will fade from him. I thought you knew that."

"But if the bond breaks, then why am I not sick as well?"

"Not yet," Cordelia said.

Allegra felt a piercing fear hold her. The bond would take them both. The blood would thin, and the immortal spirit she carried within her would be extinguished. No wonder Cordelia had come today. Allegra hadn't known—or she did not want to know. She knew enough already and still she was going through with it. Her own blood had shown her visions of the future. Comatose on the bed. Her child growing up without a mother. And Ben . . . who knew what would happen to Ben. . . .

"I did not come all the way to San Francisco to judge you, Allegra, or berate you for your poor choices. But I do ask that you see him before the end. You owe him that much."

Allegra told Ben there was an emergency back home, and that she would return as soon as she could. She left for New York that evening, and the next morning paid a visit to Charles in his grand new home on Fifth Avenue.

She had no memories of the past that did not have him in it. She had no life, no identity apart from the lonely figure sitting in the dark, in that palatial bedroom. This was the room she had picked out, had decorated, had lovingly imagined they would make their home. It saddened her to see him in it, so alone. She had done this. She was the one who had left him.

Charles Van Alen heard her enter, the soft tread of her feet on the felt carpet. "Cordelia sent you," he said, closing the book on his lap.

"Yes. But I came on my own. I didn't know," she said. "I didn't know what would happen if I didn't renew the bond. I didn't know it would hurt you like this."

"Why are you here?" Charles coughed.

Allegra sat by his bed. "I did not want you to suffer," she said, taking his hand, which had withered since the last time they had seen each other. "I did not want you to suffer because of me."

Her heart ached. Charles had given her the freedom she had asked for, and in return he had sacrificed himself. She had assumed she was free; but she would never be free; not with a Heavenly Bond at stake. The Code of the Vampires had been written for a reason—to keep not only humans but also vampires safe from harm. "There has to be another way," she said.

Charles shook his head. "There is only one way."

Allegra nodded. She thought as much and despaired. She could not love two men at the same time, and so she had chosen the one who made her happiest. But now, seeing the consequence of her actions, she did not know what to think, what to do. She hadn't expected Charles to suffer. She had thought the risk was all her own. "You can stop this," she said, putting her other hand on top of his. "You are stronger than any of us. You are Michael of the Angels. . . . You are stronger than the bond."

"Return to me," he whispered. It was a request, not an order. He was begging for her love.

"Then tell me what I want to know," she said. "Tell me what happened in our past that we became so estranged. Help me to find my way back to you."

She caught a flash of the blood memory, and for a moment she saw him as he had been: as Michael, Protector of the Garden, the one who had claimed her for his own, back when the world was new. She remembered his strength and his power, but most of all she remembered how she had been drawn to his innate sense of justice, his goodness, the pure light that emanated from his soul. He was the chief archangel of the Lord. He had triumphed over the dragon, had thrown Lucifer and the rebel angels out of Paradise. The Hand of God. He had chosen earth over Elysium to be with her.

For the length of her immortal life she had felt worthy of his love, had returned and reflected it. But something had changed between them ever since Florence in the fifteenth century. And since then, in every cycle, she had grown distant from him. She did not know sometimes what she loved anymore: the man or the myth. The angel who had led the armies of Eden or the boy who was lying in this bed, looking sickly and pale, and yet so dear to her heart still.

So dear to her still.

But she was tired of living in the past, tired of being in the dark. She wanted him to be the light that he was, to be the angel whom she had loved with all of her heart, when nothing had ever come between them.

"Tell me what happened, my love," she begged. "Help me to come back to you."

"Yes, yes. I will tell you everything."

Allegra bent down and kissed him on the lips. It was the first time she had kissed him this way in this lifetime. They had been saving this for their bonding—for their return to each other.

Charles circled Allegra's waist, and she let him pull her down to the bed.

FORTY

The Key of the Twins

Schuyler came back with a second pot of tea to find Jack contemplative and Catherine continuing to eat her biscuits. She poured them each another cup, trying to think of what to say to Catherine that wouldn't be rude or offensive. How was it that she had been sent to warn the gatekeepers—when perhaps she should have been warned *about* them. Aside from Lawrence, the Order of the Seven was a motley crew: Kingsley, the Silver Blood; Catherine, the baby killer. . . . Schuyler's mind whirred. There was more. "There's a healer here . . . a Venator from Amman. He says he is your brother."

Catherine frowned. "My brother?"

"Yes."

"What else did this Venator say?"

"He said the Coven in Amman is destroyed, and that a Silver Blood was behind its destruction, as well as the destruction of all the Covens. And he told us he knew what you guarded. Forgive me—that's why I thought he was your brother, because he knew your secret."

"I would not trust this Venator. He is no brother of mine. My brother died in the War of Heaven."

Schuyler thought hard. She had accepted that Mahrus was telling the truth, and even went so far as to think that he might be Onbasius, the healer from Rome, who had been part of the Order of the Seven and a gatekeeper himself. But of course that wasn't right, because of what Allegra had told her from the beginning: one gate per family. No. Mahrus was not Onbasius and no keeper; and according to Catherine of Siena, he was a liar.

Schuyler told Catherine of what the Venators had learned—that Mimi Force had been attacked by the blood spell in the glom, and that the Nephilim had targeted Deming as well. The Venators told her they had never discovered why the Regent had been attacked, but she thought it might have something to do with information they'd found in Paul Rayburn's files—notes concerning a star key that unlocked one of the Gates of Hell. She asked Catherine about it. "The files said that the star key unlocks the Gate of Promise. Have you heard of this key? Do you have it?"

"They have the translation wrong. It is called the Key of the Twins, not the Key of the Star," Catherine said. "Easy enough to get it confused. Nephilim aren't known for their deep intelligence."

"So that's why they attacked Mimi. . . . They thought she was the key somehow. And Deming, because she was a starborn twin. They were searching for meaning, trying to make things fit," Schuyler said. "But why would they need a key if they're already using humans to bring women through the gate?"

The gatekeeper hesitated for a moment before replying. "I suppose if you are Allegra's daughter and worthy of the secret of the seven, you will find out soon enough anyway."

"There's more that my mother didn't tell me?"

Catherine put her teacup down so it rattled the saucer. "The Gate of Promise is a bifurcated path. It leads to two different locations. This one, in Giza, guards the underworld. The other is hidden from me. I do not know where it is or where it leads. But I do know one thing: whoever holds the Key of the Twins is the true keeper of the Gate of Promise."

FORTY-ONE

Secrets of the Underworld

*T*horoughly ravished, Mimi thought she would never feel so tired or spent or satiated. Every muscle in her body ached. She was bruised with kisses and lovemarks, but there was a pleasure in knowing they had enjoyed each other utterly; that they had more than made up for all their time apart in discovering new and secret delights. She had to find her breath; she was panting. They could do this all day and night, and she had a feeling that, at least in the near future, this was exactly what they would do. Love was like a drug, a physical addiction. She wanted Kingsley near her at all times, wanted to feel his skin next to hers, to know he was real.

"Water?" Kingsley asked, hauling himself to a sitting position. He looked down at her and squeezed her shoulder affectionately.

"Please."

He wrapped himself in a sheet and whistled as he made his way to the kitchen. Mimi changed into a silk robe, feeling a bit cold in the room now that he was gone.

Kingsley returned with two crystal glasses filled with water and handed her one. He jumped back into bed.

"You know, the first moment I got here, I tried to get out. I got all the way to the gate. But I couldn't walk through," he told her. "Croatan blood will do that."

She snuggled next to him, and he gently stroked her hair as he told her his story. "I tried everything. I bargained with Helda. That's why I took this post. I thought if I could prove myself useful, I could win some favors. But the years passed—you know time is different down here—and nothing happened. I pretty much gave up. Then I saw you. I thought I was dreaming at first."

"Typical." She smiled. "You never believe what's right in front of you."

"I'm used to disappointment," he said, draining his glass and putting it on the side table.

"Do you even want to come back with me?" Mimi asked, fearing his answer and thinking of the flower blooming in the wasteland. "What about all the stuff you're doing down here—and the way you feel up there . . . with the voices. The Corruption will be part of you again."

"I know," he said. "I thought about it."

"Really, when?" she teased. "When did you have the time?"

"Right now," he said. "And it's okay. I can deal with the Corruption. I've dealt with it my entire life."

"Are you sure?"

"I have never been more certain." He kissed her bare shoulder. "I want to go home. I want to be with you. The underworld can survive without me."

She nuzzled his cheek, the happiness returning again.

"So we just walk out of here, that's it?" Kingsley asked.

"That's the plan," she said, pinching his nose. He was truly so handsome. She sighed. Her own handsome devil.

"Seems too easy," he mulled. "Helda really said I could leave? She's not going to stop us?"

"Hey, I've got some pull around here," she said. As the Angel of Death, Mimi reminded him that the darkness was part of her birthright.

"I can see that." He smiled again. "All right, then. If you're sure this is going to work—"

"Shush!" Mimi said, pouting. "Let's not be negative. Get dressed and let's go. We've got a train to Limbo to catch."

Oliver did not seem surprised to see them together at breakfast. He tactfully did not mention anything when they appeared at the table, glowing with satisfaction and bubbling with energy. "So we just take some train? That's it?" he asked.

Kingsley frowned. "It's a little more complicated than that, but we'll figure it out when we get there. I don't know what the demon told you," he said to Mimi. Then he looked at the trolls who were standing at attention around the room, their hands at their backs. "Leave us," he ordered.

He regarded Mimi and Oliver seriously. "There's something you guys need to know. I've been meaning to tell you, but I wanted to wait until I was sure."

"What is it?"

"There's been . . . unusual activity down in the ninth."

"Lucifer?" Mimi asked.

Oliver forced his bread down his throat. The thought of the Dark Prince was still frightening. He had seen what happened at the bonding, when the Croatan had revealed themselves and captured Schuyler, pulling her into the glom.

Kingsley nodded. "It's got to be . . . I think he's trying to break out again."

"Fine. We'll just kick him back here when he does." Mimi shrugged and ripped her croissant in half, as if imagining it was their enemy.

Kingsley shook his head. "No. I've heard that Lucifer has grander ambitions."

"Like what?" Oliver wanted to know.

The Duke of Hell frowned. "I've heard rumors that they've created new weapons that can be used against the divine—even more powerful than the White Fire of Heaven—and that he is gathering his demons for battle."

"So if it's war he wants, he'll have it. This is it, then. Apocalypse. We'll ready the horses," Mimi said.

"No. Lucifer has no more interest in the mid-world," Kingsley said, looking around nervously, as if spies were all around.

"No? Why not?" asked Oliver. "Humans have ruined it too much?" He smiled at his joke.

Kingsley did not find it amusing and did not respond to the crack. "I fear it's something much more precious." He paused to let it sink in. "The Dark Prince is preparing to conquer Paradise."

"But how?" Mimi asked. She tossed her half-eaten croissant back on her plate, having lost her appetite at the news. "That's impossible. Paradise is closed to the Fallen. If the angels cannot be redeemed, how can the demons and the Corrupted even get close to Eden? There's no way. They won't be able to find it. No one can."

"I don't know. They don't trust me enough to tell me their plans," Kingsley said, frustrated. "But they are confident of victory."

hen Allegra returned home to Riverside Drive, Ben was waiting for her. He was sitting on the stoop and he had his hands folded in his lap. "I know where you were last night," he said. "I know you went to him. . . ."

"It's not like that. . . ."

"It's all right. Please. It's killing me. I don't even know what to make of it. I don't *want* to know what to make of it," Ben said. "But it's sick, whatever is between you guys. It's not . . . right."

"Ben, please."

"But hear me out—" Ben coughed into his handkerchief. Allegra saw that the cloth was red with blood. He'd started coughing last week and was supposed to go to a doctor, but had been too busy to take care of it. Allegra would have to remind him. It was beginning to worry her so much that she didn't even want to think about it.

She led him inside the town house, and they sat together in Cordelia's formal living room.

"Allegra," Ben said. It hurt her to hear her full name from his lips. He'd never called her that before. "I will love you no matter what. I don't care that you were with Charles last night. I don't. I just want you," he said.

Allegra swallowed her tears. She couldn't do it, she thought. She couldn't. She'd been so sure when she'd left Charles that she would renew her bond with him again, that she had chosen the right path, but now, seeing Ben, her resolve wavered. She couldn't leave Ben. She loved him too much. Just then, the upstairs phone rang. It was the Conclave line, that only the Venators and Wardens used.

"Ben, I'm so sorry. I have to take this. I think it's important."

Ben waved his hand. "Go ahead," he said, coughing again.

She ran upstairs and picked up the receiver. "Yes?"

"Martin here. Sorry to bother you, but I thought you might find this interesting," Kingsley said. "I wanted to tell you before I left for my next assignment and forgot about it."

"This isn't a good time," she said. "Can it wait?"

"When is?" The Venator sighed. "Sorry—I promise this won't take long, what I have to say."

"Get on with it, then."

He cleared his throat. "So I looked into that thing you

told me about—the diseased Red Bloods?"

"And?"

"I couldn't find anything on it, not in any of the official files."

Allegra bit her fingernails. "No?"

"Forsyth laughed. He said he'd never heard of such a thing. Said I was letting the voices in my head drive me crazy," Kingsley said, not sounding terribly insulted. Over the centuries, Allegra knew, he must have gotten used to the barbs and comments from the Blue Bloods. "I didn't tell him I heard it from you. I didn't want you to get in trouble."

"He's lying. There was a body in that van. I saw it."

"Yes," Kingsley said. "I found the ambulance records, the one for the clinic that the Conduits use. Here's the thing: the records show there was a dead body in that van, but I checked San Francisco; there aren't any familiars who have been reported missing or recently deceased."

Allegra could not believe what she was hearing. Charles had told her to her face that it was a human familiar in the body bag. She had seen it herself—she tried to remember— the body had certainly looked human. "So what, then?"

"I don't know. I can't get any answers. But I asked around a little more and . . . I don't know what to make of it, but apparently there've been a few vampires missing." Kingsley exhaled.

"Missing?" No. It couldn't be. Allegra thought of her fear that had led her to check the body. The fear that those

274

who hunted the vampires were loose in the world again; an enemy they had eradicated centuries ago. It couldn't be happening again. She thought of Roanoke and the missing colony. And there'd been others over the years—one or two here and there—vampires who'd gone off-Coven, maybe, or did not report to the Wardens. It was nothing, Charles had assured her. There was nothing to fear. She'd had her doubts—she'd had so many doubts over the years, she realized, but she'd done nothing about them. All those doubts about what had truly happened in Florence; the secret Charles had been keeping from her.

"Yes. A few of the new Committee members who'd just been inducted can't be accounted for."

"What did the Elders say?"

"They won't speak to me," Kingsley said. "Anyway, I don't know what to make of it. I'm sure it's nothing. Maybe a couple of kids playing hooky. But I thought I should tell you. You'll tell Charles, right? I mean, he should know that someone's not telling the truth."

"Yes. Yes I will." Allegra said. They said good-bye and hung up.

She returned downstairs, almost surprised to find Ben sitting on the living room couch. "I'm so sorry, but I have to go to Charles right now."

"I understand," Ben said bravely. Allegra wanted to comfort him, but she had no time to explain.

FORTY-THREE

Bluebeard's Castle

*S*am laid out the map on the table and briefed the team on their rescue mission. They were in the necropolis, huddled in the small room inside the Venators' quarters. It was almost a week since Deming had been kidnapped, and Mahrus had joined them as well, after returning from a short trip to Jerusalem to check on the Coven there. Schuyler decided not to confront Mahrus with what Catherine had told her for now, as she did not know if she believed it.

"Catherine says the castle is located on the edge of Limbo, right at the mouth of the river Styx," Sam said. "There are only two entrances to the castle. The drawbridge over the moat is the main one, but there's a second, secret entrance from the Palace of the Zaniyat Babel that leads directly to the dungeons. The Harvest Bonding is set for Lammas, and as suggested, we'll move the day before.

Catherine will leave all the doors unlocked in the basement of the brothel so that we can get through. There won't be a new batch of girls until next month, so the place will be pretty deserted, she said."

He pointed to the next place on the map. "Once we're in the dungeon, we make our way up to the castle. It'll be heavily guarded on the outside, but inside there'll be just the usual crew of domestics. Probably a few trolls, nothing we can't take care of. Deming should be held here." He pointed to the highest tower. "The Bluebeard room."

"Bluebeard—you mean like the fairy tale?" Schuyler asked.

"Not every fairy tale is made up," Jack explained. "It's Baal's . . . 'nickname.' He's had numerous brides."

"The brides—they're all dead? Like in the story?"

"What do you think?" Sam said testily. "From what Catherine tells me, most human women can only bear one demon birth. Many of them die in childbirth, and even when they do survive, they don't live very long."

"Especially if the Petruvians kill them," Dehua said.

"Dehua and Ted will lead the attack and subdue the trolls. Jack, you and Schuyler will keep watch while Mahrus and I go to the tower and get Deming." He rolled up the map. "Clear?"

The team nodded and prepared to descend into the underworld.

* * *

It didn't take long to realize that the map was wrong. They were deep in the castle dungeons when Jack heard Sam curse as he slung the roll under his arm.

"What's the matter?" he asked, walking up to the Venator. Jack was already on high alert since he could not dissuade Schuyler from joining the mission. Like Sam, he didn't want any mistakes this time. The risks were too great.

Sam handed the map to Jack, who unrolled it and squinted at the drawing. It showed the dungeon as a series of broad rings that mimicked the walls of the castle above. Short hallways connected the rings, making it easy to move quickly through any part of it. But the dungeon in which they stood had little to do with that plan. Massive stone walls blocked the rings, forcing the team to make a winding path through the stone-lined corridors.

"I don't like this," Sam said. "We should have been out of the dungeons by now. All of these little blockades are forcing us deeper into the circle, with no guarantee that we'll be able to get out."

"You think this is deliberate? That they planted the wrong map for Catherine to find?" Jack asked.

"I don't know, but there's something wrong. The dungeon is empty; no one is in any of these cells." Suddenly there was a loud noise from somewhere deep underground.

"What was that?" Schuyler asked.

"Stay close," Jack said. Everyone was nervous now. Sam tried to lead them out of the circle, but they found themselves in front of another massive stone wall.

"We need go back the way we came," Jack said. "They're steering us somewhere we don't want to go."

"No!" Sam protested. "We'll find a way through. This is our only chance—" He stopped mid-sentence as he followed Jack's gaze to the left, where the dark corridor was flooding with trolls.

Their silver eyes and dark skin glowed with unearthly light, their collars glinting. The trolls began to jabber excitedly.

With nowhere to run, the group formed a tight circle as they braced for the trolls' assault. "They're nothing but a bunch of dimwits," Sam muttered. "Nothing to be scared of."

"There's only one way out, and it's *through*," Jack said. He removed his sword and pushed his way to the front of the group. Next to him, the rest of the team did the same, their silver blades shining in the darkness.

The trolls faltered for a moment; silver was the only metal they feared. But they had been trained to fight, and they rushed forward, teeth and claws bared.

"Jack!" Schuyler yelled, as the largest troll flew at him.

"I've got him!" Jack said, gritting his teeth. He held out his blade directly as the troll attacked. He bent his knee to drive it upward through the beast's sternum, using the troll's own momentum to ram it into the wall.

The group fought as ferociously as the trolls, but for now, neither appeared to gain the upper hand. The Venators were not in their element. They were in unknown territory, and they could soon be overpowered. There were only six of them, but there might be hundreds of trolls.

Jack tried to collect his thoughts. They'd just been ambushed and he needed to take stock, try to find some advantage. The trolls had chosen a broad stretch of the corridor to attack, as it gave their large numbers an upper hand and the ability to come at them from all sides. Jack swiveled around and found a small narrow passageway, a tiny space created by one of the blockades, which was only a few feet behind them.

"Behind that wall!" he called, leading them to the crevice.

Sam shot him a crazed look. "But we'll be trapped against the blockade!"

"Exactly," Jack replied. "They'll be forced to attack us one by one!' There was no time to argue, and the team followed as Jack pushed backward, and they fought their way into the dead end.

"We'll take turns," Mahrus ordered, understanding the strategy. The space was so tight that only two of them could fight at a time. One fought the right side, while another covered the left. They were able to slow down the charge of the trolls, and choreographed every move. When it was their turn, Schuyler and Jack fought as a team. Schuyler would slash below while Jack went in for the kill, his silver blade forcing the trolls to the ground.

They were doing well when their group was suddenly attacked from behind as several trolls burst through the back wall.

Jack cursed. He'd forgotten the trolls' inordinate strength to crush rock. "Sam! Ted! Cover the back!" The trolls kept advancing, forcing the team to make a tighter circle. "We've got to surprise them when they come out, back to the wall!" Jack cried.

Sam and Ted pushed hard, turning their blades sideways. They beat the trolls to the ground, pushing them to the side as the six of them moved back toward the wall. The smell of death and blood filled the air. They were fighting well, but Jack knew the trolls had more in store. He found his answer when he looked up and saw the trolls falling into the cavern from a hole they'd made in the ceiling.

"Watch out!" he warned as a dozen of them crashed onto the team, forcing Sam and Ted to the ground, knocking Dehua off balance, and striking Mahrus in the head.

The trolls rained down and inserted themselves between the companions, driving them apart. Jack and Schuyler fought back-to-back and lost sight of the others. "Jack, there's too many of them. There's no way we're going to fight our way out of here. They can just keep sending more of them," Schuyler said. "We've got to find Deming and get out."

"Okay," he said, slashing at a troll's torso. "Let's go."

"No. You need to stay and fight; keep them off the rest

of the team. I'll find her and bring her back."

Jack turned to look at her. It was what he feared most—and she was suggesting it. "No! I can't let you go alone."

There was a noise from the depths of the dungeon: a dark low growl that sent shivers up Schuyler's spine.

"What is that?"

"It's a Hellhound. . . ." Jack said, paling slightly. "Unleashed from the ninth circle."

"Then they'll need you down here. I'll be quick. I promise." There was no time for good-byes. Schuyler weaved through the pack, leaving Jack behind.

"Over here!" she heard him call from behind her. He was drawing the trolls to his side to cover her escape.

Schuyler followed the trolls' slimy trail through the dungeon, guessing correctly that it would lead her to the exit, and she found a winding stair that led upward. That had to be it. She took the steps three at a time, running up to the tower. She could hear the sounds of battle below, and the roar of Abbadon unleashed—Jack had transformed into his true shape. There were several landings on the way up, and Schuyler tried a few doors. She opened the first one to find a skeleton hanging from a noose. She stifled a scream. Bluebeard's castle, she remembered. The second contained a coffin. The third . . . Schuyler did not open the third. There were more, seven in all, and the final one was on the highest landing.

The door was painted red to indicate the Harvest Bride. The newest bride, sacrificed on the eve of Lammas, to bear the child of the demon.

Schuyler said the words that unlocked it. The door flew open, and she ran inside the room.

"Deming! We're here!"

But the room was empty. Deming had already been taken to the Harvest Bonding.

FORTY-FOUR

Runaway Train

"This is the end of the line." Kingsley stepped from the train as the subway doors opened in front of them. Mimi and Oliver followed him to the platform. Mimi noticed it was the same one they had taken when they'd first journeyed to Tartarus.

"What now?" Oliver asked, peering around the empty station. "It looks like the tracks loop back into the city."

"Exactly. Hell's a closed circuit. None of its paths lead to the surface." Kingsley explained that they would have to find their way out of the tunnel and locate the above-ground train, which followed the only path that led out of Hell.

Mimi looked at Kingsley questioningly, wondering why he was so nervous all of a sudden. It was just a matter of catching a train, after all. "Let's go. What are we waiting for?"

Kingsley hesitated. "This is what I meant earlier when I said it was complicated. You can't just walk on. The train's crawling with a hundred trolls, and demons guard every door. It's Charon's line. The only way souls are taken to the Dead's kingdom, faster than the old ferries. The train arrives full, but always leaves empty. I think they'd be a little suspicious if they saw the three of us hijacking our way back to the surface. Once you're down here, you're supposed to stay down here."

"Great!" Oliver said, smacking his forehead.

"Helda never mentioned this!" Mimi fumed.

"Why would she?" Kingsley said amiably, not the least bit disturbed.

"So we're stuck here!" Oliver grumbled. He'd had about all he could take of Hell. He was ready to get back home, back to earth.

He *was* going home, right? Mimi had been acting odd that morning. . . . She hadn't met his eyes when he'd said something about looking forward to sleeping in his own bed again.

"Not quite." Kingsley walked the length of the platform and found a staircase at the far end of the tunnel. "We're going up. Come on, we need to move quickly."

The stairs took them to an empty sidewalk on the edge of the city. There were no cars on the street, and the buildings looked empty and abandoned. Metal screens were drawn across the storefronts, and black bars covered the upper-story windows. Right above them was steel scaffolding that stretched three stories into the sky, casting a web of shadows across the street. The structure housed a platform on either side, and railway tracks that disappeared far into the north.

"That's the train we want." Kingsley pressed his back to the cold metal grille that covered the closest store window. Mimi and Oliver followed his gaze. The black tower was covered in dense barbed wire, and a mountain of trash clogged the bottom half of the tower, closing off all of the stairs.

"How does anyone even get in or out of that thing? It looks impossible," Oliver said.

"The trolls just bash through, pulling the souls with them. Like I said, it's a one-way train. No one boards from this end, and the return train is always empty." Kingsley glanced up as a train roared into the station, its engine releasing a billowing cloud of black smoke. It lurched to a stop, the wheels sending red hot sparks flying into the air.

Oliver watched as the doors opened and a crew of trolls popped out, carrying the dead with them. Suddenly the platform was filled with guards and their captives; the place went from ghost-town empty to rush-hour jammed in only a few seconds. The trolls kept walking straight down, disappearing into an underground stairway. Meanwhile, the train sparked into motion, its ancient engine firing a second dark cloud into the air as it powered out of the station, speeding forward underneath the thick black smoke.

The three of them watched it leave.

"What now?" Oliver asked.

"Hmm, not quite sure," Kingsley said, scratching his chin.

"I think Hell's starting to rot your brain," Mimi said, shielding her eyes and peering down the line. "See how it's passing through that building?" She pointed to a dilapidated brick building a few blocks from the station. "We can hop on the next train once it's outside the station. It's only a few blocks out; the train won't yet be at full speed."

"Did you see that thing leave the station?" Oliver asked her. "There's no way I can run that fast."

Kingsley smiled. "Let's do it."

Oliver shook his head. "You know I can't move like that. Got any other ideas?"

But Kingsley was already running ahead, and Mimi glanced back at Oliver as they dashed down a side street. "Don't worry. I'll hold your hand."

Oliver grimaced for a moment, then fled after them.

They ran across a pair of abandoned lots covered in junk and overrun with weeds. Mimi held her nose as they leapt over the wrecks of rusted-out cars and refrigerators. "Hurry, Oliver!" She looked back. The next train was just about to rumble into the station.

Kingsley disappeared ahead of them through a broken opening in the side of the building. Mimi followed him up and over an iron fire stair to the third story, Oliver lagging behind. Kingsley picked up a chair and threw it so that it shattered the glass of a tall window, bursting the pane. "Come on, it's time to jump the train."

Mimi and Oliver gathered behind him at the window. Oliver turned to Mimi. "I can't do this."

"Yes you can. You have to," Mimi said. "I can't leave the underworld without you," she said, which was the truth, but not in the way Oliver thought. There was still the matter of paying Helda.

Ahead of them, the sound of the approaching train grew louder as a gust of air pushed its way toward them. Kingsley poked his head out the window to look. "You jump first, I'll take Oliver," he told Mimi.

The train was upon them; there was no time to argue. Mimi leapt from the window onto the roof of the train. She glanced up and saw Oliver shaking his head. "JUMP!" she yelled. "HURRY!"

Kingsley pushed off from the brick, grabbed Oliver squarely by the shoulders, and propelled them both through the air until they landed not too far from where Mimi was crouching. To Oliver's eyes it was all a blur, a quick flash of metal and brick, and then they were on top of the speeding train.

"We've got to move—look behind you!" Mimi yelled, the wind tossing her blond hair into her face. "Oh god, I think they're Hellhounds."

Oliver turned to see. Mimi was right. Those weren't trolls. The three massive wolflike creatures that were chasing them were far too large and frightening to pass for the troll underclass. The hounds moved swiftly and silently, running up the empty building to where the trio had made their jump. Oliver cursed as he scrambled behind Mimi and Kingsley, who were shinnying down the side and entering the train car through a window. He had no choice but to follow, and Kingsley and Mimi pulled his legs through the window to safety.

"What now?" Mimi asked. "If they get on this train, they'll take us back to Tartarus for sure. We've got to run."

Kingsley drew himself up to his full height, and his voice was angry. "The Duke of Hell isn't about to run from a few mangy hounds. They will heel."

Heavy thuds echoed from the roof of the train. Mimi backed herself up against Oliver, shielding him. Kingsley might not fear the hounds, but they could easily snatch Oliver. The air seemed to shimmer for a moment, and then a pair hounds passed through the roof of the train and stood in front of them.

The hounds grinned at the three escapees. They had lupine faces, and unlike the lumbering trolls, they were sleek and swift and handsome. They wore the silver collars, but the chains attached to them were broken. Oliver thought he had never seen a creature as frightening. They were man and wolf, and their smiles were vicious.

"Going somewhere?" one of them asked.

"Go back to Leviathan and tell him I've left." Kingsley's

nostrils flared, and his voice was commanding and thunderous, armed with the full power of his position.

"Left? But we're here to fetch you," the Hellhound replied. "You're to come back with us."

Mimi noticed that doubt had begun to creep into their rough, barking speech. They were still in Hell, and Kingsley was still their master, but they stood their ground.

"GO!" Kingsley roared. "NOW, I SAID!" The Duke of Hell unleashed his sword from his sheath and sent it flying through the air, where it struck the wall a hair's breath away from the nearest hound. "Take that as a warning," he said. "Mimi, hand me your blade."

This time the hounds trembled, and they vanished, glimmering through the walls of the train like ghosts fading from the light.

Kingsley threw himself down onto a bench and smiled at Mimi, who was glowing with pride from his performance. They held hands across the seat. Oliver was just happy to be in one piece.

"Well, I think we just earned our one-way ticket out of here," Kingsley said. "But Leviathan's not going to be happy to know I'm leaving. I know too much about what's going on down here."

FORTY-FIVE

The Archangel's Promise

"Darling." Charles stood up from the breakfast table when he saw Allegra. He looked invigorated, returned to his former strength. But his confident smile faltered when he saw the distress on her face.

Allegra strode forward and told the servants to leave them alone. Charles nodded and the room cleared.

"Last night—I thought I would give you one night so that you could be honest with me and tell me what happened. I believed you last night, Charlie. I believed everything you said."

Last night, when they were together, he had sworn that nothing had happened in Florence; that she knew the whole truth, and this feeling she had—that something terrible had happened—was just her guilt manifesting itself as fear. He said he would never lie to her, had never once lied to her.

She believed it was her guilt at her mistake that was keeping them estranged. He had asked her to forgive herself so that together they could continue to keep their world safe. She had healed him, and she could feel the bond strengthen between them with each kiss they exchanged.

Last night, after he had pledged his honesty and his love, they had returned to each other. She had thought she'd come to the end of their separation at last. But now it seemed they were standing at the precipice once more.

"I told you the truth. I don't understand—who have you spoken to?" he asked.

"What have you done, Charles? Who was in that ambulance? What really happened between us in Florence?" She clenched her fists. "I cannot be part of a lie. I don't know what's true, I don't know what to believe. But I'm starting to think that maybe Cordelia and Lawrence were right all those years ago."

"You're throwing Roanoke in my face again? Is that it?" Charles accused. "You know there was never any other substantive evidence of—"

"No matter what you say, I know you're hiding something, and you're not sharing it with me, and *that* is the real reason we are estranged. Not my mistake. Not my guilt. Something you did, Charles. Something you did has changed the history of our world. I can feel it. That is the reason why I don't love you the way I did before. Because even if I don't remember what happened, I *know*."

"Allegra, please. Listen to yourself. This is preposterous—these things you are accusing me of—how can you hate me so much. I promised you I would keep our people safe, and I have."

"You are going to destroy us with your blindness and your pride."

"The gates are holding! I gave my strength to their creation. There is nothing to fear."

She did not hear him. "You will destroy us until we are nothing but shadows of our former glory. We have lost so much already. Paradise is closed to us forever and still you do not understand," she cried. "You're not the same person you used to be. Something's happened to you . . . and you won't let me help you."

Charles's tone turned icy. "Allegra, why are you here? If you will not return to me, then why?"

"I don't know. I think I just wanted to see you again for the last time."

"You will bond with your human familiar, is that it?"

"Yes."

Charles held his head in his hands and rubbed his temples. When he spoke, his voice was dark and terrible. "Do what you want, but know that I am destroyed if you bond with him. You will never see me again. We shall be estranged forever. I will not be able to survive this, Allegra. Know that my life is in your hands. You have seen what the bond can do."

"It's too late, Charlie. You've lied to me for the last time. You made your choice. This is mine." The bond will claim its own. Perhaps she would die, and perhaps Charles would as well. She did not know. Regardless, it was up to her to find a way to stop whatever he had set in motion, whatever he was keeping from her, whatever was causing vampires to disappear. She was Gabrielle the Uncorrupted, Queen of the Coven. She had a duty to her people. She did not know if she would succeed, but she had to try to undo what he had done.

As Allegra walked out of the room, she was sure of one thing. She would never see Charles Van Alen—Michael, her former beloved—again. Not in this world and not in this lifetime or any other.

It was not only Charles's immortal heart that broke that day.

FORTY-SIX

Dangerous Harvest

*D*eming Chen kicked off her jeweled heels. She'd run so far she had no idea she was still wearing them until she stumbled on a stone in the indoor courtyard. During her week at the castle, she had learned several things. Most important, that it was better to be quiet. She had fought, shown her claws and her strength too early, and so she had been chosen for this punishment. She'd heard that Dehua and Schuyler had been able to get away from their ladies-in-waiting, who had been blamed for the loss, and she was annoyed with herself for having made things harder on herself by attacking too soon. She should have waited until she was alone with only the Red Bloods instead of trying to skewer that ugly toad of a demon who'd picked her for his bride.

She'd weathered an entire week in the company of those simpering ladies, who hated her already because her friends had escaped and gotten them into trouble. The women pulled her hair when they combed it, and laughed at her inability to walk in the high-heeled slippers. Her groom, the demon Baal, had visited her once she had been transformed into a proper little whore: her hair a glossy black, lips a pouty scarlet, breasts rouged and powdered, lifted and presented in the skin-tight halter.

Baal was large and terrifying, with two great horns on his wide forehead, and a long black beard. He towered over her, but Deming was not afraid. When he inspected her form and cupped her breasts, she spit in his face. But he had only chuckled.

"I will enjoy this," he'd said. "Once you are mine, you will learn to love me, my sweet fallen angel."

Deming bided her time and waited for the right moment. She let the ladies-in-waiting grudgingly feed her plums and peaches; let them curl and set her hair. She'd weathered the beauty treatments and the simmering resentment.

Her bonding gown was white, the color of death, the symbol not lost upon the Blue Bloods, who traditionally only wore white at funerals. This was no wedding dress; it was funeral attire. The demon did not care that she wasn't human and would not be able to bear him any Nephilim. She had been sold to him as a novelty—the chance to bond with one of the Fallen.

The Virgin Eve, the traditional night before the bonding, was her chance, she knew. The ladies talked of nothing else but the feast that awaited the Silver Bloods and demons in Tartarus. On the Virgin Eve the ladies would return to the brothel for a celebration of their own, their work done for the week.

Deming saw the opportunity once she was alone, but a troll had been sent to guard her. She'd made quick work of the monster, using its own collar to choke it to death. She hid his body in one of the rooms leading up to the tower—the ones with the dead bodies of Baal's former brides.

She started running and did not stop. But the dress was hard to run in, so Deming tore off the hem at the thigh and kicked off her heels. She was barefoot, but now all she had to do was find the path back to the gate and she would be free.

She was almost at the entrance of the drawbridge when she heard the sound of screaming coming from inside the castle. Her rescuers. Damn it. Didn't they know she could take care of herself? This was only going to complicate things. She made her way back to the great hall and practically bumped into Sam.

"Deming!"

"Sam!"

The Venator cracked one of his rare smiles. "You're . . ."

"I'm good," she assured. "Aside from some unwanted groping, I'm okay. You think I'd let a demon touch me and live?"

He hugged her tightly. "I know. I wasn't worried. . . ."

"Let's get everyone and get out of here. I just found out something—one of the trolls told me I wasn't meant for Baal after all. He was just checking me out for someone higher up who wanted me for himself," she said urgently. The troll who'd come to fetch her had spilled the beans with a smug smile, which had made its death even more satisfying.

But before Deming could say anything more, there was a silver flash and a loud boom from the great hall, which shook the castle to its core.

Deming and Sam turned around.

Jack had been mistaken. It was not a Hellhound that had risen from the deep.

They saw a great horned beast, larger than any demon, looming over the melee. "That's not a demon," said Sam. "That's a Croatan."

"That's what I was trying to tell you," Deming said. This was Malakai, the Steward. On earth he had been known as Forsyth Llewellyn, Lucifer's strongest ally, and his appearance in the underworld meant that he was even stronger now, as it proved that he was able to breach the wall between the worlds freely and that no gate could hold him. After taking Deming he would take her blood spirit as well, and planned to consume her strength into his.

The Silver Blood reeked of death. His foul stench filled the air. He had a bull's head, and when he laughed, his yellow teeth glistened with saliva. His forked tongue was pierced with a dark bronze ring. His face was covered with dark fur and clotted with blood. When he screamed he breathed the Black Fire.

Sam and Deming ran toward the battle to help their friends, their swords drawn, but it was too late. The beast's spiked tail was already buried in Mahrus's chest.

The Venator fell to his death.

Forty-seven

The Porter's Fee

"We're going to have to jump off again, before it gets to the end of the line. The fewer hounds we see, the better. I don't know how long they'll listen to me if I'm leaving," Kingsley told them, as the train began to slow down. The land outside was the same dusty desert as from the beginning of their journey, Oliver noted. He wasn't looking forward to performing another superhuman trick, which came so easily to the two vampires; but he supposed he didn't have a choice.

"Ladies first," Oliver said, letting Mimi have the window. She pulled herself to the edge and then flew off, rolling into a ball as she fell onto the sand.

She looked up at them. "It's not bad! Come on!"

Oliver tried to do the same, but instead of rolling, he fell hard on his ankle, which twisted on the landing.

Kingsley leapt next, and fell on his feet, standing, of

course. He helped Oliver up. "Is it broken?" he asked, meaning the ankle.

"No. Just sprained, I think," Oliver said, limping a little.

They walked away from the tracks and soon came upon a familiar-looking checkpoint—the gas station and sawhorse guarded by the two trolls that Mimi and Oliver had first encountered on their journey into the underworld.

"What about them?" Oliver asked.

"Those guys work for Helda. They don't answer to Leviathan," Kingsley said. "Hey," he said mildly to the trolls.

The trolls let them pass without comment. They looked a bit bored.

Mimi let Kingsley walk on ahead, staying with Oliver, in the guise of helping him with his sprain. "Lean on me," she said.

"Thanks," Oliver said. "I'm glad you got what you wanted."

"Not quite yet," Mimi said. She felt her hands go a little numb at what she was about to do. She hadn't really given it much thought until now, since it was so distasteful, even for her. Oliver had been a good friend throughout their entire adventure. But she had no choice. It was time to pay the porter. A soul for a soul. Mimi prepared to do her worst. "Listen, before we can go, there's something I need you to do for me," she said, without looking at him directly. "I hope you understand it's not personal."

Oliver sighed. He'd had a feeling something like this was going to happen. He liked Mimi, but he trusted her as far as he could throw her, and during his time in the underworld he had carefully weighed his options. He knew he didn't have very many, but he had been hoping that somehow Mimi would change her mind, that she would find another way to get them out of Helda's kingdom. But it was apparent from the determined set of Mimi's jaw that this would not be the case.

"You're going to leave me here," he said.

Mimi did not flinch. "Yes."

"Does Kingsley know?" Oliver asked, watching the erstwhile Duke of Hell banter with a few trolls hanging at the gas station. It was all so much fun for everyone else, wasn't it, Oliver thought, trying not to feel angry. He knew what he had gotten himself into. Mimi had given him a choice in the beginning and he had chosen to descend into the Kingdom of the Dead with her.

"No. He doesn't know that part of it. I didn't tell him," Mimi said. "I don't think he'd let me do it if he knew."

"Probably not," Oliver agreed. Kingsley was a chivalrous kind of guy, and Oliver bet that his pride would never allow him to accept his release at the life of another, and a human at that.

"So . . . is this going to be a problem?" Mimi asked.

Oliver tried not to laugh. Mimi was such a piece of work. What a selfish little bitch. She didn't care what she did or whom she hurt, as long as she got what she wanted. "You're serious about this, aren't you?"

"I told you not to come with me," she said, sounding like a child who'd been told they weren't going to celebrate her birthday after all. "It's your fault for trusting me."

He brushed her arm away from his shoulder. His ankle still hurt. If he had to stay down here, what was all that jumping for, then? All that sneaking out of Hell? Oliver looked around. The underworld, when you thought about it, wasn't so bad, really. Maybe he could get used to living in slight discomfort; hook up with one of the sirens; get used to living with the smell of the trolls.

"Maybe I should let you. It's not as if I have anything to live for up there anyway," he mused. Wasn't that why he had come down with Mimi in the first place? Because he had no more purpose? Because he wanted to do his part to save the Blue Bloods? The Covens were crumbling, the vampires were retreating, Schuyler was gone. What did he have left?

He was resigned but felt his temper begin to rise. He'd thought he and Mimi were friends. He'd believed she would not throw his life away like a crumpled piece of paper. Didn't he mean more to her than that? "How can you do this to me?" he asked, point-blank.

"I really wish I didn't have to," Mimi said.

"There's no other way, is there?" he asked.

"No." Mimi looked down at her feet. Now that they had finally come to the end, she wished with all her heart that there was another way; that she had made it happen differently; that she had tried harder to dissuade him. She had let him come to his doom since he had come willingly enough, and it meant she'd didn't have to go through the challenge of having to kidnap a Red Blood for this purpose. "Does it help if I say I'm sorry?" she asked.

"A little," he said, cracking a ghost of a smile.

"I really am sorry. If I had a choice, I would bring both of you back, but I can't."

Oliver shook his head. "All right, then, lead the way. I might as well get used to my new home. Just make sure they don't put one of those collars on me, all right? They look itchy."

FORTY-EIGHT

Soldier of the Lord

The healer's body collapsed to the floor as the Silver Blood reared to strike again, his towering form casting a long shadow over the group. The beast carried a black sword in one hand and in the other a jagged club. As he raised the weapon into the light, its true form appeared. The wooden club was studded with the skulls of his victims, a grisly weapon that warned attackers of their fate.

Abbadon, his black wings outstretched and his claws dripping with the blood of trolls, rose to the challenge. He stood unafraid as the bull-headed Croatan roared toward him, the demon's eyes blazing a furious color of red. The creature was nearly twice his height, and Jack crouched low to get a better leverage on him. He thrust his sword sideways through the bull's throat, splitting his neck, the blood gushing and hissing as it hit the ground. He felt the club crash against his back, its jagged face lodging into his armor.

Jack pinned the black sword to the ground, leaving the beast defenseless as he made his final push upward. He sawed the head off the demon, sending the mighty horned dome tumbling to the earth. Malakai's face was a mask of disbelief. Then the body exploded as the Black Fire took another life. The creature who was Forsyth Llewellyn, the Dark Prince's closest ally on earth, and the destroyer of the Covens, was dead.

"Everyone hold each other," Abbadon ordered. The group linked hands, Schuyler grasping Abbadon's claws. With her other hand she held on to Mahrus's right wrist.

Abbadon's strength lifted them up and out of the borderlands, through the glom, and back into the other side of the gate, back inside the pyramid.

Mahrus lay dying in Schuyler's arms. His face was the color of ivory, like a beautiful marble statue.

"Oh my god," she said. "Oh my god."

The Venator's eyes fluttered open, and he looked at her and smiled. "It is all right, my child. I am going home," he sighed. "I am sorry I could not stay longer to help you on your journey." Then his body was covered for a moment in a brilliant white light.

"This is not one of us," Jack said, kneeling by the body of the fallen Venator and placing two coins to keep his eyelids closed. "This is not one of the Fallen."

The Venators kneeled and crossed themselves before the body.

"Who was he, then?" Schuyler asked.

"I don't know why I didn't see it before. But none of us recognized him. This is Raphael of the Muses," Jack said. "A soldier of the Lord. A true angel of Heaven. Catherine's brother. He must have survived the war only to find death on earth." His name was Mahrus AbdelMassih: the One Protected by the Lord, Servant of the Messiah.

"So if he's a true angel from Heaven and not one of the Fallen," Schuyler said, "how did he get here? The paths between heaven and earth were closed with Lucifer's Rebellion."

Then she remembered what Catherine had said. The Gate of Promise was on a bifurcated path. One path led to Hell. The other one . . .

Where did it lead . . .

Could it be . . . ?

FORTY-NINE

The Exchange

"What's going on?" Kingsley asked. He slouched against the wall of the gas station. "You guys are up to something. What is it?"

"Don't be jealous," Mimi said, coming to embrace him. "Oliver and I were just having a little chat."

Oliver snorted, but he did not disagree.

Kingsley nodded. "All right. So Helda's in there. . . . I guess we should say good-bye?"

"Wait here. I think she just wants to see the two of us," she said, motioning to Oliver.

They walked into Helda's office. It looked exactly the same as before, with the messy desk full of file folders, books, receipts, ledgers, and envelopes. Helda was the same stern old lady with a pen behind her ear. She studied the two of them.

"This is the soul you barter for the soul of Araquiel?" she asked, opening a ledger and beginning to make a note.

"That's me," Oliver said.

Mimi bit her lip. She looked at Oliver, tired and weary in his safari jacket and dusty jeans. How long had they been down here? Then she peered out the window, where Kingsley was sitting on a bench, waiting for her so they could start their new life together.

She loved them both. One as a friend, the other as her mate. She had wanted to deny her affection for Oliver, but she knew there was no way she could have gone down to Hell, found Kingsley, and been in this position without him. She owed him so much.

"Well?" Helda asked, pen raised. Once she wrote Oliver's name in the Book of the Dead, there was no going back. That ink did not wash off. It was written forever.

"Hold on," Mimi said. "I need to tell Kingsley something." She ran out of the office and banged the screen door behind her.

"Everything all right?" Kingsley asked.

Mimi held his hands. "You know that I love you, right? More than anything in the world. I just want you to know that."

"Of course—why—what's going on?" Kingsley asked, starting to feel a sense of panic.

"And you love me, right? No matter what. You love me," she said.

"I love you," Kingsley said. "I love you." He stood up and looked her in the eye. "What's this all about, Force?"

"Okay." Mimi said. "I just wanted to make sure. That you remember that I love you, no matter what happens."

"What's going to happen? Mimi. Tell me what's going on."

In answer, Mimi kissed Kingsley hard on the lips. Then she flew back into Helda's office before she could change her mind, leaving Kingsley confused and a little frightened.

"Oliver, I need to speak to Helda alone," she said when she returned.

"Right," Oliver said, excusing himself. He walked out to find Kingsley looking annoyed.

"What's going on?" Kingsley demanded.

"Beats me." Oliver shrugged.

Helda rapped her fingers on the table. "Well, Azrael, what will it be?"

Mimi could not believe she was going to do what she was about to, but she'd learned something about herself in the time she'd spent in the underworld. She could not give up Oliver. She couldn't consign him to this dark fate. No one would ask that of a friend. She wouldn't be the girl Kingsley loved if she did.

"You need a soul for his, don't you? Any soul," she said casually, as if it had just occurred to her. "So that Araquiel can leave the underworld." And her friend could leave Hell unharmed. There was no other way.

"Yes."

Mimi bowed her head. "Then take mine."

The New York Times

Weddings

ALLEGRA VAN ALEN *and* STEPHEN CHASE

Allegra Elizabeth Van Alen and Stephen Bendix Chase were married yesterday evening at a private home in San Francisco. The ceremony was performed by Judge Andrew R. Hazard, of the Ninth Circuit, a family friend.

The bride, 23, is a vintner in Napa and graduated cum laude from Harvard. She is the daughter of Cordelia and Lawrence Van Alen of Manhattan. The bride's mother is a member of the Central Park Conservancy and the Blood Bank Committee. The bride's late father was a professor of linguistics and history at Columbia.

The groom, 25, is an artist whose work is represented by the Vespertine Gallery in San Francisco, and included in the collection at the San Francisco Museum of Modern Art. He is a graduate of Stanford University. He is the son of Ronald and Deborah Chase of San Francisco, Napa, and Aspen. His father is an artist. His mother, known as "Decca," is on the Board of Trustees at the SFMOMA, the San Francisco Opera, and the San Francisco Ballet. The groom's great-grandfather founded the Bendix Group, a multinational company with steel holdings and oil reserves that was sold to British Petroleum in 1985.

imi Force, Azrael, drove through the desert plains of the Sahara el Beyda, the white desert. The rolling dunes of white powder resembled snow-covered hills and valleys. It was a place that was as beautiful as it was desolate. Unearthly towers of chalky white earth rose on all sides, and the soft creamy stone, worn from centuries of desert wind, formed mushroom-shaped towers of white salt.

She did not want to be late for her assignation with Jack.

As Mimi put the pedal to the floor, she felt the heat and excitement rise in her veins. This was it. After all this time, she would finally have her revenge.

The underworld and all that had happened there was but a distant memory. She had woken up in her bed at the Oberoi, to find Kingsley Martin, of all people, seated by her bedside. He told her she'd fainted on the way out of the underworld, and he'd carried her back to her room.

"What the hell are you doing here?" she'd screamed. "Get out!"

The ridiculous idiot had tried to convince her that she was in love with him. What a laugh! With him? The Silver Blood traitor? Kingsley Martin? Oh, he was handsome, all right, but beyond his good looks, there was nothing that she found even remotely appealing about him. What great love was he talking about? The boy was out of his mind.

Mimi Force had no love left in her body. There was only one thing on her mind when she woke up. Revenge. She would destroy her brother and slay him at the blood trial.

Kingsley had turned pale. "What did you do to yourself? What did you give Helda?" he demanded. "Mimi. Tell me!"

She had laughed. "I will tell you nothing, as I owe you nothing. Now, get out of here before I call security."

Then another ridiculous thing happened: that moronic human Conduit of the Van Alen mongrel—what was his name—Oliver Something-Stupid—had come in blathering about how he'd just gotten news that the New York Coven had disbanded—and that all the Covens worldwide had gone dark—and they had to return to the city immediately to see what they could salvage of their community and history. She'd thrown him out of her room as well. When did she ever take orders from a Red Blood?

No. How convenient that the moment she'd finally cleared her room of all those jokers, Jack had gotten in touch.

Mimi, let's end this, he'd sent. *The white desert. Blood trial to the death.*

She clapped her hands in joy. Finally. She would get what she deserved. She would dance over his blackened corpse tonight.

Azrael would finally have her revenge.

In a way, it was the best thing that could have happened.

FIFTY-ONE

The Love of a Lifetime

Without even realizing it, the small hotel room in Cairo had become a home, a haven for her and Jack, Schuyler thought. She made coffee for them every morning with the little machine, and they shared breakfast together on the small desk. She would miss this place; just another thing that she would keep in that memory file of her life with Jack.

Their last night together they had loved each other wordlessly, letting their bodies say what they could not bear to speak out loud; and even then she had tried to pretend that it was not the last time. That it was another ordinary night, just one of many to live for. But as they fell asleep in each other's arms, neither moved away for a moment, as if they were each trying to memorize every curve and surface of the other.

The next morning there was no putting it off any longer.

Jack was determined and would not be swayed. Something had changed in him since they'd met Catherine. There was a new resolve in him, and she did not want to add to his burden. She had been wrong about her illness, she realized now. She'd led herself to believe it was something wonderful and hopeful, because she did not want to think of what it meant otherwise. That she was dying. It had all been doomed from the beginning, just as Lawrence had warned her. There was never a happily ever after for them, that was all too clear.

She helped him into his jacket and buttoned the top button. Her fingers were shaking.

Jack clasped her hands in his and held them to his lips to kiss her fingers. "Trust me to return to you," he said.

"I will wait forever," she promised. "However long it takes." But Schuyler knew that whatever the outcome of the day, even if Mimi was destroyed and Jack lived, there would be no victory. Jack would never be the same after killing his twin. Mimi was a part of Jack, and killing her would kill a part of him as well. "Catherine could not help us?" She had placed so much hope that the gatekeeper would know how to free them from their bond.

Jack shook his head. "Whatever happens, whatever you hear about me, know that there is a reason for it."

"What are you going to do?" Schuyler asked, feeling a different kind of fear. Jack had never spoken like this before.

"I cannot say without putting you in even more danger," he said, and his face was so heartbreakingly sad that

Schuyler threw herself upon him to embrace him even more tightly. "You are so important in this war," he told her. "You must survive to lead us. With the gates failing, there is no darker time in our history. But you are Gabrielle's daughter, and I believe that you will bring the vampires to redemption. My life is immaterial."

"I'm so sorry. I'm so sorry for loving you, I'm so sorry," she said, and the tears began to flow freely, soaking his jacket. "But it was such a wonderful dream, my love," she whispered. "Such a wonderful dream."

"I am not sorry for a moment," Jack said fiercely. "It was worth every moment, every second that we were together. I would not change it for an immortal lifetime."

They kissed one last time.

Then Jack Force left for the Sahara to meet his fate.

FIFTY-TWO

The Battle of Abbadon and Azrael

*S*he squinted her eyes, shielding them from the bright sunlight that glinted off his hair and his sunglasses. Jack always did look dressed to kill, Mimi thought, finding she still admired him even after everything that had happened between them. "Abbadon," she greeted, getting out of the Jeep.

"Azrael." He nodded, as if they had bumped into each other at a coffee shop.

"What kept you so long?"

"I was delayed." He shrugged.

"Well." She tapped her foot. "Shall we get this over with?"

Jack nodded his assent.

They faced each other. Azrael, the ferocious and frightening Angel of Death, and her twin brother, Abbadon, the Angel of Destruction.

Then Mimi disappeared.

Jack gazed out at the crystalline sands, searching. The white desert was far from the crowds of Cairo, a fitting and secluded spot for a final confrontation. No one could hear them. No one would come to anyone's aid. This was a fight to the death. The blood trial.

He found Mimi crouched on top of one of the sandy rock towers. Behind her, the orange rays of the setting sun dimmed below the horizon. The warmth of the day faded as a cold wind swept across the desert floor. He watched Mimi's shadow, the dark angel waiting for battle. She's making me come to her. She's forcing me to make the first strike.

So be it. If there had been another way, he'd have taken it long ago. But there was no getting out of this. Azrael had to die in order for his love to live.

In an instant he was upon her. Striking at the rock where she stood, he shattered the pillar with his blade. A cloud of white dust filled the air; stone and sand ricocheted off his chest as the pillar collapsed in front of him.

Mimi laughed as she rode the collapsing column to the ground. "Is that all you can do, Jack?" she asked. "Or do you not have the courage to strike me directly?" She raised her gleaming sword and swung for his throat, the blade nipping his skin. First blood. A tiny stream trickled down from his neck as he fell backward.

"Strike back!" Mimi screamed with rage as she swung once more, and Jack did nothing but dodge the blow.

He lunged for her, but at the last moment his sword turned sideways and struck at the soft stone, sending a shower of jagged rocks toward Mimi. The air filled with the exploding powder of glittering seashells.

"You'll only make this harder if you refuse to fight me," Mimi said, panting heavily. "Either way, this ends tonight. Why not fight for what you want, Abbadon. If you love your little Abomination so much, then you must fight!"

"If that's what you want," Jack said, as he transformed into his true form, sprouting black feathered wings on his back and horns on his head, a true angel of the darkness. He towered above her, his black sword glinting with ebony sparks. His powerful energy whipped the sand into a tornado at his feet.

This is it, he thought. What he had dreaded for so long had finally come to be.

Mimi shrieked as she became Azrael, golden and terrifying, and Jack swung his deadly blade and made a clean swath across her chest.

She changed back into her human form and bit down hard on her lip. She would not give him the pleasure of hearing her scream. "That's more like it," she laughed. Then she was Azrael again, and Abbadon threw her against a tower. She slammed through the white stone and into the next so that the columns collapsed, falling like dominoes around them.

Abbadon lifted one of the tower-sized rocks to crush

her for good, but Azrael flew upward into the dark sky, with Abbadon close behind. They flew up and up, and the desert swirled like a snow globe underneath them. Still they climbed higher, and Azrael attacked, flying in a wide arc. She slashed at Jack and he parried, the two of them dancing around each other in a violent ballet.

There was no more taunting. No more conversation. There was only the pure, magnificent rage of two creatures once blood-bound, now bent on destroying each other.

From afar, the battle dance looked beautiful to those with eyes that were fast enough to follow the action. The two angels fought silently, moving with deadly speed as they cut and dodged through the cold night air.

Abbadon cut Azrael, and she fell from the sky. Her immense feathered wings stopped beating, and on the ground she was Mimi again.

She was bleeding from the head and chest, and she stared at Abbadon with so much hatred. She had forgotten how strong he was, that this was a battle she could not win. She was no match for the Angel of Destruction.

Jack reverted to his human form as well. The sight of that glorious creature falling from the sky tugged at his heart. Could he really do this? He had to. He must. His heart hardened. Do it quickly, then, he told himself, as he launched at her one more time. With every blow, he could feel her weakening beneath him. Her sword bending to his until her wrist snapped and it fell away.

Mimi cried in pain. She could not hide it anymore. She was losing. Jack was too strong, and she knew her life was over. She steeled herself for the end. She reached for her weapon, trying to grasp for it in the sand. . . . She would not die this way, unarmed and helpless.

Jack raised his sword again, but this time, when it came down, the tip of the black blade only cut the edge of her shirt collar.

I can't, Jack agonized. I cannot kill her. I never could.

FIFTY-THREE

Time in a Bottle

*I*t was time to leave Egypt. Schuyler had packed her bags and was on her way to the airport once again. She could not stop thinking of Jack, but she had to be strong—it was all on her shoulders now. The demons were at the gates. She had to do her part, carry on the Van Alen Legacy, and find the true Gate of Promise.

At the terminal she bumped into a familiar face. "Ollie?"

"Sky?"

"Ollie!" She laughed and embraced him. "We've got to stop meeting in airports."

He kissed her cheek but saw that under the smile her face was drawn with the deepest sorrow. "Where's Jack?" he asked.

She shook her head. "It's just me now. I'll tell you later, okay?"

He nodded, not wanting to pry and not letting his heart hope. He would be there for her as a friend.

"What are you doing in Egypt?" she asked.

"Same as you, I think. We just came from the underworld."

"Who's we?" Then she realized. Mimi. Of course. That's why she was here. Jack had said he was going to meet her in the Sahara.

"It's a long story. I'll tell you when we get to the lounge," Oliver promised. "What about you?"

"Let's grab a coffee and we'll fill each other in," she said.

Schuyler told him what she had learned so far of her legacy, and Catherine of Siena's secret about the bifurcated path. "The Gate of Promise is a path to Paradise."

"Of course." Oliver nodded. "No wonder it was so hard to find."

"It's why Michael put up the gates instead of destroying the paths. Because he suspected that one of them could lead back to Heaven," Schuyler said. Everything had clicked into place. She felt goose bumps forming on her arms as the enormity of the true task her mother had set before her sank in.

Oliver looked awed, and for a moment neither of them said anything. Finally, Schuyler broke their reverie. "Where are you headed?" she asked him.

"Back to New York," Oliver said. "I need to make sure my family is okay."

"What's happened?"

"You haven't heard? The Coven's gone under, and even the Conduits aren't safe. Everything and everyone associated with the vampires is being targeted."

"Your parents?"

"Safe for now, but they want me to join them in hiding."

FIFTY-FOUR

Abbadon's Sacrifice

"What are you waiting for?" Mimi screamed. "DO IT!"

She was helpless on the ground, and for a moment she wanted nothing more than her own death. She wished for it with all her might. She gazed up at the dim stars and tried to imagine the end of everything—freedom from the bond and all the hatred that had sprung from it. She wished for the end, but it did not come.

Jack had hesitated.

While he was debating, Mimi saw an opening and took it. The pain in her chest gave her newfound strength. *I'll not perish in this desert.* She had nothing left; why give up the one thing she still had—her life? Jack may be a fool for love, but she was not.

She struck back at Jack, beating his sword with her own, regardless of the pain in her wrist, as her vampire body worked to heal quickly. She sent his blade spiraling downward to the desert floor, the gleaming steel disappearing into a cloud of sand and crushed rock.

Mimi tasted victory, but she knew it was false. It had been too easy to disarm him. "What game are you playing?" she demanded. "FIGHT!"

"I need no weapon to fight you." Jack was resolute. He could not kill his twin, but with his death, the bond would free Schuyler, and she would heal. He would sacrifice his life for hers. It was what he had planned all along. It was his solution to an impossible choice.

Mimi flung herself upon him in one final rage, pressing the blade's edge to his throat as she powered him downward onto the sand.

She heard a perilous snap as he hit the jagged rock, and knew his back was broken when he hit the rough stone. Still she pushed until the blade began to cut at the skin on his throat.

A moment earlier, victory had been his, but he hadn't taken it. He couldn't kill her, and that was his weakness. But Mimi did not share in his humanity, and she bore down on him with all her anger and strength, channeling the black heart of her rage into the blade.

Every muscle in her body tightened, and sweat poured over her brow. Anger coursed through her face. "Die!" she cried, and heaved the sword upward for the death blow. But when it fell, it struck the ground next to him.

"GODDAMNIT!" she screamed as she flung the sword backward over her shoulder. She was as weak as he was. She could not kill her brother. Mimi collapsed onto the hard stone.

The battle was finished.

FIFTY-FIVE

The Hidden Gatekeeper

"Where will you and your parents go?" Schuyler asked.

"I'm not sure yet. Our whole life is in New York. I don't think they can really survive out of the city." Oliver smiled. "How about you?"

"I don't know either," she said. "Is that . . . Kingsley Martin?" she asked, seeing the dark-haired Venator making his way toward them with three huge cups of coffee.

"I forgot to tell you, I'm here with Kingsley. Mimi got him out of Hell. But she had to sort of give up something to do it. I think it was her soul or something."

"She had one?" Schuyler asked with a small laugh. But Oliver did not join her, and she knew something had changed. They were still friends, but their experiences had transformed them. "I'm sorry," she told him. "I didn't mean to make light of things."

Kingsley sat between them and set down the drinks. "Hey, Schuyler."

"Hey," she said. "We've already got coffee."

"Oh, this is all for me." Kingsley smiled. "So here we are. Hazard-Perry keeping you up to date?"

"Sort of," Schuyler said coldly, not sure if she trusted the smooth-talking Venator.

"It's okay. Kingsley's cool," Oliver assured her. "He's one of us now."

"Glad I have your stamp of approval," Kingsley said. "Anyway, I just bumped into my old team. The Lennox boys are here with their wives—didn't know the guys had it in them to pull that kind of tail." He winked. "Anyway, they told me what happened down there, with the angel being killed and all."

Schuyler frowned. "His name was Mahrus."

"Raphael," Kingsley said. "Never liked me. But that's neither here nor there." He took a long sip from his coffee. "Look, I checked in with a few more of my Venator friends around the globe. Things are pretty bad everywhere, it seems; Covens falling and all that. But there's something more important. Did you tell her, Oliver?"

Oliver shook his head. "No, but you can."

Kingsley told Schuyler what he'd learned during his time in the underworld.

"That's it, then," Schuyler said. "I think the Nephilim—this whole business with taking the girls, as terrible as it is—I think it's just a distraction. Even the destruction of the Covens is just a way to keep the vampires looking the other way. . . ."

"You're absolutely right," Kingsley said, slamming down his cup. "It's a trick."

"Because, according to you, and what they tried to do in New York—find the key of the star, which is called the Key of the Twins, by the way—is the same thing that we're doing. They want the Gate of Promise."

"And I think they've found it, which is why they were so confident," Kingsley mused. "Now all they need is the gatekeeper."

FIFTY-SIX

Blood Trial

They lay on the sand for what felt like the longest time, letting their vampire strength heal their wounds. Finally Mimi sat up. She felt strange—different—there was something happening—her body was healing—but there was something else as well.

Her soul had returned.

She had felt it right at that moment when she'd hesitated before killing Jack. In that split second when she'd decided she couldn't kill him; when she had staked her sword into the ground instead of in his chest. She had won it back with that singular gesture of forgiveness. She'd won it back, the spirit that she had given up in the underworld so that Kingsley could return with her to earth, and Oliver could keep his life. It had been returned to her. This is not Helda's doing, she thought. Helda was not so generous. Mimi did not know to whom she owed this great gift. She was just grateful for another chance.

As an immortal she could live forever—she did not need her soul to survive—and so had given it up without knowing the consequences. But when she felt its return, she understood what she had lost. Her love. Her reason for living.

What happened? Where was Kingsley? Had he managed to escape from Hell? Had she succeeded? She couldn't remember anything. Her heart hurt thinking of him. She wanted to see him so badly, to make sure he was safe and sound.

Mimi looked at her brother. Jack was breathing heavily, and he had an ugly cut on his face. They had faced the blood trial and still the bond lived between them.

"Are you okay?" she asked Jack, who sat up, groaning.

"A few bumps and bruises, a broken back, but nothing fatal, it's healing quickly. Luckily we're vampires." He smiled. "I'm glad you didn't kill me."

"Yeah, yeah. But what do we do now? Since we obviously failed at destroying each other."

Jack stood up and helped Mimi to stand as well. "There's only one way out of this bond."

"You don't mean." Mimi blanched.

"Yes," he said. "Our former master is the only one who can unmake what was made."

The bond was bigger than them—bigger than their wants and desires—and they had no choice.

"Maybe it's for the best," Mimi said. "There's something going on down there. Maybe we can stop it from the inside."

"Double agents, you mean?" Jack asked with a smile.

"Sounds kind of dorky when you put it that way, but yes." She brushed off the sand from her jeans. She wanted to see Kingsley again before she went back down into the underworld, but she knew that was not possible. Still, she could feel that he was alive—on earth—and that she had succeeded in bringing him back. As long as the bond lived, neither she nor Jack could be with those they loved. "Well, I'm ready if you are."

"No time like the present," Jack agreed.

They disappeared into the glom, and just like that, the Twin Angels of the Apocalypse went back down to Hell.

FIFTY-SEVEN

Gabrielle's Secret

he Key of the Twins. Schuyler's mind raced. She thought of everything that her mother had told her about the Van Alen Legacy and the Order of the Seven. The Key of the Twins.

Allegra Van Alen and Charles Force. Michael and Gabrielle. The strongest angels who had ever lived. The Uncorrupted. The Archangels of the Light.

"They Key of the Twins is Michael and Gabrielle's key," Schuyler said, a little awed. "The Almighty left a path open for them because they were vampires by choice and not sin. A way back home."

"How do you know this?" Kingsley asked, looking a little awed himself.

Schuyler could not explain. It was something Allegra had said all along, right from the beginning—in those dreams Schuyler had had of her mother, and during their last conversation before Allegra sent her on this quest to fulfill her legacy. She realized this was her true legacy, a secret so important, Allegra could not tell her herself. She'd trusted Schuyler to find out on her own. The Van Alen Legacy was part of it—searching for the Gates of Hell would lead her to discover this. It was all there, a puzzle whose pieces were hidden, but were slowly locking into place. Allegra had said of Charles: *There is something broken in the universe that only we can fix together. That is part of your journey as well.* And what was the last thing Allegra had told her? *My daughter, I am in you. Never forget that.*

"It's in . . . me," she said. "My mother was the keeper of the Gate of Promise. I know that now. It's right. That's why there were two gates—because she hid one from the Order." Allegra had hid the knowledge of their salvation in her daughter. Whatever made Allegra the keeper—she had given it to Schuyler for safekeeping.

The Order of the Seven had been sent out into the world to find the Paths of the Dead and build gates to keep the demons in the underworld. But what if one of them had found something else . . . not a path to the dead but a path back to Eden. What then? Why had Allegra not chosen to use the key herself? What was she hiding? Why did she hide it in her daughter?

Gabrielle's daughter will bring us salvation, Lawrence had told her. *She will lead the Fallen back to Paradise.*

It was all up to her. Schuyler Van Alen was the keeper and key. The Key of the Twins.

"We have to find it before the Silver Bloods and Nephilim do. And we have to defend it. Oliver, Kingsley . . . you have to help me."

"Already there, Sky," Oliver said. He looked up from notes that Lawrence had left, and read the passage that had led them to Cairo. "'On the shore of the river of gold, the victor's city shall once again rise on the threshold of the Gate of Promise.' The Thames is named after Isis, the golden goddess. And as for the victor's city—the City of London was established by the Romans in A.D. 43."

"What do you say, guys?" Schuyler asked.

"Londontown," Kingsley mused. "Good place as any."

"I'll get our tickets changed," Oliver said, standing and feeling exhilarated to find himself useful again.

Schuyler felt her heart calm. There was so much to do before the end. She thought of Bliss out there—she had been charged with finding the wolves—but from what she had seen of the Hellhounds, she knew that her sister had a tough task ahead of her. They would need the Hounds of Hell in the end, if they were to destroy the Silver Bloods, her mother had said. When the time came, when the battle was fought, she hoped she would find Bliss by her side.

Kingsley gathered their empty cups and tossed them in the trash. Schuyler took a moment to herself while she was alone. She could not feel Jack in the glom anymore.

The telepathic bond between them had gone dead, and she did not know if he was alive or dead. She had to carry on without him. She had promised him that. Just as before, she would have to find a way to survive, and she was glad she would have her friends with her this time.

FIFTY-EIGHT

Bonded Servants

he Dark Prince sat on his golden throne. One day, not far in the future, he would no longer need this facsimile of Paradise. One day, he would return to his former glory.

"I was wondering when you both would realize that the Uncorrupted will never appreciate you like I do." Lucifer smiled when he saw the latest additions to his royal court.

Abbadon and Azrael shone in their golden raiment. They were dressed for battle, as they had been that day so long ago, during the glorious rebellion, when Lucifer had first tried to take Paradise for his own.

Their wings beat against their backs, and their golden armor glowed like beacons in the night. Their faces were calm and serene, extraordinarily beautiful. His lovely dark angels.

Lucifer sat in his white robes, gleaming, shining with a

light more wondrous than anything they had ever seen. This was the Morning Star. The lost prince of Heaven.

They walked up to the throne and knelt at his feet.

"We come to pledge our allegiance in return for an unmaking," Abbadon said.

"Our swords are yours to command," Azrael added.

"What proof do I have of your loyalty? You betrayed me once before," Lucifer demanded.

Jack was prepared. "You shall hold our souls hostage until we are free. When our debt is paid, we will regain them along with our freedom from the bond and each other."

Mimi nodded.

"So be it." The Dark Prince smiled. With Azrael and Abbadon at his side, his return to Paradise was assured. "Arise, my friends. Welcome back to the fight."

EPILOGUE

The White Darkness

*A*llegra waked into the White Darkness. It was over twenty years since she had broken her Bond. Not long ago, she had left her two daughters back on earth with their tasks, and she had journeyed down to the center of Tartarus. She found Charles in a smoky nightclub. They had not seen each other since that night when she'd left him in New York.

"There you are," she said gently.

Charles wore a sharp black suit and was sitting in front of a piano, idly playing the keys. "How did you find me here?" he asked.

"It's one of our favorite memories, isn't it?" Allegra looked around. "1923. The Cotton Club. Before the fire."

Charles sighed.

"Shall I play you something?" Allegra asked, sitting next to him. "Will you sing for me?"

341

Charles nodded. He stood to take the microphone and began to sing. "'Unstop the day, you'll rise again . . .'"

Allegra listened, her eyes glistening with tears as she played. When he was done, she clapped.

"Shall I tell you the story? Of Florence," Charles asked. "I do not know if you are strong enough to hear it."

"Begin from the beginning," Allegra said. "I only know my side."

Acknowledgments

Thank you to everyone at Hyperion for all your wonderful support over the years—your blood is definitely BLUE; especially to my AWESOME editor, Emily Meehan (Yay!). Love to the entire team: Russell Hampton, Jeanne Mosure, Suzanne Murphy, Stephanie Lurie, Christian Trimmer, Laura Schreiber, Jennifer Corcoran, Nellie Kurtzman, Andrew Sansone, Ann Dye, Simon Tasker, Dave Epstein, Elena Blanco, Kim Knueppel, and Drew Richardson. Many thanks always to my agent and dear friend, Richard Abate. Big thank you to my sister and assistant Christina Green, and Kady Weatherford, who joined the team this year. A huge debt of gratitude to my research assistant, Jessica Robertson Wright, for the Cairo help. Love to all the fans on the Blue Bloods Facebook, Twitter, and online fan pages. Love to the DLC and Johnston families, especially the Blue Bloods readers: Mom, Mom J, my in-laws: Christina and Steve. Most of all, love and thanks to Mike, who writes and lives the books with me; and Mattie, who makes it all worthwhile.

For more about Ingrid and the witches,

read the Beauchamp Family series

Witches of East End

Available now

Serpent's Kiss

June 2012

For more about Bliss and the Hellhounds,

read their first adventure in

Wolf Pact

September 2012

Look for the first Blue Bloods novel,

beautifully illustrated and brought to life.

Blue Bloods

The Graphic Novel

January 2013

Watch out for the explosive finale in the Blue Bloods series.

All your questions answered . . . All the mysteries explained . . .

Friends reunited . . . Hearts broken . . . Will Bliss return

with the Hellhounds? Will Schuyler save the Blue Bloods?

Who will live? Who will die? Find out in . . .

Blue Bloods

The Gates of Paradise

The seventh and final novel in the epic saga

January 2013